A Change to the Plan

BY
PAMELA MOULTON

To my partner, John,
for giving me the time and space to
make a dream come true.

To my siblings, Delia, Laurie, and Roy
for your unconditional love and support.

To my friends, Doug, Chrissy, Colleen, Desiree, and Ellen
for being brave enough to read an early draft
and to share your feedback.

Chapter One

Flickering light from the dripping candlesticks reflected the emotion in Katerina's gold-flecked hazel eyes. As the man across the table smiled tenderly and raised his champagne flute, the background noise in the restaurant's private dining room faded to a soft hush. Dressed in a dark classic suit with his wavy brown hair uncharacteristically subdued, he had never looked more handsome. She'd loved Michael for as long as she could remember, since childhood.

"To the woman I want to spend the rest of my life loving," he said with gentleness and a touch of pride.

"To Amy," the guests at the table chorused in unison, raising their champagne flutes. From what seemed like a long distance, Katerina heard her own voice chiming in with the good wishes and tasted the sweet dryness of champagne in her mouth.

The celebration dinner passed in a blur of images—Michael's proud smile and the expression of maternal love in the warm blue eyes of his mother, Helen; familiar faces of old friends; the sparkle and luster of the diamond solitaire nestled in its classic setting; snowy white tablecloths, waxy pale petals of fresh hydrangeas, and so many candles. The images could have been lifted from Katerina's dreams, except for the contentment so unmistakable on Amy's pretty face. That was most certainly not part of her dream. She closed her eyes, willing the image to disappear, but when she opened them, the blonde interloper was still sitting in *her* chair and wearing *her* ring.

She relied on every bit of her self-control and pride to keep her plastic smile firmly in place while responding to the conversation and praying for the evening to end. Katerina was aware of the looks of curiosity directed her way. Even old friends couldn't help but be captivated by a front-row seat to Michael's latest epic desertion, and dealing with the sympathetic expressions was hard.

"Kat, welcome back to Seattle. Is this for good or just a visit?" The question interrupted her musing, and she turned to face Dan, a childhood friend.

"I am back—my apprenticeship just wrapped up." Katerina turned in her chair to face her friend and instead met the speculative gaze of the dark-haired man sitting beside him. She had the distinct and immediate impression that he was measuring her up in some way. Shrugging off the thought, she turned her attention back to Dan.

"So, paradise got old, and you missed the rain? From what Michael's told us, the resort you've been working at is incredible, and I can tell you, we've all been quite jealous." Dan looked at the people sitting around him for confirmation, and several heads nodded in agreement.

"Well, I can only say paradise is not the same experience for the on-site staff. I don't think I've ever worked so hard to make something appear effortless!" Katerina smiled wryly, shrugging her slim shoulders.

"Just what do you do for a living?" The question came from the dark-haired man she had noticed earlier. His expression was neutral, but again Katerina felt the almost tangible sensation she was being judged, and that the points weren't adding up in her favor.

Unconsciously sitting up straighter, she replied in a cool tone. "I'm a sous-chef, currently between positions, as you've just heard. And what do you do? I'm afraid I didn't catch your name?"

"My name's Jack Logan. I'm a partner with a local real estate development firm." His voice was smooth and polished, full of the confidence that Katerina associated with arrogance.

Katerina nodded politely, but her smile lacked any real warmth. Someone on her other side engaged her in conversation, allowing him to study her.

She can stand on her own two feet, Jack thought. The woman might be down, but she had spirit, and he admired that. She was beautiful, too. Those incredibly colored eyes dominated her heart-shaped face and delicate features. She wore her dark hair up, exposing a glittering array of small diamond studs that climbed the rims of her delicate ears. Her black dress clung to her body in a sexy, yet understated, way. The overall image she presented was one of confidence.

His cell phone buzzed, and he excused himself, walking to the lobby to take the business call he'd been unable to reschedule. The noisy restaurant and kitchen made it difficult to hear well, so he stepped down a dimmed hallway. The conversation progressed better than Jack had been expecting, and at his client's request, he waited on hold for two engineers to be conferenced in to close the loop on some technical issues for the project.

From his vantage point in the hallway, he observed Katerina heading toward the coat check. She was a woman who would always turn heads. Her petiteness surprised him; she didn't look as if she stood more than five foot six in her heels. Projecting such a strong presence at the table, he had expected her to be taller. He admired the lithe athleticism in her walk and the toned, sculpted look of her small frame. For not the first time that evening, his interest in her was piqued. Ms. Katerina Gascay was certainly not your typical passed-over love interest.

She walked by without noticing him as he stood in the dim hallway, and Jack caught a faint trace of her perfume, reminding him of spring. She handed her coat check ticket to the waiting attendant just as her cell phone rang.

"Hello," Jack overheard her say. "Oh, thank God it's you! No, I'm just leaving dinner now, and Marnie, I can't just stand back and let Michael make this mistake. I know he still has feelings for me. Marn, can you hold on a sec?" She shrugged into her coat and, handing the attendant a tip, she headed toward a less populated area and out of Jack's hearing range.

But Jack had heard enough. Katerina didn't intend to give up without a fight. He waited until he saw her drop her cell phone back into her evening bag before he stepped out of the hallway. He saw a flash of recognition in her eyes, and she nodded at him and began to head toward the door.

"Katerina!"

At the sound of his voice, she turned, looking back with a polite but guarded expression.

"Yes?" she asked, as his long strides closed the gap between them. He stopped in front of her, close enough so she was forced to tilt her head back to meet his eyes. A chunk of her dark hair had worked its way free, softening the severity of the

French twist. Again, of its own volition, his mind noted how attractive she was. He also noticed the haunted expression in her eyes and the lines of strain around her mouth. It was as if all her earlier vitality had been drained from her.

The fragility she exuded almost caused Jack to question his resolve. But damn it, he was not an impartial bystander, and she was not as innocent as she pretended to be. "Katerina, I couldn't help but overhear you just now on the phone say that you can't stand by and let Michael make this mistake." He heard the sharp intake of her breath, but when she replied, her tone was deceptively soft and held both a hint of defiance and challenge.

"What I'm quite sure of is my private conversations are none of your business. Now, if you'll excuse me." She moved to pass him, and he stepped forward to block her path, towering over her. She glanced quickly at his dark, good looks and the cold flatness in his gray eyes. He projected an air of authority, and Katerina's previous energy seemed to evaporate in the face of his intensity.

"Wait, Katerina, I'd like to know just what you plan to do about this so-called mistake." His voice, though quiet, held a silken thread of warning. He expected her to respond with anger and defensiveness, and was taken totally by surprise when instead her tough façade crumbled, and her eyes sparkled with unshed tears.

Her reply was husky and broken, "Look, I don't know who you are or what skin you have in this game. But what I do know is, I have to be sure this is what Michael wants." Stepping around him, she headed toward the door.

This time, Jack didn't try to stop her. Instead, he found himself admiring her self-possession and feeling reluctant guilt for having caused her more unhappiness.

Chapter Two

The next morning dawned uncharacteristically bright for December in Seattle, and Katerina stretched lazily, enjoying the languorous state between sleep and wakefulness. Opening one lazy golden eye, she gazed at her familiar surroundings and then with an unwelcome jolt, the reality of recent events landed hard.

She always found the morning to be a safer time to analyze situations. Somehow, in the light of day, it was easier to separate emotion from the problem at hand. Today was an exception. As if suddenly blessed with the gift of total picture recall, she saw Amy—the tall, pretty obstacle to her own happiness—and she replayed how the blonde's eyes had lit up each time she'd looked at Michael. She also recalled the accusation and condemnation in Jack's expression. *What right does a total stranger have to judge me?* Katerina knew she hadn't imagined the confusion in Michael's eyes, and she certainly hadn't imagined his whispered request to meet him for lunch.

This was so far from the perfect homecoming I'd envisioned. Many times, over the last year—despite the warm tropical breezes and the affluent atmosphere of the Australian resort where she had lived and worked—she'd dreamed of when she could return to her life in Seattle. An improved version, one where she was actually happy in her relationship and her career choices. *This is all my fault—how could I have thought that recklessly accepting an apprenticeship halfway around the world would work?*

The sheer need to escape her black thoughts drove Katerina to push back the heavy feather duvet and climb out of her warm bed. Reaching for her robe and slippers, she padded out to the kitchen to make some much-needed coffee. The sputtering and spitting of the coffee maker signaled the end of the brew cycle, and she curled her toes in happiness as she inhaled the rich, dark scent of the French roast. Despite the sorry state of her love life, it really was good to be home. Australia might have the Great Barrier Reef, but they didn't know the first thing about good coffee.

Her phone rang as she savored her first cup. She could barely make out her mother's cheerful voice coming through the phone with what sounded rather like the enthusiastic accompaniment of a mariachi band. "Darling, welcome home!"

"Mother, where are you calling from? I can barely hear you." Katerina found herself shouting to be heard.

"Oh darling, your father and I are in Cozumel. The cruise ship just pulled in, and I wanted to catch you and welcome you home. We're so sorry to miss you for the holidays, but this was just too good to pass up—I knew you'd understand. You do, don't you darling?"

With insight born of long practice, Katerina could visualize the look on her mother's face, which would be a combination of impatience and guilt. Her mother's priorities would always favor her own interests. "Mother, of course I understand. You sound as if you're having a wonderful time. Tell Dad 'Hi' for me."

"Marvelous, darling. All our love, Merry Christmas, and Happy New Year!" Her mother's voice faded along with the band, and the connection went dead.

With a sigh, Katerina set the phone down and picked up her coffee cup. She'd had her lifetime to learn that nurturing her only child was not in her mother's repertoire of talents. Honestly, Kat had thought she'd moved on from feeling hurt by her parents' indifference, but today she felt an unfamiliar sense of anxiety. While her mother and father had provided her with an upper-middle-class lifestyle, it was Paul and Helen Doran who had applied the Band-Aids to her skinned knees and given her big hugs when life handed out unwelcome surprises. Katerina knew just how fortunate she'd been to grow up next door to the Dorans.

As she sipped her coffee, she tried to quell the burst of anxiety and ground herself instead, focusing on the simple joy of being back in her familiar condo. She cherished this space despite its tiny size and quirky shape. She'd loved it from the first moment she'd seen it. It fulfilled all the mandatory requirements, was inexpensive, downtown, and had charm to spare—a fact her best friend had been totally unable to appreciate. "No one can live in 600 square feet with no closets," Marnie had stated practically. Michael had been concerned about the safety of the urban neighborhood, but Katerina had been adamant. Her career as a chef meant long hours, and lots of late nights. Typically, the nicer restaurants were in downtown Seattle, and it made sense to live in that proximity.

Size had been an obstacle, but Katerina had relished the challenge. On a shopping spree through old second-hand furniture stores, she had discovered a truly unique floor mirror with stepped corners and raised beadwork. The mirror stood almost seven feet tall and wider than a typical doorway. She had lovingly removed the grime and tarnish to return it to its original gleaming silver. Propping it in the corner against her large bay windows created a feeling of openness.

Her splurge had been working with a closet design company to create floor-to-ceiling storage and closets which hid a Murphy bed. When closed, the raised, molded cabinetry created an accent wall and a pull-out desk, and by adding a small but modern chair, she had another seating area. A small, ornate fireplace, which no longer functioned, now held a variety of candles varying in height and size that she lit for ambiance. Across from the fireplace was a small but comfortable couch, scattered with pillows, and two small ottomans acting as a coffee table.

The tiny kitchen had won Katerina's heart—as compact as the space was, it featured a waterfall quartz island and oversize cabinets. The builder had even included a small-scale stainless-steel hood above the equally small range. Katerina adored her tiny kitchen, and with two kitchen island stools, she had everything she needed. The builder had also modernized the small bathroom; while the shower and sink areas were small, they were functional and new.

Living in a small space, she was learning to embrace the art of minimization. No "two for the price of one" and "double sizing" allowed. With the entire space decorated in cream, white, and accents of gray, she filled the walls with oversize colorful art pieces. The tiny condo now resembled an eclectic Parisian flat—even the skeptical Marnie had been impressed.

Katerina walked from area to area, stopping to touch items she had missed during her absence. The small space was filled with the heavy, sweet fragrance of the yellow roses that

Michael had given her when he'd met her at the airport. She eyed them resentfully. *Yellow roses should have been my first clue.* Those yellow roses were a tangible reminder that unless she could undo the damage she had caused, Michael intended to marry Amy. In that instant, she felt very much alone.

A knock at the front door startled her and, peering through the peephole, she was grateful to see Marnie's pert profile. "Hey, you!" she exclaimed, opening the door wide.

"Hey, yourself," Marnie replied, pushing past Katerina, holding a Starbucks latte and waving a bag from which wafted the mouthwatering scents of biscotti and scones. "I know you've probably already made your sacred bitter brew, but I for one need a latte to take the edge off the morning."

"Marn, I can't believe you're here—did you come from Portland just to see me?"   Marnie turned and looked at her closely. "Are you okay? I know last night must have been hard." She reached over and hugged Katerina's petite frame.

"I'm okay. I'm just really happy to see you."

"There's a strict code of conduct for besties, and I'm just doing my job. Now get out of my way—there's a blueberry scone in that bag with my name on it." Marnie laid her coat over a bar stool and removed her knit cap, running her fingers through her long, honey-colored hair before settling down close to the fireplace with her coffee and assortment of baked goods. Katerina grabbed her coffee and a couple of extra napkins before joining her.

With a concerned yet stern look, Marnie brought the conversation directly to Michael's engagement. "Kat, please listen to me—you know I have your best interests at heart. About your call last night… maybe you need to accept that Michael is going to marry Amy."

Setting her coffee cup aside, Katerina locked her arms around her knees as if to steady herself. "This is all my fault. I was just frustrated and angry," she said, her gaze staring into the unlit fireplace as if it held the answers. "We were supposed to be taking a break to re-evaluate our relationship while I was in Australia, not finding a replacement for it—"

"Kat!" Marnie interrupted, reaching out and covering her friend's hand for emphasis. "I can't stand to hear you take the blame for this—Michael asked for space, and you just made it work for you, too. Listen to me, this is not your fault. Look at you two, you're in your late twenties and you've been dating off and on since high school!"

Katerina nodded, "You're right, I wasn't happy before I left. I felt like we were just treading water. Michael hated my job, the friends I made at work, the hours, all of it. His mind was closed, and he just wouldn't compromise. I have my own questions about how I can find the right place for me in this industry, but I didn't even feel like I had his support. I guess coming back, I was hoping the time apart would have given us the space to figure our relationship out."

"Were you aware that Michael was dating, let alone serious about someone else? You never mentioned it to me whenever we spoke." Marnie's curious and demanding gaze focused on Katerina.

Katerina let out a long sigh before answering. "Sure, I knew he was dating. He was evasive, but I sensed it, and we didn't talk often, so it was probably easy not to read into his comments. I just couldn't imagine he would move on without me."

"Kat, are you sure that you would really want to have taken the next step with him anyway? You just admitted to me that you guys hadn't talked much for a year, and even sensing that he was dating, you still let the situation go? If you are really in love with him, why didn't that make you crazy?" Marnie's expression told Kat that she'd better have a good answer.

"He's asked for time-outs in the past, and we've always gotten back together. I just can't see a future where the two of us don't end up together." Her voice sounded defensive even to her own ears. Pointing her finger for emphasis, Katerina added, "Marnie, you should have been there at the dinner. I know Michael still has feelings for me. I could see it in his expression and his body language. I'm not denying that he has feelings for Amy, but he hasn't resolved his feelings for me. I'm certain of that."

"Kat, I don't think you answered my question. I think you really need to understand why you were okay with Michael dating someone else. As for Michael's feelings, this isn't a new pattern. He always has feelings for you. The problem is he doesn't know what to do with them. He can't seem to commit to you, and he can't seem to get over you either. I don't know what to make of it, but I don't think it's good. He asked Amy to marry him—that's big." Marnie's expressive brown eyes held a challenge and Kat understood that this conversation wasn't the end of it. Marnie would be following up.

"Oh Marn, why has it been so hard?" A solitary tear made its slow descent from the corner of Katerina's eye, finally dripping from the end of her chin to make a wet print on the napkin in her lap.

"Honey, my opinion is that it's been hard because it wasn't meant to be." Marnie's expression turned to compassion. "I could never see how the two of you fit together. You are opposites for sure, but it never feels like the classic opposites attract. Instead, your differences just seem to be a constant source of tension."

Katerina nodded silently, acknowledging her friend's words. Marnie was right, the differences had been tearing them apart.

"I know you just got back to town, but maybe it would be good for you to put a little distance between yourself and Michael. Christmas will be here soon—are you planning on going to your parents'?"

Katerina shook her head, "No, Mom and Dad are on some sort of holiday cruise. Helen has already invited me to spend Christmas Day with them, but I just couldn't, so I told her I already had plans. To be honest, I think I'm going to check with Phillipe and see if they can use some additional help in the kitchen that day." Katerina raised her hand to stop Marnie's protest. "You know I don't like Christmas anyway, and I've spent more than one working in a restaurant kitchen."

"Well, I still don't like it… I don't suppose your parents would've been able to see beyond their own world to notice that you're going through a hard time," Marnie said with her characteristic honesty. "I wish Bill and I were going to be around. It's a no-brainer to join him on this six-month assignment to Oahu, but I wish I could be closer to you right now."

"I'll be fine," Katerina stated with determined conviction for both Marnie's and her own benefit. "I need to find a job and do some holiday shopping. Also, Helen has invited me to her annual pre-Christmas celebration dinner, and I agreed to attend."

"Do you think it's a good idea for you to be around Michael so much right now?"

"Marn, I feel as if I do need to be in his space. Being gone so long created the mess I'm in now." Katerina swallowed hard and determinedly wiped at the tears that had begun welling in her eyes. Even though Marnie was her closest friend, she didn't want her to know that Michael had asked to meet her. She didn't want to see the censure on Marnie's expressive face. She knew that Marnie thought the two of them should have moved on long ago.

Forcing herself to change the subject, she tried to adopt a more upbeat attitude. If Marnie could see through her ploy, she didn't call her on it.

Chapter Three

"Well, she's back and I've met her," Amy announced to her best friend over salads and chilled glasses of Chardonnay at their favorite downtown waterfront restaurant. She ran her fingers through her short blonde hair and gripped the napkin in her lap with nervous fingers.

"And this was at your engagement celebration dinner, right?" Deanna asked. "I'm still so bummed that I couldn't be there."

"Yes, and that was my fault. Michael and I are fast-tracking this engagement, so finding a night that worked for everyone was next to impossible! But let me catch you up on what you missed. She's even prettier than the pictures I've seen, unfortunately," Amy smiled ruefully. "She's petite, dark hair—long I guess, but it was pulled up. She just looked very chic. We are obviously complete opposites." Amy gave a lopsided smile and shrugged with feigned indifference. "She was quiet, didn't create a scene, and left early, for which I was grateful.

Deanna, I just didn't want her to come back from Australia! It's not like I didn't know about her, but I don't want her here, and I don't understand why she had to be invited." Amy finished her words in a rush of frustration and reached for her wine glass. It felt so good to be able to talk openly to her friend. She had been keeping so much inside, and she'd needed this vent session.

"I'm not sure I get that either. I feel sorry for you. You've told me that Michael and she grew up together, but they are still exes!" Deanna rolled her eyes for emphasis.

"Exactly! Michael tried to justify it to me by saying that her parents were pretty emotionally absent, and his family all but adopted her. I think Michael is trying to avoid making a big deal of this—he says his parents accept that the romantic relationship ran its course, but that she's still family. In fact, Michael's mother has her annual Christmas celebration coming up, and guess who's invited?"

"Oh God, I'm so sorry," Deanna commiserated. "Are you okay with all of this? Really okay? Amy, are his parents treating you like family, too, and is Michael making sure you feel secure? I mean it when I say that you and Michael seem perfect together—I've never seen you so happy and relaxed, and he adores you. But the Katerina thing is a lot to handle."

"Deanna, that's just it. It's been almost too easy and perfect, which makes me scared that this is our first big hurdle, having her back. I can't lie; we've had some arguments already over what Michael feels he owes her. It makes me crazy that he's still so worried about how she feels. I want to be confident, but it's scary to fight with him when she is the beautiful and available backup plan. They have such a long history. As for his parents, I guess I don't know if they will change now that she's back. They've always been so warm and welcoming and since I don't have any family of my own besides Jack, I really want to be close to them." Amy bit her lip and her expressive face looked as if her thoughts had taken her somewhere else.

"I know you told me that they had several break-ups and reconciliations. Do you know why things ended between them the last time?" Deanna asked with obvious curiosity.

"I think there'd been issues for a while, and I know Michael did not like her being a chef and they fought about that a lot. Michael told me when he asked for a break, she impetuously took a job in Australia. He also told me he'd actually wanted to end it earlier but didn't know how. I want to believe that's true. I haven't asked too many questions—I guess I don't want her in my head."

"That's probably the best approach." Deanna nodded in agreement. "Don't let her bring you down—this should be your time. How's the wedding planning? I know you were looking at places for the ceremony."

"It's going well—we were able to nail down the venue, a winery in Woodinville that will be perfect for the casual, intimate experience we want. I know we're moving fast, but we're ready and we can't think of a good reason to wait. I just gave notice on my apartment and I'm moving into Michael's condo by February first. It will save us a little bit of money and the commute won't be any worse than the one I have now." Just talking about moving in with Michael made her a little less tense   surely with moving in together coming up, they would be okay.

Deanna reached over and squeezed Amy's arm. "I am so happy for you. Let's have another glass of wine to celebrate your future!"

Chapter Four

With Christmas shopping to finish and time running out, Katerina planned to reward herself with a massage from her favorite spa once she had wrapped her last gift. *Looking forward to something indulgent will be good motivation.*

It wasn't that she hated Christmas exactly, just that it stressed her out. All those high expectations for the perfect gift, perfect outfit, etc., had her longing for her regular routine. Growing up, her mother had always disliked the holiday season and Katerina figured that was the one thing they had in common.

With the days winding down to the holidays, she decided on a gift certificate at a romantic bed and breakfast inn for Marnie and Bill, a soft cashmere pashmina for Helen in the exact shade of her blue eyes, and a gift certificate from the local hardware store for Paul, Michael's dad. Since his retirement, he was forever tinkering with something around the house or yard. She had brought back several bottles of various Australian wines that she planned on giving as gifts to some of her other friends, so she only needed to get something for Michael, and her parents.

Not surprisingly, it was Michael's gift that Katerina was having the hardest time with. She considered and rejected more items than she could easily count. And then, quite by accident, she found it. She was walking past an art gallery when she glanced in the window and spotted the painting. It was a small-scale watercolor of a rustic, weathered, and gray cottage on a lonely stretch of beach with only the softly lapping waves of the ocean to keep it company.

Without conscious thought, she stopped in the middle of the crowded sidewalk, forcing hassled holiday shoppers to maneuver around her. Steeling herself, she entered the gallery and walked to the painting, losing herself in the bittersweet memory of that long-ago summer day. The Dorans had invited Katerina to join them on an outing to the ocean. It had been a relatively cold day so instead of playing in the water, Michael and Katerina had taken a walk through the sand, eventually winding out of sight of his parents and coming upon a deserted gray cottage set back on the beach.

The cottage was little more than a shack and looked as if no one had cared about it for a long time. The two children circled the structure, finally finding an open window and climbing inside. The inside was as decrepit as the outside, but to them, the shack was a magical place. Katerina found an old broom in the corner and began sweeping the house. Michael stated with authority that sweeping was girls' work and wandered around checking windows and testing the loose boards. The two eight-year-olds, with all the confidence and innocence of children, had made a solemn pact that day. When they were older and married, they would come back and live in that house by the ocean.

Each time Michael and Katerina returned to the beach together, they would go in search of their cabin, and each time they found it a little more run down. Until finally when they were about ten, Katerina guessed, it had simply not been there anymore. Only a few scraps of weathered gray siding, buried in the sand, remained of their cottage by the ocean. Katerina could still picture Michael, pushing an unruly lock of brown hair out of his blue eyes, and declaring in a determined voice that he would build them a new cabin even better than the old one. *Damn Michael for breaking that promise!*

"Is this painting of a local Washington beach?" she asked the watchful clerk who had noticed her interest in the painting and walked over to join her.

"It is a local artist, so it certainly could be—he didn't specify the location. It's lovely, isn't it?" she offered in a subtly persuasive tone.

Katerina nodded, "Yes, it is. I'll take it, please."

The clerk nodded approvingly and removed the painting from the window and the two of them moved to the cash register. The clerk wrapped the painting in brown paper while Katerina watched. Stowing it carefully in her Jeep, she decided to call Christmas shopping complete. The painting was the perfect symbol of a lifetime of memories that she and Michael shared. But discovering it and reliving the past had come with a price— she felt physically drained and longed to just be at home. She still had to get something for her parents, but there was plenty of time for that. *It's not like I'll be seeing them anytime soon.*

Chapter Five

Michael called Katerina shortly after his engagement dinner, repeating his earlier request that she meet him for lunch. Katerina wanted to respond that she needed more time. *I've made such a mess, and I haven't figured out how to fix it yet.* Winning back her errant boyfriend despite not having resolved their combustible issue—her career—was daunting on its own. Add to that equation a fiancée and Katerina feared her plan might need to include a miracle. When Michael followed up with a text insisting that he needed to see her and suggesting they exchange their Christmas gifts over lunch, she gave in—a September wedding did not give her much time.

The day of their lunch date, she dressed carefully in a soft creamy sweater, pairing it with skinny jeans and boots. She left her long, dark hair loose and went light with the makeup, the way she knew Michael preferred. Before leaving the house, she took one more look in the mirror and hurriedly removed the three diamond studs climbing her ear lobes, leaving only a simple silver hoop. She gave her reflection a nod—Michael should approve.

Arriving early gave her time to park her Jeep and relax. This was the first time she had seen Michael alone since he had picked her up from the airport, since he'd turned her life upside down by stumbling through an awkward and apologetic explanation of his engagement to another woman.

She was seated at their table sipping a glass of Sancerre when Michael arrived. He walked toward her, smiling, one hand holding a wrapped gift, the other characteristically pushing back a chunk of wavy brown hair. His blue eyes, so like his mother's, searched out her own and held them as he stepped close to kiss her on the forehead before taking his seat.

"It's good to see you, Kat," he said, reaching over and covering her hand with his own larger one. "You look beautiful." His voice was warm and affectionate and yet Katerina could sense the undercurrent of anxiety. The realization that the man she had planned her future around felt uncomfortable with her was almost her undoing, and it took her a moment before she could respond.

"Thank you, it's good to see you, too, Michael." She imagined her turmoil was nakedly visible in her eyes and she fought the urge to look away.

It was Michael who broke the eye contact and at the same time removed his hand from hers to pick up the wine list. Katerina felt both relieved and sad when her hand was alone on the pale tablecloth. She immediately moved it to her lap, clasping it tightly around her other hand.

A waiter interrupted the moment to take Michael's drink order, and the disruption helped to cut the tension. They made small talk until a glass of cabernet was put in front of Michael.

"So, I assume your parents are in town and you're spending Christmas with them?"

"Actually, they're on a cruise. I'm going to help Phillipe out in the kitchen at the Sorbonne," Katerina replied, trying to keep her tone light and matter of fact.

Immediately, Michael's expression darkened and his gentle eyes reflected concern. "What is it with your parents!" He broke off awkwardly, almost as if he felt like the change in their relationship didn't give him the right to criticize them.

Katerina shook her head, smiling wryly, and said, "You sound like Marnie. Apparently, I didn't do a very good job of raising them."

His smile was resigned. "Same old, same old, I guess. Your parents have been in their own private world as long as I've known you. You're more than welcome to spend Christmas with my family, Kat. You know Mother would love to have you. Amy and her brother will be joining us as well."

"No, really, but thank you. I'm looking forward to seeing Phillipe and the gang. It's been a long time." Katerina was truly looking forward to it. Working on Christmas was certain to be easier on the nerves than a gathering with Michael, Amy, and their respective families. With Amy sitting in *her* chair, Kat would just be a fifth wheel. Still, it hurt to see the quick relief in Michael's honest blue eyes.

This lunch is going to be harder than I thought. Katerina struggled to think of a subject that would get her equilibrium back. "I wanted to tell you in person how proud I am of you for receiving the Teacher of the Year Award. I know how much making a difference means to you," Katerina said sincerely.

"Thanks, Kat, I know you do. Working with teenagers is a responsibility, and there are times when I'm sure they aren't getting anything I'm trying to say—whether it's school- or life-related. When this award came along, I realized I was making an impact." Michael spoke with quiet pride and satisfaction. "Incidentally, I met Amy at St. John's Prep—she's a teacher there as well," he added as an afterthought, his tone winding down awkwardly when he realized what he'd said.

Katerina fought to keep her expression neutral, but her true emotions warred between anger and despair. Did he have any concept of how hard this was for her, or worse yet, was his insensitivity a confirmation that he really had no feelings left for her? Was she so totally off-base in thinking that he was conflicted at all between his feelings for her and Amy?

Recognizing his words had upset her, Michael reached out and touched her cheek with his hand. She fought the urge to lean into the warmth and strength of his touch.

"Kat, honey, I'm sorry. I didn't mean to hurt you."

Against her will, Katerina felt the tears well up. She didn't trust her voice to speak without breaking so she simply nodded. One warm tear started a wet track down her cheek, and she quickly reached up to wipe it away.

"Oh hell, Kat, would you rather we grab something simple and be alone? I'm sorry—I thought—I don't know what I thought." His voice was full of self-recrimination and his eyes were bleak.

"That sounds good," Katerina managed to say. She swiped at her eyes again and peeked surreptitiously in her compact mirror, searching for signs of running mascara while Michael settled up the bill.

Outside, Michael carried both wrapped gifts and Katerina carried the hot dogs and drinks they had purchased from a street vendor. For lack of a better option, they ended up sitting in Michael's Audi. He started the motor to get the heater going and the two of them leaned back against the doors facing each other. They shared a laugh over the incongruity of their exodus from an expensive restaurant to go in search of hot dogs, and the mood was considerably lighter, although the small interior space of the vehicle also felt more intimate.

They munched contentedly in companionable silence interspersed with small talk. Finally, Katerina wiped her fingers on her napkin and in a soft but determined voice, broached the subject on her mind. "Why did you invite me to lunch, Michael?"

"I'm sure the situation has been hard for you," he said in a low voice, his eyes not quite meeting hers.

"I've been numb since you told me, and I'm still processing. I know we weren't happy, but I didn't expect this. I know I messed up by leaving abruptly for Australia. We were just in such a bad place and, Michael, I felt like by asking for time apart you were pushing me to quit the food industry, and I just wasn't ready to let my dream go. It's all I've ever wanted to do, and I was so afraid that I would let you talk me into quitting. I just thought we would have another chance—" The words had tumbled out of her mouth, leaving her vulnerable; she hadn't intended to say so much. But looking into his familiar face and flooded with the memories of a lifetime, she just needed him to understand.

Michael worked the plastic straw back and forth in the opening of the lid on his soft drink before responding. "Kat, to be honest, my feelings for you are too complicated for even me to understand."

Katerina forced herself to take a deep breath and willed her mind to stay clear and focused. Somehow, hearing the honesty in Michael's words helped. She ached to know why he had been able to ask Amy to share his life when he had never asked her, but she knew that confronting him would cause him to shut down. She still had a lot of questions, but if his feelings were complicated, that must mean something. It meant she needed that plan and soon.

Turning to him, she asked, "Shall we open our gifts now?"

Michael nodded, and the two of them got out of the car and opened the trunk. Reaching for the wrapped painting, she handed it to him. He carefully peeled back the paper, and as the picture was revealed, she saw in his eyes that he recognized what it represented.

He turned to her and spoke quietly, "Thank you, Kat." He looked as if he was going to say something more, but the moment passed, and instead, he handed her his gift for her.

She searched through the tissue paper in the gift bag to reveal a small blue velvet box. With the velvet box still closed, a cynical part of her appreciated the irony of what the box wasn't going to contain. But when she opened it, she was truly touched to find an exquisite silver locket on a delicate chain. Carefully opening the locket, she saw it contained a miniature picture of Michael and her on their first day of grade school. Both of them smiling widely for the camera and clasping hands.

"Thank you, Michael, it's lovely."

"Kat, I wanted to see you because I just need to know that you're okay," Michael said in a dejected voice.

"I don't know the answer to that," she responded, her voice so low he read her lips more than heard her reply. She squeezed his arm briefly and turned to leave, cutting off the chance for any more discussion—she was too raw.

Michael didn't try to stop her. Instead, he watched her go.

Chapter Six

Michael carefully balanced the dozen red roses while digging for the keys to Amy's front door. Pushing it open, he was met with the mouth-watering smell of roasting chicken. He exhaled, releasing a bit of pent-up anxiety and continued his way toward the kitchen. Maybe the home-cooked meal meant that Amy was no longer upset.

"Hey, babe," he said softly, presenting her with the roses and giving her a long, tight hug. "The chicken smells delicious, thank you."

Amy nodded, reaching for a vase to put the flowers in. "And thank you, for the roses," she said with a smile that trembled and didn't reach her eyes.

"Let me help," he offered, taking the vase from her and filling it with water. Once she placed the roses in the water, he pulled her to him and gave her another long hug. "I'm sorry, Amy. I'm sorry that my situation is adding stress to our lives right now."

She nodded slowly and asked, "How was lunch?"

"Amy, you've been incredibly understanding in all of this. I think it provided more closure for her, and I worried about you all day," Michael responded, looking deeply into Amy's eyes.

"I just want her out of our day-to-day lives, Michael. I can understand to a point, but it's just that this is supposed to be our time, and it feels like it's too much about her!" Amy's blue eyes filled with tears, and she stood stiffly with her arms crossed tightly over her chest.

"That's fair. I can't tell you how much I regret disappointing you like this." He reached across and squeezed her rigid shoulder.

She nodded, wiping her eyes, and asked, "Did she try to get you to break things off with me? I told myself I wouldn't ask you, but I need to know." The rawness in her voice was plain.

"No," Michael answered quietly. "No, she just said our situation was unexpected, and that she's hurting, but she acknowledged that she knew she and I hadn't been happy."

Amy shrugged and then added with a burst of frustration, "I'm trying to handle this, I am! But I can't promise you I won't need to talk about this again."

"I love you, Amy," Michael said, wondering if he could ever make this up to her.

She nodded again and then said quietly, "I think the chicken is probably ready to come out of the oven—I just want to have a tranquil dinner and put this day behind us."

"Let's do it," Michael readily agreed, heading for the wine opener. His mind was still full of the day's events, but he needed to let it go for now and concentrate on Amy. Later he could focus on why he had felt compelled to see Kat today. His mind flashed back to Kat's tear-filled eyes, and he forced himself to tamp the image down. For a guy who craved peace over just about any other condition, he felt caught in a web of drama.

Chapter Seven

The night of the annual Doran Christmas celebration arrived, and Jack found a parking place down the street from Paul and Helen's home. He was greeted at the door by a smiling Helen who hugged him warmly and waved him toward a festively decorated room already filled with guests. When Jack got his first look across the crowded space at Katerina in her red dress, his feet stopped moving. *That woman is pure sin...* It wasn't even that the dress was sexy, although it was, it was more that the woman herself was incredibly sexy—the graceful, yet confident way she carried herself. Her dark hair was styled in a mass of long curls and held back with a silver clip. She wore oversized silver hoops in her ears and several large silver bracelets twirled seductively on her small wrists. In a room filled with well-dressed, attractive women, she looked exotic and original. Jack found himself once again intrigued and attracted to her in a way he hadn't counted on.

He watched her sip her wine and make conversation with those around her. She seemed more at ease tonight than she had at the engagement dinner. Procuring a wine glass, he threaded his way in her direction.

"Hello, Katerina," he said casually when she noticed his approach. She looked surprised by his presence, and he suspected she didn't realize he was Amy's brother. Her look of surprise was replaced by a guarded expression as if she didn't trust his intentions.

Before he could introduce himself, Michael joined them, "Have the two of you had the opportunity to meet yet?" And then, without waiting for an answer to his question, he spoke again. "Kat, this is Jack Logan. Jack is Amy's brother. Jack, this is Katerina Gascay, an old and close friend of mine." Introductions completed, he excused himself to handle a last-minute errand, leaving Katerina and Jack alone. Jack wondered if he had only imagined the possessive note in Michael's tone.

"So, that's how you fit into this picture," she said in her low, soft voice. Her expression was refreshingly direct as if she was comfortable acknowledging that they might have different agendas and secure enough to call a temporary cease-fire.

"Yes, I didn't realize you didn't know." His reply, delivered in the same smooth tone she remembered from their first meeting, held the ring of sincerity.

"Yes, well I missed the whole beginning and middle of this romance so there are some gaps I'm still trying to fill in," she said with a strong hint of self-directed humor.

Jack's sudden unrestrained and masculine laugh earned him his first genuine smile from Katerina. The smile lit up her expressive golden eyes and brought her delicate features to life. He felt a strong pull of attraction toward her and was conscious of a disappointment in knowing that what he must say next might destroy this tenuous thread of connection. "Well, I'm glad to have the chance to see you again." The seriousness in his gray eyes contrasted with the almost apologetic smile that turned up the corners of his generous mouth. "We didn't perhaps end on the best note, the other evening."

"No, perhaps not," Katerina nodded in agreement, the spark fading from her eyes. "However, rest assured, I got your message that my motives are not to be trusted." She shrugged offhandedly, but there was a determined and stubborn tilt to her chin.

He delayed his response, measuring her with an enigmatic gaze. "To be honest, Katerina, I don't want to see Amy hurt. And—" he put his hand on her arm when he noted the mutinous expression building on her beautiful face. "I find you intriguing and don't want to see you hurt either." His handsome face had an earnest expression, taking the sting out of his words.

Her eyebrows rose in surprise, and Jack watched the play of emotions on her face. She met his gaze and held it. "I've loved him my whole life, you know," Katerina said with conviction. "There isn't going to be a happy ending to this story for both Amy and me."

Helen Doran appeared at their side and draped her arm around Katerina's shoulders, breaking the moment between Jack and Kat. "I came here to steal you away for a moment, dear. I can never help myself from taking advantage of Kat's help in the kitchen," she explained to Jack. "Why, even when she was a child, I knew she was destined to be a chef when I caught her serving Michael mud pies garnished with fresh basil from my garden and served on her mother's good china. I have to tell you"—Helen lowered her voice and added in a confidential tone—"I've been too busy chatting with guests, and I've managed to get behind on some platters. I recruited Amy's help as well."

Helen reached over and patted Katerina's shoulder with affection. Katerina forced herself to breathe deeply and maintain her smile, which felt like a mask. She knew Helen loved her, but she had an admittedly childish reaction to hearing that Amy was helping in Helen's kitchen. The gentle squeeze of Jack's hand on her bare arm caused her eyes to catch on his steady gaze. In that simple look and gesture, somehow, he gave her the strength to pull herself together. She swallowed past the lump in her throat. "Of course, Helen, I would love to help." As she walked toward the kitchen with the woman who was the only real mother figure in her life, she turned back and caught Jack's eyes still on her.

Helen ran her kitchen with the precision of a military training mission. Everything in the large, well-ordered kitchen was polished to a high gleam and organized down to the spices lined up alphabetically in her spice rack. As Katerina entered the room with already rocky emotions, she spotted Amy arranging crackers and cheese on a large platter. Amy had already usurped her in Michael's life. Did she also have to lay claim to her childhood kitchen?

"Hello Amy," she said, tamping down her frustration and hoping her voice sounded natural.

"Oh hello, Katerina," Amy returned with a nonchalance that didn't come off with complete success.

Katerina couldn't begin to wrap her head around appropriate small talk for the two of them, so she just walked to the faucet and began washing her hands.

Helen's voice cut in, interrupting the awkwardness, "Kat, honey, can you please decant the wine and then arrange the brie and fresh fruit on my good silver platter? I'll be right back to help you."

"Of course," she responded, walking to the counter, knowing exactly where the wine opener was kept. She had grown up helping Helen in this same kitchen, and it was as familiar to her as her own.

As she opened a couple of bottles of Cabernet Sauvignon, she glanced furtively in Amy's direction, curious to learn more about the woman Michael had chosen over her. Amy wasn't wearing much makeup, and her blonde hair was styled in a blunt chin-length bob that framed her face and suited her natural look. She wore a long, eggshell blue dress which showed off her curvy figure without being overtly sexy. Added to that, if her job at a prep school was any indication, Amy must have gotten an advanced degree and was, in Michael's eyes, responsible. Katerina felt a pang recognizing that Amy fit more comfortably into Michael's "type" than she did.

Michael entered the kitchen to retrieve wine, and paused awkwardly, giving Amy a quick kiss on her cheek before retreating quickly with the bottles in tow. Katerina pretended not to notice, keeping her eyes down while she arranged various fruit selections on the platter. She wondered if the two of them had felt even half as uncomfortable as she did.

As if she could read her mind, Amy's voice interrupted her thoughts. "Katerina, I realize your return is unsettling to Michael, but you need to know that he does love me."

Katerina turned to face the other woman, unsure how to respond, but meeting Amy's eyes, she saw strained determination.

She paused for a moment and then spoke from her heart. "Michael and his family are important to me," she said, hoping it was equally clear that she wasn't going anywhere.

Helen bustled back into the kitchen, breaking the tension. Leaning in quickly to assess their efforts, she shooed both girls out of the kitchen to join the others.

•○○○○○○○○◯◯○○○○○○○•

As Amy re-entered the living room, filled with the assembled guests, Jack could see she looked stressed, and he reached out a hand and grabbed her arm. "How're you doing, sis?"

"I'm okay," she said softly, but Jack's skeptical look said he wasn't buying it. "Really, I'm okay," she said with more authenticity. "I know Michael loves me, but she's quite an act to follow. You have to admit she isn't what you picture when you talk about the girl next door."

Jack chuckled despite himself. "Just remember that Michael chose you, and don't let her shake your confidence. I'm going to get another glass of wine. Can I get you anything?"

"No, but thanks, and also thanks for the pep talk." She squeezed his hand lightly before moving off to join Helen, who was beckoning to her.

A moment later, returning with his wine glass, he noticed Katerina talking to Paul and that Helen had just joined them. Even for an outsider like himself, it was clear that the three had a close, affectionate relationship. From the little bit Amy had shared with him, he knew that Paul and Helen were like second parents to Katerina.

Recognizing Dan, one of Michael's friends from the engagement party, he moved to join him. The group included a few other people he didn't recognize. "Hey, Jack, good to see you again," Dan said with the same easy style that Jack remembered. "This is my wife, Sue, and this is Todd and Rachel

Jergen. Guys, this is Jack Logan." Everyone nodded and smiled as the introductions were made. Dan continued, "Michael, Kat, Rachel, and I rode the school bus together from kindergarten until Michael was old enough to drive."

"And then Dan and I rode the school bus because Michael and Kat wanted to be alone," Rachel said wryly, and the group shared an awkward laugh.

"I should have mentioned that Jack is Amy's brother," Dan said pointedly.

"Oh God, I'm sorry," Rachel said, giving Jack a sheepish look. "I didn't realize since your last name was different."

"Please, don't apologize. Our parents married when I was a teenager," Jack explained with a shrug and a smile that said no harm done.

"I do apologize anyway," Rachel said. "It's clear to all of us that Michael and Amy are very happy. It's just if you grew up with Katerina, you had to believe that she had some kind of superpower—every time Michael took one of his 'pauses,' she managed to get him back. So, it's just amazing to think that Michael is marrying somebody else." Her voice began to drop off and Jack had the distinct impression that one of the other three friends was giving her the strong hint to shut up. Looking at Katerina across the room, Jack smiled again, trying to put Rachel and the group at ease. "So, she packs a big punch?" he asked lightly.

"Well—I guess no one here is going to bail me out of this," Rachel said with an awkward laugh and an apologetic grin to all of them. "Katerina is one of my oldest friends and I love her like a sister, but I think it's fair to say that marrying Michael was always the plan." There was reluctant laughter in agreement from the others.

Jack and Katerina weren't seated close together for dinner. Through no fault of his dinner companions, his gaze was more than once drawn to her. As he had noted earlier, she seemed much more comfortable and animated around her old friends tonight. Her lively presence and quick wit intrigued him and there was no denying he found her very attractive. Once, when he caught her eye, she nodded at him and a smile teased the corner of her red lips. If he was honest with himself, he would have to admit he found her more interesting than anyone he had met in a long time.

∞∞∞∞∞∞○○∞∞∞∞∞∞

Across the table, Katerina was aware of Jack's eyes on her. She felt off-balance from their earlier conversation. He hadn't turned out to be what she'd expected, and for some reason that unsettled her. She watched as he turned to laugh at something Rachel was saying. The combination of his dark, good looks and his easy conversational style seemed to be a woman magnet based on the reactions of the females around the table. Even Helen was preening a bit, she noted with amusement. Her eyes drifted back to Michael who was sharing a tender look with Amy, and she felt some of her enjoyment of the evening ebb.

With a jolt, she realized that with Amy here, for the first time in recent memory, maybe ever, she, Kat, would be leaving the party early and not staying late to help Helen clean up the kitchen. Was she just a guest now in the house that had always been her home? Her hand tightened on her wine glass, and she took a quick sip to settle her nerves. She wondered if Amy would be able to see through Helen's baseless bluster that she didn't need any help. Kat sighed and considered. *Maybe Marnie is right. Maybe I'd be better off spending some time away.*

With dinner completed, the group began dispersing—some gathering in the family room, enjoying coffee, and others leaving for home. Sipping his coffee, Jack noticed that Katerina seemed to have grown quieter, and he caught her eyes on Michael more than once. He turned away to respond to a question, and when he looked over in Katerina's direction, he saw her heading toward the front door. Excusing himself, he followed in her direction. He wasn't entirely sure of his purpose, but something drove him to say goodbye to her. For all her self-confidence, she had a certain vulnerability.

As he rounded the corner, he saw Michael lay his hand on Katerina's bare shoulder with comfortable familiarity. Katerina's expression of naked pain made Jack feel like a voyeur, and he hung back, not wanting to intrude.

As Michael turned away to get her coat, Katerina's eyes met Jack's, and she saw what might have been disappointment or condemnation in their cool, gray depths. She'd felt a connection with him tonight, and now it was clear she'd reinforced his earlier mistrust, she thought with a confusing sense of regret. *Well damn him!* Katerina shrugged defiantly and accepted her coat from Michael.

"Let me walk you to your car," Michael offered.

"No, that's not necessary," Katerina protested quickly, conscious of Jack's judging gaze. "I'll walk the lady to her car," Jack offered behind them, and Michael turned in surprise. "Sure, all right. Good night then, Kat," Michael said uncertainly.

"Goodnight, Michael," Katerina replied, as Jack opened the front door and stood back, allowing her to go first. The night was clear and cold, and Katerina could see her breath as she exhaled. She turned suddenly to Jack and spoke in a determined but low voice. "Your offer to walk me to my car really wasn't necessary, you know. Nothing was going to happen between Michael and me."

"I'm sorry you're hurting," Jack said gently. He was standing so close to her that she had to tilt her head back to see his face. He stood there for a moment with an expression on his handsome face that she wasn't able to interpret. Then he brushed the corner of her lips with his thumb. "Goodnight, Katerina," he said softly, stepping back and opening the door of her Jeep.

Chapter Eight

The minute Katerina entered the back entrance of Sorbonne's, she was met with a whooping holler from Phillipe. He immediately rushed over, giving her a big hug and lifting her off her feet. "Oh, Kat, you are a sight for sore eyes!" he exclaimed in his heavy French accent.

"It's wonderful to see you, too, Phillipe," Katerina said, laughing at the older man who was the head chef at the Sorbonne and had been such an important mentor and friend. "How are Nadja and the family?" she asked, knowing his family was the center of his world.

"Good, very good. Nadja tells me that another baby is on the way," he said, lifting his chin proudly.

"Phillipe, what is this, number five? I'm losing track." Katerina shook her head in mock exasperation, and Phillipe grinned sheepishly.

"Ah, it is good to see you," he said again, and then his tone turned to admonishment. "But what are you doing asking to work on Christmas Day when you should be taking advantage of the chance to enjoy the holiday for once?"

She grinned up at him as she took the large white coat he handed her. She layered it over the simple tank top she had worn underneath her winter coat. Working in a kitchen was hot work, and you quickly learned not to dress warmly. "Phillipe, I figured the only way I could get into a good kitchen would be if they were desperate for help. I'm truly out of practice—you'll need to keep your eye on me tonight!"

"Nonsense, ma chérie, it's like a bicycle—once you learn… However, we do need to talk about what you think you were doing, leaving good solid chef work to hang out at pampered resorts!"

Before she could reply, the back door opened and more of the staff entered. There were a few more hugs, and looking around at her old friends, Katerina smiled. *I made the right decision to spend Christmas here today.* It would be hectic, she knew, but it would keep her mind busy and that could only be a good thing. Her former role as sous-chef had been replaced by Marcus when she had turned in her resignation, and Katerina was more than content to simply play a general fill-in role wherever she was needed.

The kitchen was beginning to fill up, and Katerina found that interspersed among the familiar faces were a lot of new ones. Restaurant kitchens tended to be a male-dominated space, and Katerina found herself again one of the few women in the kitchen.

Phillipe re-entered the room and in his booming voice called everyone to order. "Merry Christmas, all," he announced with a big smile. "Tonight is going to be hectic, and expectations will be justifiably high. The specials are duck à l'orange and entrecôte de bœuf with Roquefort butter. The regular menu is of course available as well. We also have a former employee, Kat Gascay here. Kat previously had Marcus's role, and tonight she has graciously offered to stand in wherever she's needed. Due to the complexity of some of the sauces for tonight's specials,

I'm going to have her assist Marcus, and all other roles can adjust accordingly. Questions, anyone?"

In a matter of minutes, the process was well underway, with the prep cooks busy setting up for the evening ahead. Freshly scrubbed vegetables and herbs were lined up on the stainless-steel counters, waiting to be incorporated into the evening's dinners, and previously prepped produce waited in the cooler. Katerina listened in as Marcus reviewed the evening's recipes with the line cooks, while Phillipe appeared to be everywhere at once, his voice calling out directions and cautions as needed.

Antoine, the executive chef, entered the kitchen to review the menu against his wine selections for the evening. When he saw Katerina melting butter for the beginnings of a Roquefort butter sauce, he immediately came over and gave her a quick kiss on both cheeks. "My dear, you are as lovely as ever," he said with his customary European flair.

"You're too kind," Katerina protested, smiling at the sophisticated Frenchman. "It's good to be back. I appreciate the opportunity to be here tonight."

"Nonsense!" Antoine replied. "The pleasure is all ours."

Phillipe called out to Antoine and Katerina turned her attention back to the butter browning in her oversize saucepan.

The night was a blur of sights and smells. A large working kitchen had always seemed a magical place to Katerina. The leaping of the flames as the line cooks grilled and broiled the meat. The bubbling sauces, watched over by Katerina and Marcus and tended by a select few line cooks. The constant and harried calls to the prep cooks to run to the refrigerator and bring out this or that. And, of course, Phillipe's voice directing over every shoulder. Katerina dodged the dishwashers who routinely dashed in to retrieve dirty dishes and pans and sighed in pure satisfaction. She had missed this more than she realized.

As the night grew later, the orders began to slow down, and Katerina had her first moment to catch her breath. She pushed a chunk of dark hair that had escaped both her ponytail and her hairnet, and smiled at Phillipe, who was headed in her direction.

"Ma chérie, you have a visitor here, and I insist that you go because we can handle it from here."

"Phillipe, what are you talking about?" Katerina asked in bewilderment, looking in the direction of the door he was gesturing toward. "I'm not expecting anyone," she insisted.

"Well, my dear, he asked for you by name, and he is tall, dark, and handsome, if I may say so myself. Perhaps he is your Christmas gift." His voice was filled with amusement.

She had told Michael she would be working tonight—had he come to wish her Merry Christmas? Katerina walked to the door and pushed it open, hoping to see his smiling and apologetic face. Instead, she had a quick view of Jack's broad shoulders and dark hair gleaming in the recessed lighting of the dim hallway. With a low groan, she backed up, letting the door close abruptly. Okay, she was not ready to deal with this right now. Mentally, she scolded herself for allowing herself to imagine it would be Michael.

Phillipe approached and touched her arm. "Kat, is something wrong? Should I ask the gentleman to leave?"

"No, no, thank you. It's okay—just a little complicated," she replied with a reassuring smile.

"Well, ma chérie, complicated sounds, at the very least, interesting." He leaned over and kissed her cheek briefly. "Goodnight, my dear, and I do want to talk to you soon," he called over his shoulder.

Chapter Nine

Katerina exchanged her stained white coat for her jacket, removed her hairnet, and grabbed her purse. Then she stood for a moment, taking a deep breath, before opening the door and stepping into the dim hallway where Jack was waiting.

He was leaning back against the wall, and as she approached him, he gave her a mocking smile which seemed to imply that he was as surprised to be there as she must be to see him. He was dressed more casually tonight than he had been in their previous encounters. The snug-fitting faded jeans emphasized the length of his legs. His dark hair was ruffled, as if he had been running his fingers through it. Pushing his long frame away from the wall, he stepped close to her, and looking down into her eyes, he simply said, "Merry Christmas, Katerina."

Despite herself, Katerina felt again a mutual connection with this man that she couldn't understand, but along with that connection was frustration at the way he always seemed to be watching and judging her. "Merry Christmas yourself. This is certainly a surprise," she responded dryly. "Are you here to make sure that I'm not getting into trouble?" she asked, her smile tinged with sarcasm.

"I was hoping that you might be interested in having a drink?" he suggested with a persuasive grin on his handsome face, but his eyes were serious as he looked into hers.

"Thanks, but I don't think that's a good idea. To be honest, I don't think we have anything to talk about, and it's late." Katerina moved as if to walk back through the door into the kitchen.

"Katerina, wait." Jack reached out and grabbed her hand, squeezing it briefly before releasing it. "It's Christmas, can we call a truce?"

Her earlier frustration melted a bit at the genuineness in his gray gaze, and she found to her surprise that the idea appealed to her. Maybe it was just nice to know that someone wanted to be with her on Christmas. "I'm not sure what's open tonight, given that it's Christmas. Also, I'm afraid I need a quick shower to get some of this grease off me and look even halfway presentable." She gestured casually at her pulled-back hair and smiled ruefully but without any self-consciousness.

Jack looked impressed by her self-possession. "How about this—why don't I follow you to your place, you can take a quick shower, and we can take it from there. Or if you prefer, I can grab a bottle of wine on the way and we can stay in, if you're comfortable with that."

Katerina paused, considering his offer and acknowledging to herself that she had mixed feelings about whether it was really a good idea. It was an intimate situation to be in with someone she didn't know well; however, he had been welcomed into the Doran family. The desire for some company won out. "Why don't you come to my place, and there's no need to stop for wine. I have plenty of good Australian wines if those appeal to you at all. You can just follow me—I'm parked out back here." Katerina pointed behind the restaurant.

"It's a deal. See you in a few," Jack replied, touching her shoulder briefly before moving off toward the front entrance.

Looking in the rear-view mirror at Jack's smoke-colored Mercedes following on the deserted, rain-slicked city streets, Katerina couldn't help but wonder why she had agreed to this and why she felt drawn to this man. In their short acquaintance, he had shown that he didn't fully trust her intentions, and given his relationship to Amy, could they even be friends?

The proximity of her condo interrupted her musings, and she pointed him toward a parking space in front of the building while she drove into her underground parking space. When she entered the front entrance, he was waiting for her, and she let him into the secured building. "I live on the third floor," she explained, gesturing toward the elevator. As the elevator made its slow ascent, Katerina glanced at her watch.

"I hope it's not too late for you," Jack said, noting her gaze.

"No, it's not too late at all—unfortunately, you get used to late hours in this business. I was wondering if it was too late for you. Are you working tomorrow?"

"I am, but I was planning on going in a bit later. The holidays are pretty slow at the office," he explained.

The elevator came to a stop, and, unlocking her front door, Katerina opened it and stepped inside.

Following her, Jack had the immediate impression that her condo was as unique and surprising as the woman herself. The space was small, for sure, but the mood was so saturated and rich looking, and the pops of contemporary accents were the perfect balance. "I'm impressed," he said as he took in the furnishings and art.

"Thank you, I've been really happy here." Katerina moved over to the fireplace and grabbed her long electric lighter as she knelt to light the candles.

"Let me do that," he offered, extending his hand to help her up.

"Thanks, maybe I'll open a bottle of wine and go take that shower."

"I'll get the wine, too. Why don't you just take that shower so you can unwind?"

"Okay, you've got yourself a deal. The wine opener is in the first drawer on the right, and feel free to grab any bottle you like. Give me about ten minutes," Katerina replied, heading in the direction of the bathroom. Her smile looked forced, as if she was second-guessing her decision to invite him over.

Jack made quick work of lighting the candles and moved into the kitchen to handle the wine. He opened a bottle of Shiraz, and grabbing the bottle and two wine glasses, he returned to the sofa. Katerina had a leather tray propped on the ottoman, which had coasters, so he figured that was a safe place to set the wine glasses down. He poured them each a glass. As he took his first sip, he heard music coming from the speakers above and recognized the smoky, sultry sound of jazz. He settled back, taking in the large colorful art on the wall. Geometric patterns, some pop art—an eclectic collection, but it worked.

During dinner with the Dorans, he'd learned she was spending Christmas working. He'd surprised himself by driving to the restaurant to see her. He still wasn't sure what he'd planned to accomplish—if anything. He wasn't in the habit of getting involved in anyone else's relationships, and yet he felt strangely as if he had a role in this saga, too.

He heard the water shut off and the sound of her blow dryer. The bathroom door opened, and she came out, running her fingers through the still partly damp strands of her long, dark hair. He had always seen her with her hair pulled up, and he caught his breath at this new image of her. She was dressed in an oversize button-down shirt worn over a pair of navy leggings, and her freshly scrubbed face was bare of makeup. She looked soft, natural, and incredibly sexy.

"Hey, I'm back," she said, sinking down beside him on the couch and accepting the glass of wine he handed her. Jack watched her swirl the dark ruby liquid in her glass and take a sip, savoring the first taste. He felt the slow, tight building of desire as he watched her obvious enjoyment of the wine. The fact that he found her attractive was a complication none of them needed, but if he was completely honest, wasn't that partially why he was here?

"So, Katerina, how did you decide to become a chef?" he asked, wanting to know more about her and trying to get his mind off how those navy leggings hugged her well-toned legs.

"Well, now that's a mystery to everyone who knows me," she said, laughing. "My mother is the ultimate take-out queen. Growing up, we always ate out or had something delivered. She had no interest in cooking and typically the only groceries in our house were chips, drinks, and frozen dinners. But for some reason, even as a small child, I was fascinated by putting ingredients together—you know, the consistency of different things and even how you served or presented it. When I was about seven, I think, Helen and Paul bought me the Kenner Easy Bake Oven, and I never looked back. I was the only kid on the block who spent her allowance on cooking and baking ingredients." She smiled easily at Jack's genuine laughter.

"So, I guess I'm not sure how your business works. Do you go to college to learn to be a chef, or do you just work in a restaurant?" Jack pressed, genuinely curious to better understand her.

"You can do either or both, actually," Katerina explained in her soft, low voice. "Some people start as dishwashers or prep cooks—you know the guys who wash and prepare all the raw ingredients and such—and just work their way up the line. Others, like myself, go to a culinary institute to get some formal training, which gives you a bigger perspective and allows you to step in at a higher level. Several excellent chefs have gone both routes."

"So now that you're back, are you planning on staying and working for a local restaurant?" Jack found himself uncomfortably interested in her response as much for his own reasons as for any impact on Amy's situation.

"I don't know," Katerina said with a frown marring her brow. "To be honest, I'm questioning what I want to do. There are things I enjoy about the restaurant business, but it's very removed from the actual customer, and I miss that a lot. I guess I'm hoping to recreate my satisfaction in cooking for good friends, or at the very least be able to create my own flavors and menu." Katerina's face wore a wistful expression.

"And now, what about you?" Katerina asked, setting down her wine glass, wrapping her arms around her knees, and hugging them to her chest. She looked relaxed, and yet Jack sensed an inner tension.

"What about me? What would you like to know?" he replied with a lazy smile, casually stretching out his long legs. His collared shirt was open at the neck, and he looked completely at ease.

"How about starting with how you ended up with the role of protecting Amy's interests?"

Jack choked back a low chuckle at her directness and responded dryly, "Well, I guess I inherited the role when our parents passed away several years ago in a car accident. Amy was only a junior at the university and was still living at home. Their deaths were especially hard on her, and I've tried my best to be there for her."

"I'm sorry to hear about your parents," Katerina murmured, reaching out a hand to briefly touch his forearm. As she removed her hand, Jack clasped it for a moment in his much larger, masculine grasp, giving it a gentle squeeze before releasing it.

He took a sip of wine before responding. "We're certainly closer since our parents' death. I was thirteen when my mom married Amy's dad, and she was only six, so we didn't spend a lot of quality time together growing up. It wasn't until the accident that we connected on an emotional level. She's a good kid with a solid head on her shoulders."

"Kid?" Katerina asked with a wry smile.

"I guess that does sound strange given that the two of you are pretty close in age." Jack acknowledged her point, but added, "Forgive my presumption, but Amy has a naivety that makes her seem younger than her years, and with you, it seems the opposite. You seem to have confidence and independence beyond your years."

After a moment, she spoke with the quiet strength and honesty he was learning were her trademark. "I probably owe that to being the only child of parents who would probably have chosen not to have any if they'd felt that society gave them that option."

That explains a lot, Jack reflected on the obvious protectiveness and affection that Paul and Helen Doran demonstrated toward her. "Hey, let me get you some more wine," he said, noting her empty glass.

After he refilled their glasses, Katerina turned to him and asked, "So, what about your love life? You know so much about mine," she added ruefully,

He gave a low chuckle and tipped his wine glass in her direction. "Fair enough," he said. "I guess I just haven't met the right woman yet."

"Now, why does that sound like the easy way out?" Katerina asked with a disbelieving grin.

"It's the truth," Jack insisted. "For a while, I probably just wasn't ready to be serious about anyone, and I had Amy's needs as a distraction. So, for one reason or another, I just haven't met the one. Seeing the relationship between my mom and Amy's dad set a very high bar for me. Another way to say it is that I haven't yet met a woman who's made me feel as if I couldn't be happy without her in my life." His words were casually delivered, but he seemed to be looking at her with an intensity that made her feel as if she needed to catch her breath.

Pulling her eyes away, she took a small sip of wine, and then with a low sigh, she turned to face him. "So, Jack, why are you really here tonight?" she asked.

"Would you believe me if I said I'm not sure?" he replied. "I find you intriguing. Every time we talk, I am surprised and impressed by something I learn about you. While I can't call myself impartial exactly, I would like us to be friends." Even as he said the words, Jack knew that his feelings for Katerina were already more complicated than that.

He leaned forward and brushed her cheek lightly with his fingertips. Her skin was soft to the touch, and he smelled the fresh scent of melon shampoo or soap. He felt her stiffen at his touch, but she didn't move away, only tilted her head back to meet his eyes and smiled sadly.

"Jack, I'm not sure that's possible, but somehow you make me wish it was."

"Katerina, it never hurts to have a friend. And now, I'll let you get some sleep. Thank you for letting me enjoy your company." At the door, he wished her a Merry Christmas and, with a cryptic smile, let himself out.

Locking up behind him, Katerina stood for a moment, leaning against the door. Even though she'd been unwilling to admit it to Jack, she, too, felt uncomfortably drawn to him. Initially, she always felt on edge, but as their few conversations had progressed, he seemed to have a calming effect on her. She shook her head in annoyance—she didn't see where a friendship between them could lead. Worse, he'd shared information about Amy that made her seem sympathetic, and that made Amy feel more real.

Chapter Ten

Michael idly bounced the tennis ball with his racket while he waited for Amy to finish refilling her water bottle. She screwed the lid on and took a big gulp before turning to him with a wide smile that had victory gloat written all over it. "I guess you need to practice more if you want to challenge me," she said sassily, using her own racket to steal the ball he had been bouncing.

In response, Michael reached over and pulled her close, kissing her smiling lips. The tennis ball bounced away as Michaels's arms tightened and the kiss became more urgent. "I'll challenge you all right," he said huskily. "Give me five minutes to drive us home, and I will have you crying uncle," he said with a growl.

Laughing playfully, she grabbed his hand and pulled him toward his parked car. In record time, they entered his condo, pulling off their clothes as they made their way down the hall to his bedroom. Their lovemaking was loud and both silly and sexy, and Amy did indeed cry uncle twice. Later, they showered and made love again as the hot water and suds ran over their slick bodies.

Feeling a different kind of hunger—this time for lunch— Michael foraged through his bare pantry and managed to find some stale bread and peanut butter. They decided to toast the bread, and Michael opened his mostly empty refrigerator to offer Amy a beer.

"We are going to have actual groceries when I move in here, you know." Amy shook her head with amusement, finishing her sandwich and heading back to his pantry. "I can't believe you've survived on your own," she said, removing a box of open and presumably stale crackers and tossing them into the trash.

"Babe, having you here will be an upgrade for sure," Michael teased, pulling her in for another kiss. "Let me clean up these dishes, and why don't you start taking inventory of the space so we can get an idea of how many of our things we should plan to get rid of during your move."

"Good plan," Amy agreed, wandering off in the direction of his bedroom.

Michael finished in the kitchen and followed her into the bedroom just in time to see her pulling the small painting Kat had given him for Christmas off the shelf where he had placed it. He had known it would be wrong to hang it but hadn't yet figured out what to do with it.

"What's this?" she asked, holding it out to him. "I don't think I've seen this before." Amy's face held only curiosity, and Michael braced himself for her reaction to hearing the details of the picture.

"That was a Christmas gift from Kat," he said in a neutral tone, hoping Amy would just let it go.

"When did she give it to you?" Amy asked it softly, but in the quietness, he heard a building intensity. "Not this year—she wasn't there on Christmas Day, right? She was working?"

"We exchanged gifts the day we met for lunch." Michael said the words with a sense of doom.

"I feel like you lied to me." Amy's blue eyes filled with tears, and Michael felt again a mix of frustration, guilt, and weariness. She stood in his bedroom, her arms held stiffly at her sides, and a judging set to her lips.

"Amy, I admit it looks bad, but I didn't mean to hurt you. I just didn't think the decision through well enough, and then I didn't want to upset you. I was going to show it to you," he insisted.

"What did you give her?" she asked in a shaking voice.

"A locket with our first-grade picture in it."

"Jewelry, you gave her jewelry?" her voice rose, and the sobs started in earnest.

"I thought it was showing that she was my past." Michael was conscious of the pleading note in his voice.

"So, your idea of providing closure was exchanging gifts?" Amy's tears had turned to anger. She replaced the painting on the shelf in Michael's closet. "I don't want to see it again, so I hope you find someone to give it to," she said stiffly, rubbing at her tear-stained cheek.

Chapter Eleven

K aterina sat in her living room with a messy compilation of computer printouts for online restaurant postings spread on the couch beside her. She held a large red pen to use for circling any promising leads. *For all the good this has been.* Frustrated, she laid the pen down in exchange for her coffee cup.

She hadn't found anything to circle—nothing yet that even halfway appealed to her. She had no desire to go back to being a chef in a large restaurant, no matter how prominent. She had already proven to herself that she had the food chops. She was a damn good chef, but the experience she craved was having a voice in the food that was served. She was honest enough with herself to know that she did not want to run her own restaurant. She was looking for something smaller and more personal. She flashed back to Marni's observation that she seemed to be at a crossroads. *That's the truth.*

One thing she knew for certain, though, was that she needed to find something to do soon, even if it didn't meet her definition of the "right job." She was determined to protect her savings account, and she needed something to keep her busy.

Plus, she had too much time on her hands, which led to brooding about her love life, and she was still no closer to coming up with a plan for that either. She had tried to convince herself that Michael's engagement was no different than their earlier pauses, but a small, knowing voice told her it was. The engagement was public, and that made it different. Michael didn't like to be the center of attention, and he had never been comfortable when Katerina brought increased focus to them. She had accused him more than once of managing his life around the goal of being in the background.

The large engagement dinner had almost certainly not been Michael's idea, but the fact that he had taken part in it said volumes. But was he still sure enough about marrying Amy now that Katerina was back in town? He hadn't convinced her of that fact yet—and until he did, she couldn't leave it alone. She and Michael had grown up knowing they would always be together; he would come to his senses soon. New Year's Eve was in a couple of days, and she knew she would see him then. Maybe that evening would give her some additional insight for pulling her plan together.

Frustrated, depressed, and consumed with the need to burn some anxiety, Katerina abandoned her job search and changed into workout clothes. *A strenuous workout is just what I need.* She laced up her white gym shoes, and ten minutes later she was at the local gym, heading for the weight room to exhaust her body until her mind couldn't focus on anything but her screaming muscles.

Almost an hour later, Jack spotted her there. He had thought she looked good before but seeing her in black spandex and a tank top was another level. Katerina was sitting on a weight-lifting bench performing a set of military presses with free weights. Her erect posture and form highlighted the muscular definition in her arms and shoulders. Impressed with her execution, he waited until she'd completed the last rep and replaced the weights before he approached her. "Aha, so that's how you keep that shape despite being a chef," he said in a teasing voice coming up behind her.

She turned quickly toward his voice, her dark ponytail swinging over her shoulder. When she recognized his face, she rewarded him with a cocky smile that turned up the corners of her full mouth. "The real trick is to avoid eating anything I cook for the restaurant," she said, laughing.

Jack found himself entranced by her infectious grin. "Do you have time to join me for a smoothie?" he asked, hoping to prolong this unexpected encounter. It had been several days since they'd shared a drink on Christmas Day, and he'd found himself thinking about her more than he'd expected.

"I'd like that," Katerina agreed, letting him lead her to the small sitting area inside the gym that served smoothies and other healthy concoctions.

∞∞∞∞∞∞◯◯∞∞∞∞∞∞

Katarina sank gratefully into the chair Jack pulled out for her. She'd put in a good workout, and she was tired. She was also conscious of how inexplicably happy she was to see his handsome face. Somehow running into him had managed to turn her lousy morning around. *Maybe Jack was right that I need a friend right now.*

"So, what can I get you?" As he spoke, he reached forward to brush a loose tendril of dark hair off her face. Their eyes met, and she felt an unfamiliar spark of awareness that made her look quickly away.

"Peanut butter smoothie, please."

"Got it," Jack responded, but when he returned with the smoothies, the mood was broken.

Katerina convinced herself she'd only imagined it. Accepting her drink and taking a quick sip, she asked, "So, I didn't realize you worked out here—is this your regular gym?"

"Yes and no. I just moved downtown from Bainbridge Island about a year and a half ago, so I joined this gym then. I still actually spend a lot of time on Bainbridge, so I keep a membership there, too." As he replied, Jack stretched his long legs out in front of him and worked some kinks out of his shoulders.

Katerina found herself admiring his well-proportioned and muscular body. *What is wrong with me?* She forced her attention back to the conversation. "Bainbridge Island is a beautiful place, but how do you like commuting by ferry?"

"It's kind of relaxing, but it just got to the point where it was more convenient to have a place closer in, too. I entertain a lot of clients, and it becomes a long night if you add on a commute to the island," Jack explained, pausing to take a sip of his smoothie. "How's the job search going?"

"Frustrating. Nothing seems to be speaking to me. To be honest, I was here at the gym trying to burn off some frustration." She grinned at him as if she was confessing to something bad, and Jack grinned back in amusement.

There was a lull in the conversation as each of them turned their attention to their drinks. But the silence was comfortable, and neither of them felt any pressure to fill it with small talk.

Jack and Katerina lingered at their table for another ten minutes or so, casually talking about nothing in particular. He noticed her dry sense of humor and that she seemed to feel comfortable in his company.

Finally, when he could delay no longer, Jack pushed his chair back. "So, may I call you Kat?"

"Of course, everyone except my parents calls me Kat."

"The name suits you. I'm glad we ran into each other today, but I better get myself moving I still have a long day ahead."

"Thanks for the smoothie, and it was really good seeing you, too," Katerina said, her genuine smile bringing that intangible spark to her pretty face.

They each rose from their chairs, and Jack fought an urge to touch her before she walked away. An inner voice cautioned him to take it slow. A burst of frustration accompanied the inner voice—she was a beautiful and available woman, and he wasn't used to putting this much thought and caution into his interactions with the opposite sex. He sighed as he watched her walk away, enjoying the sway of her hips in spandex. *I may need a cold shower after this.*

Kat showered quickly, and as soon as she got back to her apartment, she texted Marnie.

Kat: Hey, can you talk?

Marnie: Calling you now.

The phone rang and Kat answered, "Aloha."

Marnie laughed, "Nice touch, how are you?"

"Let's start with how you are. You're the one in Oahu."

"It's the usual—in the 80s and it's sunny. This Pacific Northwest girl does *not* know how to handle all this sunshine."

"How are you spending your time while Bill's working?"

"Well, there's the time I spend worrying about my bagel shop, and the time I spend calling and micro-managing my brother about running my bagel shop. Eventually, I manage to get out and take a walk. The beach is breathtaking, and I've never seen waves like these."

"Do you and Bill get to spend any quality time together, or is he buried with work?"

"He's pretty buried. His client brought him here to help them take their business public, and it's all-consuming right now. We knew it wasn't going to be a vacation for him."

"That's too bad. Weekends, too?"

"Some, but it's all good—I'm glad to be here, and opportunities like this are rare. I know I'm lucky, and as much as I give my brother, Jeff, a hard time, I'm grateful we work together, and that he was able to step in and run the business." Marnie paused. "But how are you doing? Kat, don't sugarcoat it just because I'm not there to see your face." Marnie's tone was light, but Kat knew her friend wanted an honest answer.

"I'm doing okay, Marn. I really am. I know it's different this time with Michael, I do. And I know you think I'm stubborn, but I'm still working through issues. One interesting development, though, is that Amy has a brother. We've spent a little time together, and he wants us to be friends. I like his company, but I'm not sure it's a good idea…" Kat's voice trailed off as she talked.

Marnie laughed, "Oh, Kat, you don't know how to do simple, do you? That does sound complicated. I am fully behind any relationship you want to pursue if it makes you happy. Friends, I don't really know the answer to that. In my experience, women are more likely to see value in being friends with men than vice versa. Do you think he's hoping it turns into something more?"

"Maybe? I think there might be an attraction on his part."

"Be honest with me, girlfriend… only on his part?"

"Okay Marn, he is handsome, but the more I get to know him, he just seems like a nice guy, and I honestly like being around him."

"Just be careful, Kat—please. He may have mixed loyalties, and Amy might not be so happy about the two of you being 'friends.' But you already said it's complicated. Hey, sorry, Kat. The valet is back with my car—I've got to go."

"Thank you, as always, for your wise, married-woman counsel," Katerina said, smiling to herself.

"Love you, girl," Marnie replied with a laugh.

"Love you back," Katerina responded, ending the call.

Chapter Twelve

From his downtown office, Jack had a spectacular view of Puget Sound. Even on a gray, cloudy day, the view of that large expanse of water was breathtaking. But as Jack looked out his window, he didn't even notice. His mind was still focused on the telephone conversation he'd just had with an acquaintance. Ed Dracon ran a successful bed and breakfast and knew that Jack was transitioning his childhood home on Bainbridge Island into a B&B, too. Ed had called to see if Jack was interested in taking on a longer-term guest, a published author of mystery novels. The woman was looking for a quiet place to work through the editing process of her latest novel and was willing to pay a premium if she could be guaranteed a longer-term and exclusive stay. Jack hadn't immediately turned the offer down, but from a practical standpoint wasn't sure he could pull things together fast enough.

With only one very basic experience as a backup to Ed's overbooked inn, he was still learning the business and hadn't yet completed all the remodeling and decorating work he had planned. To be prepared for the busier late spring and summer season, he needed to stay on track with his renovations. The guaranteed income and the premium price from the author would be welcome to help finance his new venture, but he'd need to make sure his prospective guest didn't mind him moving forward with his remodeling plans. His mind began to work through the list of things he would need to do. First, he would need to hire an inn sitter to run the place, as well as someone to do some general cleaning and prep work. Reaching for a piece of paper, he scratched out a quick list of to-dos and then turned his attention back to the demands of his day job.

Later that evening, as he fixed himself a quick cheese omelet at his downtown condo, he again considered the opportunity Ed had offered him. One of the biggest obstacles he could see would be finding the inn sitter. From Ed's description, it sounded as if the author was looking for room and board including all meals. Jack didn't think that Beth Milner, the woman who had worked for him the year before, would be interested in taking on such a big role. Last year, she had helped Jack by coming in to prepare breakfast for his guests and had taken care of check-in and check-out, but Jack himself had moved back into the house on the island to be there during the nights. He didn't think that the previous pieced-together arrangement would work well for a long-term guest.

He decided to make a few calls the next day to see if he could find someone interested in filling that position. *Running a bed & breakfast inn would be easier if I actually lived there myself, but that just isn't practical for me right now.* Jack had wanted to keep the large rambling home he had grown up in, and turning it into a B&B had seemed to be a way to make it pay for itself. So far, if he was honest, it was costing him money, but he loved that house and couldn't imagine selling it. *I should get out there this weekend.* He needed a more comprehensive list of the issues left to handle if he was going to move forward with the author guest.

Chapter Thirteen

Katerina found a parking space on the crowded street near her friends' home and paused to admire the beautiful house outlined in white lights for tonight's celebration. Her friends lived on Mercer Island, one of the more affluent neighborhoods on the east side of Seattle. *It's almost like being in a fairytale.* In the darkness, Katerina admired the artistry and for the first time that year, felt the stirrings of a true holiday spirit.

Jim and Melissa were old friends, and their traditional holiday party was always a great time, with dancing, free-flowing drinks, and mouth-watering appetizers. It was just that marking off a new year left Katerina entirely too conscious that the new year could end with Michael marrying someone else. Pushing her dark thoughts to the back of her mind, she stepped up on the large, beautifully decorated porch and rang the doorbell.

After a moment, the door swung open, and Katerina was enveloped in a big bear hug from Jim. "You'll break her," Melissa exclaimed as Jim gave her one last squeeze before releasing her.

The party was in full swing, and typical of Jim and Melissa's casual irreverence for their expensive home, people were milling about, precariously balancing heaping plates of food and glasses of red wine. "Oh, Kat, it's good to see you. It's been such a long time," Melissa said, leading her in the direction of the bar and the tantalizing smells of food.

"It's good to be home," Katerina agreed, smiling at her friend and giving her arm a gentle squeeze. "I really missed everyone." She accepted a glass of red wine from the uniformed bartender while Melissa, with an apology, left her to greet another guest. Katerina wandered around the beautifully decorated rooms, enjoying the chance to see old friends she had missed.

Eventually, as she had known she would, she encountered Michael and Amy. They were standing quietly in an otherwise empty room looking out a large window at the bright lights of the Seattle skyline. Michael's arm hugged Amy close and she was leaning against him. It was a very romantic setting, and Katerina inwardly cursed her bad luck for choosing this room to enter. She seriously debated her chances of backing out of the room without being noticed, but some sound must have betrayed her because they both turned and looked in her direction. She was immediately conscious of an elevated level of tension from the two of them.

"Good evening, you two," she said brightly, praying that her voice sounded more natural to them than it did to her own ears. "Beautiful view, isn't it?" she asked, inwardly berating herself for her triviality. *Ugh, at this rate I'll be talking about the weather next.*

"Yes, it is," Amy's voice was strained and decidedly cool. Turning her back on Katerina, she once again focused her attention on the view.

"Good to see you," Michael said awkwardly. The look he gave her was a mixture of apology for Amy's dismissive attitude and a pleading for understanding.

Feeling awkward herself and not just a little put off by Amy's attitude, she returned Michael's look with an expression that she hoped conveyed her ability to take the high road even if Amy wasn't capable of it. "Well, I'll leave you then," she said, turning away, but not before she saw Michael's look of regret.

Damn him and his regret! She turned quickly and left the room, running straight into a strongly muscled chest. "Oh, I'm so sorry," she exclaimed, glancing up to see who she had bumped into and finding herself looking into a pair of amused gray eyes.

●──∞∞∞∞∞◯◯∞∞∞∞∞──●

"On the run?" Jack asked lazily, reaching out an arm to steady her.

Katerina's tense face brightened suddenly, and she looked actually happy to see him. "Oh, I didn't know you'd be here!" she blurted.

Jack tried not to act surprised by her enthusiasm. "I know Jim from some mutual business interests, and he invited me when he realized that Amy was my sister." *But I'm not going to admit out loud that I only accepted hoping to see you again.*

"Well, your sister's in there," Katerina pointed with emphasis to the room she'd just made her rapid exit from.

Jack sensed from her tone more than her words that something had upset her and most likely it had to do with the uneasy balance between Michael, Amy, and herself. Jack was beginning to feel sucked into the vortex himself. What was getting more unclear was whose cause he was championing, and for what reasons. "Well, come on then," he said, guiding her in the direction of the doorway.

"Oh, no!" she said quickly, trying to back away.

"You're tougher than that," he said with that same lazy amused tone, and before she could stop him, he had pulled her with him into the room. Although Michael and Amy were still alone in the room, the romantic mood was gone—instead, it appeared they'd been arguing. Amy's pretty face wore an expression of petulance and Michael looked as if he was trying to placate her.

They both stopped talking at the sound of someone entering the room. Michael wasn't quick enough to hide the surprise he felt at seeing the two of them together. Kat's head jerked down to look at her hand Jack still held, and she pulled to release it from his grasp. With an amused smile, he resisted her tugging for an extended moment and then finally let it go.

"Good evening," Jack said in his deep, easy voice. "Kat was kind enough to let me know where you were so I could say hi."

"Hey, Jack, good to see you, and glad you could make it," Michael responded. Beside him, Amy smiled tightly, and then her face resumed its earlier petulant expression. If she was surprised to see Jack and Katerina together, she didn't show it.

"Well, we're going to go grab a couple of glasses of wine— we'll catch you two later." Jack headed for the door, reaching for Katerina's hand again and pulling her with him. This time she seemed willing enough to follow him.

A few feet from the door, he stopped, and looking down at her, laughed. "Well, the two of them don't look to be good company right now and it is, after all, New Year's Eve. Let's go get that wine."

"Hey, you can't blame me this time. All I had done was walk into the room and said, 'Hi,'" Katerina protested half seriously, but her eyes sparkled with mischief. Her spirits seemed to be lifting in his presence.

"Well, I'm sure that looking as good as you do, that was probably more than enough." His tone was dry, but the heat in his eyes made her catch her breath.

"Well, Mr. Logan, you cut quite a fine figure yourself this evening." Katerina teased him in return as she led the way to the bar where they sipped wine and sampled the large selection of food offerings while enjoying each other's company.

∙◦◦◦◦◦◦◦◦◖◗◦◦◦◦◦◦◦◦∙

A little later, with two new glasses of wine secured, they made their way down to the lower level of the house where Jim and Melissa had hired a DJ and cleared out the large room for dancing. Kat and Jack stood for a moment watching the dancing before he set his wine glass down. Pausing as if he was weighing the consequences of his actions, he spoke, "May I have this dance?" His eyes were serious.

"I would like that," Katerina replied, looking up into his handsome face. Despite her love for Michael, she couldn't deny that she was developing feelings of some kind for this enigmatic man. Their gaze met and lingered and a slow delicious sense of awareness grew between them. Katerina found herself almost uncomfortably aware of the masculinity of his broad shoulders and long lean frame and the obvious look of appreciation in Jack's eyes as his gaze traveled over her form-fitting silver dress—so deceptively demure until you noted the high slit on the right side.

Katerina loved how time seemed to stand still while they danced. Neither of them felt the need to speak, but she sensed they both felt the intensifying bond between them. A song with a more upbeat tempo began to play, finally breaking the spell that seemed to enthrall them both.

"How about taking our wine out onto the deck to cool off for a moment?" Jack asked, still holding Katerina, but finally removing his hands from her hips as he indicated a large deck facing into the lights of the Seattle skyline.

"Sure," she replied, aware of her mixed feelings as he released her.

Rescuing their wine glasses from where they had left them earlier, they threaded through the crowd until they reached the deck. With a gentle hand on her back, Jack guided her to a corner of the deck where the wind was partially blocked. The cool air felt wonderful on her heated skin and the view was breathtaking.

"Is it too cool for you?" Jack asked, trailing a gentle finger down her bare arm.

His touch set off a spiral of sensations and she shivered more in reaction to him than to the coolness of the night. Misinterpreting her shiver, he removed his jacket and reaching forward, laid it around her shoulders. She was engulfed in the scent and the warmth of him. She turned toward his profile. His lean, chiseled features were outlined by the light of the moon, and whether it was the wine, the moonlight, or simply him, she spoke without conscious thought. "You are making me feel things I'm not ready to feel."

First, she became aware of his stillness, and then she heard the soft, amused sound of his chuckle. Turning toward her, he drew her close in the circle of his arms and laid a kiss on the top of her head. Within his arms, she had the most unsettling sense of coming home.

"Well, if it makes you feel any better, this isn't exactly what I had expected either, although I won't deny I did find you attractive the first time I saw you. I don't want to be the cause of any more confusion or pain for you, Kat."

Even as he said the words, Jack knew they were true. Looking down at her beautiful features, he knew this woman drew him in as much through her honesty and strength as she did through her beautiful face and sexy body. When they'd been dancing, Jack had lost count of the number of songs that were played. He was lost in the feeling of Katerina's exquisite body in his arms. She was the most intoxicating paradox he had ever encountered. Her skin was as soft as silk and yet there was no hiding the sleek muscle tone so evident in her bare arms and back, and in the teasing glimpse of those toned legs through the tantalizing slit of her skirt. She was so strong and self-assured and yet vulnerable at the same time.

He glanced down at the top of her dark head, and as if she could feel his gaze, she raised her head to look up at him with those spectacular golden eyes. They stood enjoying the view for another few minutes, sipping their wine in companionable silence and then, offering his hand to her, Jack suggested they head back into the warm house.

From the crowded dance floor, Michael had an unrestricted view of Katerina and Jack on the secluded deck. He felt blindsided by the two of them having some kind of relationship and acknowledged to himself that he had been searching for them in the crowd. Michael caught himself sighing out loud at Katerina's sexy dress. Some things never changed and among them was Katerina's ability to attract the attention of every eye in the room. He had never been comfortable with the attention she generated.

Outside on the deck, Jack's acceptance and respect for her feelings had helped to make Kat feel more at ease. But she felt confused by her reaction to this man. How could she love Michael and yet be so comfortable with, and yes, intensely attracted to Jack? She hadn't seriously dated anyone other than Michael, so maybe this reaction to Jack was simply the reaction she would have to any new man who paid attention to her. Even as she finished that thought she knew it wasn't true; there had been other men in Australia who'd been interested. There was something different about her feelings for Jack.

As they re-entered the house, Katerina saw that Michael's gaze was involuntarily drawn to her face from across the room, and their eyes locked in a silent exchange. She felt Jack stiffen next to her and glanced at him. Jack and Michael had just made eye contact and it was hard to read the expression on Michael's face. Jack laid a steadying hand on Katerina's shoulder as if he'd felt her steps falter slightly.

As Katerina followed in the direction that Jack indicated, her feelings were in chaos. Michael had seen her and Jack on the deck, but she hadn't been able to read his expression. Maybe seeing her with someone else would be the catalyst he needed to realize his mistake. *Maybe that will help me get Michael back. But if that's what I want, why do I feel so confused now?*

As she followed Jack toward the enthusiastic sounds of karaoke, she tried to shake off her troubling thoughts. *Obviously, I love Michael.* But she was very conscious of the dark-haired man by her side and how her pulse seemed to beat dangerously faster each time their bodies brushed together in the crowded room.

As the midnight hour neared, most of the guests began making their way to the dancing area and Katerina and Jack managed to squeeze into a small spot. If Michael and Amy were anywhere near, Katerina was too aware of Jack to notice. As the signal came that midnight was upon them, Katerina found herself longing for Jack to kiss her. She raised her gaze to his and saw the answering flame in his own eyes. Finally, he lowered his head, and she couldn't hide the shiver of longing as his lips met hers. His kiss was nothing more than a gentle brush of his lips against her own, but Katerina's lips tingled from the soft teasing contact. She was aware of the bittersweet knowledge that despite what she had said earlier, she'd wanted him to really kiss her. Jack continued to hold her close as the shouts and celebration of the new year erupted all around them.

Chapter Fourteen

The Washington State ferry pulled up to the Winslow dock on Bainbridge Island and despite the heavy gray skies and cool drizzle, Jack stood on the deck until the last minute, enjoying the view of the water and familiar shoreline. This place would always be home to him, and every time he returned, he was conscious of how much he missed it. He began to make his way down to the level where the cars were parked. Balancing what was left of his coffee with one hand, he opened his car door, slid into the seat, and waited for the slow unloading process to begin. Eventually, his turn came, and he drove off the ferry, arriving at the house in a few short minutes.

As always, just the sight of the large two-story shingled house with its gabled roofline gave him the satisfied feeling of truly being at home. Jack had grown up in this large house with only his mom for company until his early teens. He had lost his policeman father to gunshots fired during a domestic disturbance while he was still a toddler. Jack did not remember his dad, but his mother had done her best to bring him to life with pictures and her stories. He had good memories with his stepdad and Amy in the home as well, and he cherished them all.

Jack longed for the day when it made sense for him to move back to the island—if even on a part-time basis. When he had bought his Seattle condo, he had fully intended to split his time between the two locations. Island life and ferry schedules just weren't very conducive for casual dating. Without conscious thought, he pictured Katerina and wondered what she would think of the house.

Forcing his thoughts back to the job at hand, he got out of the car, and with his notebook in hand, decided to start his to-do list with a tour of the outside. He had landscapers regularly looking after the yard and it did look healthy and well-kept, so there was nothing really to handle there. The previous summer he had added a small gazebo in the back with a hot tub, which was currently empty. It would need to be cleaned and filled with water and chemicals. He wrote that on his list as he walked, but after completing the perimeter of the yard he hadn't found any additional items.

Opening the front door, he stepped inside, marveling at how a house seemed to take on a musty, deserted smell so quickly when left un-lived in. He stood in the entryway, which opened into the living room on the right, and to the left he caught a glimpse of the study through the new glass-paned doors he had recently installed. A light layering of dust seemed to cover everything, but he already had general cleaning on the list, so there was nothing new to note.

He gave the living room a critical view, noting the furniture and decorations. The large fireplace created an inviting space, but decorating was not his strong point, and he realized he'd selected furniture with comfort in mind more than style. *It feels like it's missing something.* He moved on to the kitchen, checking the appliances, noting that everything seemed to be in order.

He made a quick pass through the study which he intended to turn into a reading room. Along with the new glass doors, he had added floor-to-ceiling bookshelves, but it needed more books and some comfortable furniture. He continued to the den with a fireplace. *I'd love for this to be a game room, even though right now it just looks like a man cave.* He finished walking through the downstairs. Besides the kitchen, dining room, living room, study, and den, the original downstairs featured a powder room and a large laundry room.

Jack had added a large bedroom with a private bath, which was intended to provide the inn sitter with some privacy, and since all of the guest suites were on the second floor, they had more privacy as well. Since his fledgling B&B business was in the start-up phase, he was the only one who had used this room, and he hadn't bothered to do anything more than move in the necessities of a bed, dresser, and chest. Stepping into the room, Jack had forgotten how bare and unfinished it looked. The walls were still covered in primer and the bathroom also needed paint. Smiling to himself, Jack added the inn sitter's room to his list of to-dos. In its current state, it might scare prospective candidates away.

He made his way upstairs, to the original four bedrooms. He went first to the room at the far end of the hall, which had once belonged to his parents. The room had been remodeled to the point where it bore little resemblance to its earlier state, and he rarely thought of it in connection with his parents anymore. It was the best room in the house. *This should serve the needs of the author nicely. It has an eastern exposure, which should give her the most daylight—if there is any to be had.* He chuckled to himself, looking out at the heavy overcast day so typical of the Seattle area. The room also had a large stone fireplace that he had recently converted to gas, and an updated private bath, which now boasted a large soaking tub and separate glass shower. *The bathroom could use a new paint job.* He added it to the list.

Next, he inventoried the bedroom next door. He had added a separate bath to this room, and it, like the new bedroom and bath on the first floor, needed a paint job and to be outfitted accordingly. The last two rooms did not have their own baths but shared a bathroom in the hall. He stepped into the bedroom on the left which had been his. The room had different furniture now and like his parents' room, it was difficult to see any of his personality in this room. *It still feels nostalgic though,* Jack decided, looking at the distinctive slant to the ceiling and the large dormer window. He remembered lying in bed as a boy and looking up at that angled ceiling.

Making his way back downstairs, he added a few final touches to his list. He was glad that he had come out to the house to double-check his memory, but it was pretty much as he had remembered. The list of things to accomplish was more cosmetic than construction-related and should be able to be pulled together within a short time and with minimum disruption to his guest. *I should probably just hire a decorator to help me pull the style together.* He realized it would be expensive but likely make him money in the long run—if the B&B was appealing, he would get more business.

The larger issue by far would be his ability to find a live-in inn sitter on such short notice, and one both willing and capable of providing three meals a day. Suddenly, he remembered Katerina's comment about enjoying cooking for a few good friends. He wondered if she would have any interest in temporarily filling in as an inn sitter until he was able to find someone on a more permanent basis. *I'd get to see more of her, too, while I'm out here fixing things up.*

The more he thought about it, the more the idea appealed to him, and he was impatient to discuss it with her. Using his cell phone, he called Helen Doran, hoping to get Kat's phone number. If Helen was surprised by his request, she didn't mention it, and with Kat's number in hand, he dialed, hoping to catch her.

"Hello," she answered on the third ring. He was uncomfortably aware that just hearing her soft voice made him remember what it had been like to dance with her in his arms.

"Hi Kat, Jack here," he said, trying to banish the erotic picture from his mind and focus on the reason for his call. "How've you been?"

"Hey Jack—I'm doing good, thanks." Her voice had a surprised, questioning tone.

"I'm calling because, well, do you remember I mentioned my place on Bainbridge Island? So, last summer I turned it into a B&B, and I have an opportunity I'd like to discuss with you. I'm wondering if we could get together sometime this weekend. I apologize for the short notice, but this opportunity is something that just came up recently. And— to be honest, I would also like to see you again," he added. Even as he said the words, he was aware of how true the statement was.

There was a short pause before he heard her reply. "Sure." After a moment, she added, "It probably doesn't do a girl's reputation any good to admit that she doesn't have plans on Saturday night, but I'm not doing anything tonight if that works for you." Her tone was dry, and again he found himself impressed by her ability not to take herself too seriously.

"Well, if it makes you feel any better, I don't have anything going on either," he admitted. "But I probably can't get there much before eight o'clock." He was conscious of the fact that he was very much looking forward to seeing her tonight, even if she turned his B&B offer down.

"Okay, since it's going to be later, I could just plan on serving some appetizers and wine. We could just meet here at my condo around eight?"

Jack realized she sounded hesitant to suggest something that might become intimate, so he tried to stay upbeat and casual. "That sounds great. I'm out here on Bainbridge Island now, and that will give me plenty of time to get back to Seattle. I'm looking forward to seeing you." He added the last comment knowing that he was probably pushing her, but unable to stop himself.

After a slight pause, she answered, "I'm looking forward to seeing you, too."

Jack found himself grinning widely as he said, "I'll see you at eight o'clock and I'll bring the wine."

Returning the phone to his pocket, he locked up the house and headed for his car. He had intended to stay on the island for the night, but instead, he was now in a hurry to get back to Seattle and work through the details of what he could offer Kat that would entice her to accept his position as a temporary inn sitter. With their meeting set for eight, he still had time to hit the local hardware store to start purchasing some of the work items he would need.

Riding back across Puget Sound on the ferry, Jack had an attack of guilt as he considered the impact of where his interest in Kat was taking him. He seriously intended to make her an offer that would place her squarely in his life, even if just for the short term. He owed it to Amy to let her know and he sincerely hoped she wouldn't see it as an abandonment of her. *I'll drop by and see her tomorrow.* He loved Amy and owed her all the support she needed, but somehow Kat had become important to him, too. He wanted to see where this connection between the two of them was heading. He knew she still needed time to resolve her feelings for Michael, and he was willing to proceed at a slow pace and give her time. However, he did very much intend to move forward on his agenda.

Chapter Fifteen

Jack was outside Katerina's building promptly at eight, and when he called her condo from the outside entrance, she buzzed him in. He rode the elevator up to the third floor and knocked on her door, amazed to find himself a little bit nervous.

She answered the door on his second knock. Bending forward, he pressed a gentle kiss on her forehead. He was sure he didn't just imagine the quickening of her breathing and the slight flush on her pretty face when he stepped back. "Hi," he said softly, handing her a bouquet of defiantly yellow daffodils.

"Hi yourself. And thank you for the flowers—they're beautiful." She reached behind him to close the door, and Jack had the impression that she was a little nervous, too. She was dressed casually in a pair of snug-fitting faded denim jeans and a long-sleeved white T-shirt that hugged her curves in all the right places. Her long dark hair was loose and straight. She looked as casual and sexy as ever. *This taking it slow is not going to be easy.* Jack's mouth twitched from the effort not to smile too wide.

"Come on into the kitchen and I'll let you open the wine while I put these in some water," Katerina said, heading in the direction of her tiny kitchen. Jack followed with the bottle of wine he had brought.

"Mmm, something smells good," he said, sniffing appreciatively and peering over Katerina's shoulder into the kitchen which looked deceptively clean to be the source of such aromatic scents.

"That would be the crabmeat canapés in the oven. I thought we might start with those and some fresh fruit with cheese—and, of course, the wine." Katerina reached around him to grab a couple of wine glasses, and Jack found himself breathing in her distinctive perfume. The fresh scent again reminded him of spring.

Opening the bottle of wine, he poured each of them a glass and carried the glasses over to the small quartz island. Turning to watch her remove the appetizers from the oven, he said, "You have created such a unique and beautiful place here. Did you do the decorating yourself?"

"Thank you, and yes, decorating and design are another passion of mine—I think if I hadn't decided to be a chef, I probably would have worked in the design field. This place was a challenge simply because of its size, but now that it's done, I find myself getting restless to decorate something else. So be careful—my friends are usually the target of my decorating energies."

Laughing in response to her teasing comment, he said, "Well, Kat, do I have the offer for you—"

"Does that have anything to do with the reason you wanted to see me—your B&B?" Her golden eyes were curious as she brushed past him to set the platter of crabmeat canapés on the island. She grabbed another platter that held seasonal fruit on skewers and an assortment of cheeses.

"Well, not originally, but now I must admit I'm thinking outside the box, which could be dangerous," he warned, smiling at her as she efficiently set the island with small appetizer plates, napkins, and cutlery.

Finally finished, she sat down beside him and accepted the glass of wine he handed her. "Okay, now you've got me curious."

Jack paused, taking a bite of crispy toasted bread with a dollop of crab topping, and groaned appreciatively. "These are great," he said, reaching for a sip of his wine and looking across the counter at her pretty face. He debated on the best way to sell her on the idea, and finally, he just plunged in. "As I told you, I grew up on Bainbridge Island. When my mom married Amy's dad, we moved to Seattle, but our parents decided to keep the Bainbridge house. For a while, we spent occasional weekends there and summers, but mainly, I think they both felt like it was a good investment to hold on to it. For reasons I can't even fully fathom, that old house has always been special to me, and I think our parents grew to realize that. After college, they allowed me to move back there with a couple of buddies, and I eventually bought the house from them and remained there until about a year and a half ago when I decided to move to Seattle."

He paused for another quick bite of his appetizer and then continued. "Anyway, I still can't bear to part with it, and I finally decided to turn it into a B&B, partly so it could start paying for itself and partly because I knew that would help me rationalize putting more money into it—updating it, and so forth. I think I was also looking for an excuse to get back out there more often."

Katerina was nodding her head in understanding, and her expressive eyes were still curious as she listened. She used her tongue to catch a crumb of toast from the corner of her mouth, and Jack fought to keep his attention on his story instead of focusing on the erotic picture of her small pink tongue.

"So anyway," he went on determinedly, "last week I was asked if my B&B would be available for use by an author who needs quiet time to work through some editing. She wants an exclusive stay and is requesting meals. The bonus for me is of course regular revenue, but the downside is I'm still renovating the house, and I don't have an inn sitter who is available to provide that kind of service."

He paused for another sip of his wine and caught her eyes, "I thought of you, Kat, because I would like to get to know you better and because I remembered your comment about liking to cook in a more personal setting. I know you're still looking for a new opportunity, and I wondered if this as a fill-in gig would have any appeal. Also, there are a lot of decorating and finishing touches that need to be added, and after seeing your place again and hearing that you like that kind of thing, I could sure use your help in that area."

He again caught her gaze. She held the contact for a moment and then reached across to offer him another appetizer. Finally, she spoke. "Your offer sounds interesting, but I guess I do have a couple of concerns. First of all, I don't know anything about what is expected of an inn sitter. The cooking part would be fun, but I'd need a better understanding of what else is involved. Secondly,"—she reached across and laid her hand on his arm—"I'm not sure I want to be so far from Michael right now."

Jack didn't immediately react to her comment. Instead, he took a sip of wine, and when she moved to release her hand from his arm, he reached for it and held it firmly in his own. "Kat, the inn sitter part is pretty straightforward, and we can be flexible as needed. As for Michael… Kat, I guess I don't know what to say." She could hear the frustration in his voice and sensed that he was doing his best to mask it. "Michael is marrying Amy, unless you plan to come between them in some way?"

"You know, I don't need this from you—and I don't deserve it either!" Katerina interrupted him, her voice filled with fury and her eyes flashing with fire. She tugged on her hand, trying to release it from his grasp, and when he continued to hold it, he almost expected her to reach over and bite him. "I told you before—I just need to know that my being back in town hasn't made him change his mind!"

"And what about you?" Jack raised his voice, surprised to find himself angry. "What about what you deserve? Are you happy to just stand by waiting on the sidelines in case Michael realizes he's making a mistake?" He released her hand, and she pulled it back into her lap, rubbing at it furiously as if to remove the feel of his touch. "Jesus, Kat, I just can't reconcile the confident woman I'm getting to know with the woman who's willing to let herself be treated this way."

"You've heard more of my history than I'd suspected." The heat had gone from her voice, and it was pure ice, but her coolness couldn't hide the hint of sadness underneath.

"Probably less than you think," Jack growled back in frustration, but his tone was more controlled. "Amy has shared with me that you and Michael have been involved on and off since high school. I've gotten the impression that Michael was the one with cold feet. From what I've seen since getting to know you, I think he's a fool." Jack paused, waiting for her belligerent gaze to meet his sincere one. "Since meeting you, I have found you to be on my mind a lot—I mean that, Kat."

He watched the emotions flitting across her expressive face, and finally, she spoke, but her eyes were focused on her wine glass instead of him. "I love Michael. I've always loved him, but he has hurt me, and not just this time. We have a history of him backing away from a serious commitment with me." She smiled wryly and her anger seemed to have melted.

Jack reached for her hand, squeezing it lightly.

Kat continued, "He always ends up coming back, but each time it takes something out of me, and this time he has asked another woman to marry him—something he's never asked me." She shook her head as if still trying to comprehend it, and a small tear formed in the corner of her eye and began to trickle down her cheek. She brushed it away with a determined gesture.

She reached for her wine glass and took a sip before setting it down. She still didn't raise her eyes. Finally, she met his serious gaze with her own. Looking into his face, so handsome with its chiseled masculine features, she spoke. "Jack, I don't know if you and I should see each other anymore. I don't feel like we can be friends if you don't trust me and... I am confused by... well, by my attraction to you." Her expressive eyes were filled with misgivings, but her mouth slid up in a one-sided smile.

Jack leaned toward her. "Katerina, I don't want to let go of what we're building here, whatever it is. And I do trust you—I wouldn't spend time with you if I didn't. You have been honest about your feelings for Michael, and I respect that. Perhaps I was harsh, but I think you need to see the reality of your situation. Michael is marrying Amy, and even if you're successful in changing his mind about that, you need to question what it is you'll have achieved. You deserve someone who recognizes your value." He paused. "Now, as for this mutual attraction—it's not a bad thing." He grinned at her, trying to ease the tension. "Katerina, I promise to give you the space you need, but please give this a chance." He reached for a skewer of fruit, allowing her to regain her composure.

She felt, again, the comfortable sense of being with him. He seemed to have a knack for calming her emotions. She knew with certainty that she didn't want to cut him out of her life, even if she wasn't exactly sure where he fit in. "Deal," she finally said, and Jack found himself exhaling in relief and saw her face lighten. *She seems relieved, too.*

They finished the appetizers while enjoying an easy conversation that had nothing to do with Michael and Amy. Jack offered to help her clear the table, but insisting there was only room for one, Katerina sent him out to the living room to light the candles instead. In a moment, she joined him, carrying the bottle of wine and their glasses.

She set the items down on the leather tray and joined Jack on the couch. He noticed that she was careful not to touch him as she sat down, and he guessed that without the distraction of serving the food, she was a little bit nervous. For all her self-confidence in some areas, he sensed that her relationship with Michael had hurt her confidence in romantic relationships. Jack felt a certain resentment toward the other man for hurting Katerina and reluctantly acknowledged yet again that this relationship between the four of them was complicated.

"Why don't I fill you in on some of my thoughts regarding the inn sitter position?" he asked, wanting to put her at ease and hoping to nail down some sort of commitment from her.

At her nod, he set his wine glass down and reached for the leather folder he had set on the ottoman in front of him. He opened it and referred briefly to a handwritten list and then set it aside. "Let's talk in generalities first. As I mentioned, this won't be the typical B&B arrangement because we will only have one guest. The role will involve serving three meals a day, changing linens, and light housekeeping. I'll have a regular housekeeper come in weekly to do the main cleaning. I will be reaching out to the writer to make sure I understand any specific requests she may have. From the little I know at this point, she is looking for an isolated spot to work on edits to her latest manuscript. She selected the Northwest because it is the setting for her book, and she is hoping for inspiration."

Katerina nodded, sipping her wine, and Jack became even more conscious of how badly he wanted her to take this position. He looked across at the serious expression on her pretty face and tried to gauge her interest. She put her glass down and pulled her legs up, hugging her knees to her chest.

He wanted more than anything to reach over and kiss her soft, inviting lips. Instead, he searched for the lure that would make her decide to take the job. "I really could use your help in decorating, Kat. As I mentioned, I've done a lot of remodeling on it, so the place needs to be painted and decorated. It lacks the style that you've brought to your home." He watched her face intently and thought he saw a growing spark of interest.

"Room and board are, of course, included, and we can work out the details to make sure that you get some time off throughout the week. Also, I am prepared to compensate you for your decorating help in addition to your inn sitting since I would have paid for those services anyway." He named a figure that he felt was generous but reasonable, given the 24/7 nature of the position. "I know this is short notice, but the guest is asking for availability starting in four weeks and for the end period to be flexible."

Katerina was quiet for a moment, and then she turned to him and spoke, considering her words. "I think this might provide a nice change, and I appreciate your offer. I'm happy to help you with the decorating—to be honest, that sounds like a lot of fun. However,"—she turned to him and smiled with a hint of apology—"I hope you won't mind if I use your kitchen in my spare time to practice recipes. I've been seriously considering catering, so this could be a chance to research and come up with ideas."

"That's totally fine," Jack confirmed.

"Also, I'd like to share something with you." She sighed. "If we are going to be friends, I'd like you to have a better understanding of who I am." Jack nodded, and Kat resumed speaking. "A few years back, even as my career as a sous-chef was heating up, I knew that I didn't want to stay in restaurant work. With the full knowledge and blessing of my head chef, I continued working for him to get the experience and cooking skills I needed to stand on my own. I sold my condo and downsized to this one, freeing up my finances. The apprenticeship in Australia paid pretty well, and it allowed me the bandwidth to consider what's important to me in the food space. I don't have all the answers, but it's getting clearer to me. The decision to step back and simplify so that I could take risks for the future I want made sense to me. That choice did not go over so well with everyone else," Katerina acknowledged wryly.

Jack nodded again and grabbed her hand. "Thank you for sharing that with me. I do want to know you better, and I'm impressed with your confidence to keep adapting to work in an area you love." Squeezing her hand, he exhaled a sigh of relief and smiled at her. "I hope spending time at my B&B will give you some space to be creative—I was crossing my fingers you would accept. Let me start nailing down the arrangements on my end. The next step is probably to get you out there to view the property."

Jack's voice got softer, and as he locked eyes with Katerina, he thought he saw her catch her breath. "I'm glad you're up for this. I am looking forward to spending more time with you."

Katerina sat up straighter and smiled. "I'm looking forward to it, too."

While Jack could hear the sincerity in her tone, he could also sense that she wasn't completely comfortable vocalizing it. He wondered if she was thinking that taking this step was being unfaithful to Michael. Even though Michael was probably with Amy at this very moment, the woman he intended to marry, and hopefully not giving Katerina a second thought. The expression on Michael's face when Jack and Kat had come in from the deck at the New Year's Eve party flashed into Jack's mind. *Michael may be in love with Amy, but he could still have unresolved feelings for Kat…* Looking over at her beautiful profile as she sipped her wine, Jack had the unsettling feeling that Katerina was indeed someone who would be hard to let go.

Katerina interrupted his brooding with a quick nudge to his shoulder and a playful smile. "Hey, I don't know where you've gone, but how about a toast to our new adventure? And then if you're up for it—it must be still fairly early, only ten or so—we can see what's on Netflix."

"Sounds like a plan," he responded, reaching for the wine bottle to top off their glasses, but Katerina waved him off, deciding that the event called for opening a bottle of champagne she had brought with her from Australia. His mood was considerably lighter. Not only had she agreed to take the inn sitter position, but she was the one initiating that they spend more time together this evening. She could have simply agreed to take on the role and called it an evening.

She returned with the bottle and a couple of champagne flutes. He poured them each a glass of the dry, sparkling wine. Looking across at one another, they raised their glasses and Jack spoke, "To us." Their glasses clinked, and they both took a sip. The grin on Katerina's face let him know that she recognized his deliberately personal toast, but she didn't comment on it.

While Jack looked for a movie, Katerina cleared the ottomans so they could put their feet up. Jack leaned against the back cushions, and when Katerina joined him, he moved over a little bit so that their shoulders were touching. He was conscious of her initial stiffening, but then she must have overcome her internal struggle because he could feel her relax against him.

Shortly after midnight, Katerina could no longer contain her sleepiness, and Jack reluctantly removed his legs from the ottoman and faced her. She looked sexy and rumpled with her dark hair tangled around her face and her T-shirt coming untucked from her jeans. He managed to console himself with the thought that they had just opened the door to more opportunities like this one.

"Thanks for coming over tonight," she said, walking with him to the door. "And I meant it when I said I appreciate your offer." She was looking up at him with those beautiful eyes. His gaze shifted to her full lips, and he heard the soft intake of her breath. In her expressive face, he thought she might be expecting him to kiss her. But he knew he shouldn't—it was too soon. Instead, his finger traced the delicate diamond studs climbing the lobe of her right ear, and he caught her eyes with his own. "You are a sexy woman, Kat," he said, and then he simply lowered his head and brushed his lips against her forehead.

When he reluctantly released her, he thought he detected a quick look of disappointment in her eyes before she moved away to get his jacket. Shrugging his broad shoulders into his leather jacket, he turned to look down at her. "I look forward to doing this again," he said.

Suddenly, he very much wanted to see her again and soon. "Is next Sunday, a week from tomorrow, around 1:00 too soon for you to visit the property?" he asked.

She shook her head, "Not at all. That works, I'm sure we do have a lot of decisions to make."

Jack liked the way she had said "we." He drew her to him again briefly in a quick hug and then released her.

Her voice had a husky catch as she wished him goodnight.

Locking the door behind him, she leaned against it for support. "Damn you, Michael!" she said out loud, feeling more confused than ever.

Chapter Sixteen

The expression on Amy's face warred between frustration and surrender. Her blue eyes held a sheen of tears, and Jack could see that the hand not holding her coffee cup was clenched tightly in her lap.

"So, you're under her spell, too," she stated quietly, dropping her eyes so they didn't quite meet his concerned gaze.

"I am interested in getting to know her better, and I could use her talents, and she has the time right now," Jack replied slowly, watching for her reaction. So far, the discussion had progressed about how he had imagined. Amy's initial reaction to the plan for Katerina to help Jack with the B&B had been anger.

"It's just, why does it have to be her? It's not enough that Katerina is basically a part of his family, I mean her relationship with his parents is strong enough for me to know that she will be included in all of Michael's family events. Helen was showing me some pictures of Michael as a child… Do you realize that Katerina is in all their family albums? But now, you're asking me to see her at our family events, too. I need some space from her!"

Jack reached over and pulled the hand from her lap and held it in his own two hands. "Look at me, sis. The holidays are over—how many family events do we have planned?" His voice held a hint of laughter, and Amy gave a reluctant half-smile at her over-dramatization of the situation, but then her tone turned serious.

"It scares me, Jack. I mean, having her around throws me off. I think Michael is uncomfortable, and I guess, to be honest, I think he's confused about how to treat her now. They've had a lifelong relationship, much of which has been romantic. I admire him for not wanting to hurt her, but at the same time, I hate him for caring. I try not to let him know how much she bothers me because I don't want him to focus his attention on her. I'm afraid he'll want her back." The tears had started in earnest, and she pulled her hands free to search for a tissue in her purse.

"Hey, hey." Jack waited while she blew her nose and then pulled her close, hugging her tight. When her sniffling had quieted and she sat back on the couch, he caught her watery blue eyes with his own and said solemnly, "Amy, Michael has had every opportunity to ask Kat to marry him. That never happened, and I'm sure he has good reasons for why he asked you instead."

"I guess you're right," she responded slowly without conviction, "but I do think he's having some struggles with her being around. I'm sure it wasn't lost on you or Kat that I was in a bad mood on New Year's Eve. Maybe you're doing me a favor by taking her at least a little bit out of his path." Amy sniffed and wiped at a tear. "I want to be confident, but it's hard—Kat's a part of their family whether I like it or not."

Jack couldn't help flashing back to the look on Michael's face on New Year's Eve. He hadn't been sure how to interpret that look then, and he still wasn't. One thing was certain: there was nothing to gain by including Amy in his speculation. He was confident that Michael loved Amy and truly believed that Kat's return was just a temporary strain.

Jack accepted the cup of coffee his sister offered and then tried to cheer her up by asking her about her move into Michael's condo and her wedding plan updates. He felt bad that his intention to include Kat in his B&B plans had upset Amy, and he hoped he was being honest with himself. *Am I crazy to hope that Kat and I could have some sort of relationship?*

━━◦∞∞∞∞∞◖◗∞∞∞∞∞◦━━

Amy gave her brother a goodbye hug at the door and headed back into the kitchen to get another cup of coffee she didn't need. Her nerves were already shot; caffeine would only make her more jittery, but she poured the cup anyway.

Running an unsteady hand through her blonde hair, she considered the rollercoaster of emotions that the last few weeks had brought. It was clear to her that all the lows could be directly attributed to Katerina. She resented the other woman intensely for ruining what should have been some of the happiest days of her life. The joy of her engagement and the holiday season was overshadowed by the strain of trying to feel secure in Michael's love. Michael was everything Amy had ever dreamed of finding. *He makes me feel safe, secure, and loved.*

Sometimes she felt like her brother wished she would be more independent, but Michael seemed to like her relying on him for decisions. This last year had been a magical time, falling in love and making plans for the future. It wasn't as if Michael hadn't told her about his history with Kat, but somehow with the other woman so far away, it hadn't seemed like a big deal.

Now, it felt like a train wreck happening in slow motion. She trusted Michael, but it was impossible not to resent him for still caring about Kat. *I don't think he needs to feel obligated—Kat seems like someone who can take care of herself.*

Chapter Seventeen

Katerina powered down the treadmill and wiped her face with her towel. Five grueling miles and she still hadn't managed to quiet her mind. *How is Michael going to react to me helping Jack with his B&B? Will he be jealous, or just view this as another example of me being impetuous?* Maybe he would see this as another failure on her part to find a traditional job and color inside the lines. Worse yet, would he only be worried about Amy's feelings? Even with all these unanswered questions, she was honest enough to recognize that she was determined to accept Jack's offer.

Clearly, she needed another diversionary tactic to calm her roiling thoughts. As she showered, she decided the market was the perfect plan. A well-stocked grocery store was to her the equivalent of a candy store for a child. Something about standing in the fresh produce aisle and brainstorming new menu items worked as a release every time. Jack was going to pick her up tomorrow to take her to his house on Bainbridge Island. It might be both fun and practical to plan a picnic to bring with them. Grabbing her coat and keys, she closed her front door and headed to the elevator. *I'm going to enjoy myself today.*

Across town, Michael paced the living room of his condo, filled with restless energy. He had dropped by Amy's on the way home from coaching a high school soccer game, and she had filled him in on Jack and Kat's plan. After being moody and sullen all week, Amy had finally told him about Jack's visit the previous Sunday. She was upset with Jack and what she felt was another intrusion of Kat into their lives. The need to comfort and reassure her had thankfully allowed him the opportunity to cover his surprise. He needed to call Kat and see if he could stop this. The whole culinary experiment had been a trainwreck—bad hours, sketchy co-workers—and Kat had been too stubborn to admit it. Now, she was going off on another tangent and, God help him, he needed to help her see reason. He felt the familiar pressure behind his eyes—another headache coming on.

Chapter Eighteen

*J*ack headed toward Katerina's condo with light steps after she'd buzzed him in. He was looking forward to the day with her. She opened her door on the first knock.

"Hi," she said brightly, and again he felt the impact of her dazzling smile when it was given genuinely.

"Hi yourself," he said, kissing her cheek. As soon as he released her, he became aware of the mouthwatering cooking aromas in the air. "Wow, something smells great!"

Katerina smiled and pointed toward a wicker picnic basket lying beside the door. A leather portfolio was propped against it. "I made us a picnic dinner," she explained, zipping up a red jacket over her thick, oatmeal-colored sweater and grabbing a pair of gloves from the shelf in her closet. "Now, let's get this show on the road—I'm anxious to see your house."

"After you," Jack offered, opening the door and stooping to pick up the picnic basket. Katerina grabbed the portfolio and locked the door behind them.

"Thanks for packing dinner—that was a great idea. What's in the portfolio?" he asked with curiosity.

"Just some decorating stuff, paint samples, and furniture groupings that have caught my eye over the years." Katarina grinned. "I wasn't kidding when I said I love to play around with decorating, and I thought this stuff might be helpful so that I could get a better idea of your taste. I know you want to move fast on this, but we still want to make sure you like the end result. I also researched some B&Bs on the island and printed some pictures because you might want to consider being similar vs. presenting an alternative to the norm."

The inherent competence of Katerina's comments impressed Jack even more. She was a confident and independent woman, and he found that very attractive.

He had spent the morning making the necessary phone calls to the B&B association and his prospective guest, the author. He now had tentative dates and an idea of the expected amenities and service levels requested by the author. Out of curiosity, he had gotten online and discovered that she had two books currently in print. On his way to Katerina's condo, he had dropped by a bookstore to buy them for her. As he opened the car door for Katerina, he grabbed a wrapped package and handed it to her.

"What's this?" she asked, smiling up at him.

"I bought you a couple of recent books written by the author who will be staying at my B&B. Her name is Jessica Lowry. You mentioned that you love to read, and I thought it might be fun for you to read these since you're going to meet her soon."

"How fun and thoughtful!" she exclaimed excitedly, reaching up to hug him. "Thank you. I can't wait to start in on them." As soon as she had fastened her seat belt, she began tearing at the wrapping paper to study the two books. They were both romantic suspense, one set in Louisiana in the Bayou Country and the other set in Sedona, Arizona. "These both seem interesting, and I'm curious to learn what her book-in-progress is like, too—I'm looking forward to meeting her."

Jack pointed to the author's picture on the back cover that showed a young woman with curly brown hair and a wide, engaging smile. "Well, I talked to her today and she confirmed her stay at my B&B," he said, smiling.

In no time at all, they were pulling up to the ferry dock where a line of cars was waiting to board. Jack nosed the Mercedes into the line, put the car in park, and shut it off while they waited for their turn. Looking over at Katerina he asked, "So what's in that picnic basket that smells so damn good?"

"Well, we have grilled rosemary-lemon chicken, sliced tomatoes in a creamy onion dressing, French bread, marinated olives, and brownies for dessert. Oh, and I packed a bottle of wine. I thought eating at the house would give us more time to map out the details, and I thought it would be fun," Katerina explained, grinning over at Jack.

Jack found his attention pulled away from the delicious aromas coming from the picnic basket and back to the equally enticing charms of the beautiful woman across from him. The combination of her playfulness in contrast to her strength attracted him. He liked that she was comfortable taking the initiative. "Sounds like a great plan. I appreciate your willingness to take this on in such a hurry."

"Hey, right now, time is something I have to offer." Her tone was wry, and the smile they shared was companionable. "You know, it's relaxing in a way to start a friendship knowing so much about each other. It's refreshing not to be playing the typical games." The smile she turned in Jack's direction held a tinge of sorrow, and her eyes had lost some of their sparkle. Jack realized she was thinking of her relationship with Michael.

"Does it ever occur to you that maybe we feel a connection simply because of the two of us?" In the close confines of the quiet car, Jack heard Katerina's startled intake of breath.

After a while, the car in front of him began to move, and Jack's attention shifted to his driving. The silence between the two of them was charged with unspoken thoughts. They pulled onto the ferry and parked in the designated loading zone.

"How about some coffee and then heading to the top deck?" Katerina asked. She seemed determined to regain her earlier bright spirits.

He grinned widely when he caught her watching him appreciatively, and she looked away quickly. "Sounds great," he said, "but it's going to be cold up there on the deck. You sure you're up for it?"

"Yeah, at least for a little bit—we should take advantage of this rare sunny day in the middle of winter. You can't beat the view from there." She grabbed his hand and pulled him in the direction of the stairs leading up to the concession area. A few short minutes later, they were standing on the top deck, holding their hot coffee and trying to catch their breath in the cold wind.

Katerina faced into the wind with a determined look on her face. Jack couldn't help but smile at the fierce expression as she stood there gripping her coffee, her long, dark ponytail whipping around her shoulders. If that expression was any indication of how she took on challenges, look out! He reflected on the night of the Dorans' Christmas party and her friend's comment about how Katerina had always managed to get Michael back after their time-outs. But the friend had been talking about an earlier time in their lives. *Will Katerina be successful this time in getting Michael back, despite his engagement to Amy?* Jack wasn't convinced he knew the answer to that question.

Stepping behind Katerina, he pulled her back to lean against his chest, wrapping his arms around her to give her added warmth and protection from the wind. She stiffened but then relaxed, and Jack almost groaned out loud at the reaction of his body as she innocently pressed her alluring little backside against him.

They stood there silently enjoying the view of the Olympic Mountains on the western horizon and the city skyline on the east. He pressed a light kiss on the top of her dark head, and she tilted her head to smile up at him. Tightening his arms around her, he gave her a gentle squeeze and considered for the first time the chance that he might not come out of this relationship unscathed.

They remained on the deck until the outline of the island appeared on the horizon, before making their way back down to the car. Jack found himself both excited and anxious to show Katerina the house he loved. He realized it mattered a lot to him that she liked it, too.

Driving along the winding road, he could see the house as it appeared around the bend on his left. "That's it, isn't it?" Katerina said excitedly, pointing at the house. "It's just like you described it, but you never said you could see Puget Sound from your place!" she added before he could answer. He nodded, laughing at her enthusiasm.

As he pulled the car into the driveway, he asked, "Would you like a tour of the yard first or do you want to go straight inside?"

"Oh, I want to see the house first," she said, pulling impatiently on his arm. "This is going to be a lot of fun, I promise you," she said with a contagious grin.

"Fun, or just expensive?" he teased her back.

"Both," she said in a perfectly serious voice, and they both laughed, knowing it was probably the truth.

He opened the front door, and turning to let Katerina enter first, he noticed that she had walked several feet in the opposite direction and was looking at the house from the edge of the driveway.

"Did you change your mind about coming in?" he asked with lazy amusement.

"No," she said. "This might be silly, but I just always feel like the inside of a house should try and have the same basic personality as the outside of the house, so, I wanted to decide what kind of house you have." The look on her pretty face was very earnest.

"So, what kind of personality do you think my house has?" he asked more than half seriously.

"Well, it reminds me of a house you might see on the East Coast shore, like maybe Connecticut. I like the shingles, and the white trim around your windows and doors. It looks casual and relaxed, and it makes me feel like the inside should have a cozy retreat feel. I like the way the house sits on your lot. I know we'll see more of the outside later, but I like what I see so far."

"So do you enjoy landscaping, too?" he asked, surprised yet again by her.

"I love everything about making a home comfortable. I just get into this stuff—I don't really know why…" Her voice faded a bit, and Jack had the impression that something had made her unhappy.

"Come on," he said, covering the distance between them in a few large steps and grabbing her hand. "Let's go inside. Just keep in mind that what you see will be my attempts so far at decorating, and I have a feeling you will want to make some changes." Jack made a comical face, and Katerina laughed.

∞∞∞∞∞∞(∞∞∞∞∞∞

Inside the house, Katerina walked from room to room, reaching down to touch the aged patina of the wide plank oak floors. She admired the trim work and the wood casing around the windows, which had been painted white. She loved the large stone fireplace that dominated one whole wall in the den. She sighed in pleasure when she saw the large kitchen with French doors opening out to a garden patio.

She seemed undaunted by the newly constructed areas and the empty rooms. "Oh, those are the fun rooms," she assured him. "You get to start from scratch, and these rooms, even though they are new, have the same personality as the rest of the house. When we're done, you will never know they were added. Your contractor did a great job."

"That's good to hear because I was the contractor," Jack said, unable to hide his smile.

"You're kidding, right?" Katerina asked, surprise evident on her face.

"No, I'm serious—I worked construction during the summers at my stepdad's construction company, and when it came to doing this work, I guess I just feel pretty territorial about this house, and I wanted to do it myself."

"Wow, I'm impressed, and to be honest, now that I know you're handy, I'm even less concerned about our short timeframe. Between the two of us, we can get this place painted in no time, and then I can start the decorating. Depending on what we decide to do, we may have to order some stuff. But, Jack,

this is a great house—I can see why it means so much to you."
Katerina's eyes shone as she twirled around in the living room.

"What's that supposed to mean, now that you know I'm
handy?" Jack asked with amusement.

Katerina's smile looked sheepish. "I guess I thought you
would be more the type to pay for construction and painting to
be done, rather than do it yourself. If you're okay with it, it might
make sense for me to move in here early. I can handle a lot of the
painting, and that would give me another chance to think through
the decorating. It would also save time, which is a premium."

"Kat, are you sure about that? I agree that any time savings
are a valuable commodity, but I don't want to put you out. You
just got home from Australia." Jack's face showed only concern
for her.

Katerina flashed back to Michael's calls and knew with
certainty that he was trying to stop her from taking this
position—and that he wasn't pleased she and Jack were
spending time together. If she made arrangements with Jack
for her to move in immediately, it wouldn't allow Michael a
chance to talk her out of this. *God knows I need something to do,
and if this is uncomfortable for Michael, maybe that works in my
not-yet-pulled-together "plan."*

"I'm sure, Jack. If you can get me a key, I'll pack up some
things and come over on the ferry Monday."

"If you don't mind waiting until later in the afternoon, I'll
come and help you. You will want your car here, but let me
make sure you're settled in and understand the security system,
and where things are, etc."

"Jack, that isn't necessary," Katerina protested, laying her
hand on his arm. "I'm sure I can manage just fine, and it will
save you the trouble of coming back out here."

"Coming back out here is no trouble—I'm used to commuting, remember—and besides, I insist on it." He had covered her hand with his own, and now he laced his fingers through hers and pulled her toward the stairs. "Let me show you the attic. I have stored a lot of my parents' items that I kept—you might find some things up there that you want to use. And Katerina, make yourself at home. Browse around the attic, move things around, change whatever you like. This house has always been important to me, but I am under no misconceptions about my lack of skills in the decorating area."

The attic was dimly lit and dusty. Once or twice, Katerina walked into a spider's web and shuddered as she brushed herself off. She prayed that no spiders had become lodged in her hair or clothing. Jack walked in front of her, lifting back corners of sheets that had been used to shroud furniture. He opened several boxes, and Katerina caught glimpses of lamps and other accessories. It took only moments for her to lose all fear of the spiders and react like a child at Christmas. Pulling the sheet completely off a small chest, she traced her finger over its delicately carved surface. "How lovely," she exclaimed reverently, conscious of the fact that these items had belonged to the mother he had lost.

"It would be nice to see some of these items in the space," Jack said, coming to stand beside her and looking at the chest that had caught her attention. "My mother had a lot of beautiful things, and I didn't want to sell them, but I wasn't exactly sure how to use them either."

"Doesn't your sister want any of these items?" Katerina asked with curiosity.

"We both went through and took what we wanted, but to be honest, Amy didn't want all the ghosts that go with this." He waved his arm to encompass the attic brimming with boxes and indeterminate shapes.

"And you?" Katerina tilted her head up to look into Jack's eyes. "How are you going to feel if some of these things are used in your home?"

"Time has passed," he said quietly. "I miss them both still, but I would enjoy seeing remembrances of them."

"I will look around, and I bet we'll find a lot of good uses, but please just tell me if something doesn't feel right, okay?" Katerina reached up on her toes to give him a soft kiss on the cheek, and Jack held her tight for a moment before releasing her.

"Deal," he said. "Now, how about checking out that picnic?"

Downstairs, they retrieved the picnic basket, and Katerina began laying out the items. She had brought a beautiful, brushed cotton tablecloth in muted shades of peach, gray, and cream, which she laid over the kitchen table. Next, she unpacked the food, which looked as appetizing as it smelled. Reaching in the basket again, she unloaded coordinating colored picnic plates, stemware, and utensils. And last, she retrieved a fragrant cluster of heather, secured with a ribbon, and a vase to rest it in.

"Very impressive, Ms. Gascay," Jack said, looking over his shoulder while he opened the wine bottle. "You certainly have a talent for pulling the whole package together. You know, you really might be right on target with the catering idea. It seems like that could take advantage of both your cooking and your flair for style."

"Thanks, I think that's part of the appeal for me," Katerina said, laying out the place settings and giving the tomato salad a quick stir. A warm feeling of satisfaction came over her that he had noticed and genuinely appreciated her efforts. She was also surprised that he had been so quick to recognize the essence of what she truly enjoyed. Again, she had the sense that there was a depth to Jack that one might not guess from simply looking at the very handsome and confident exterior of the man.

Over the picnic dinner, Jack shared stories of growing up on the island and a sense of the small community that she would now be a part of. "There is still a small-town feel to Bainbridge Island despite its proximity to Seattle," he explained, giving Katerina a wistful smile. "I think that's why I love it here. Many residents rarely find reasons to leave the island, and since the community offers most of the major services, you can have the conveniences you are used to without going into Seattle.

"For instance, there's a decent hardware and paint store, so we can buy a lot of our supplies locally. I am guessing, however, that you may need to go to Seattle for some of the accessory and furniture shopping and other specialty items."

"I look forward to spending some time here," Katerina said, and was surprised to find that she genuinely meant it. Jack had a beautiful house, and it would be great fun to decorate it. She was also looking forward to the cooking aspects of the position. The downside was the very real fear that by being farther away from Michael, she would have less chance of making him realize his mistake. But she admitted to herself, her proximity hadn't yielded results yet. *Maybe this is the perfect opportunity to make him jealous.* She considered what Michael would say when she finally answered his calls.

With an uncomfortable start, Katerina realized that she felt guilty for the direction her thoughts had taken. How would Jack feel if he knew she had even considered this position as a catalyst to make Michael come back to her? *At least I've been honest with Jack about my feelings for Michael.*

Forcing her thoughts back to the present, she grabbed her portfolio and smiled at Jack. "I'd like a better understanding of your likes and dislikes so I can visualize the right colors and personality for the house." She began quizzing him on his preferences as he reached for a second brownie. She also showed him pictures of the other competing B&Bs' guest suites.

"I guess I'm curious about what you would do here if the decision was all yours." Jack swept an arm around to encompass the living area. "When I look at the house right now, even the rooms that are complete and furnished look unfinished somehow. Apparently, construction I can handle, but the rest is beyond me."

"Okay… if it were all up to me, huh?" Katerina took a sip of wine and was silent as she considered. Finally, she spoke. "Here's my first take on this. As I mentioned before, this house has a New England, Hamptons kind of feel to it. For me, that feels like a vacation—cozy and comfortable. Combine that with the fact that you intend to use this for a B&B, add in pampering, and I think that defines your style. I think you get there by using warm, neutral paint tones along with some darker hues than you have now." Her words began tumbling out as she got deeper into her subject. Her golden eyes were alight with enthusiasm.

"This is a resort, a getaway, and it should feel more styled than the average home. However, I think your competition is going in a heavier, and in my opinion, dated style. I would try to keep it cleaner and more modern." Reaching over to him, she grabbed his hands in excitement. "Oh, this will be such fun! We won't be able to get to everything that you ultimately want done before Jessica arrives because furnishings will take time, but we can paint and bring some style to what we have."

Jack couldn't stop himself from laughing at her animation and excitement. "Okay, I'm all in—let's go with your plan. God knows your sense of style is much more defined than mine. On my own, I can't get beyond the basic furniture requirements and the fact that the walls should be painted in something other than primer."

───≈∞∞∞∞∞∞◯◯∞∞∞∞∞∞≈───

Katerina was already out of her chair, pacing back and forth through the connecting kitchen and dining room. With a satisfied smile, Jack followed her lead; he had a good feeling about this partnership.

On the ferry ride back to Seattle, Katerina and Jack confirmed their plans for her move to the island house. She was still keyed up with excitement and tried to put to rest Jack's fear that he was imposing on her by having her stay there and get a head start on some of the painting on her own. Finally, he gave up the argument, sensing that she was determined, and promised instead to help on the weekend.

When he pulled his car up to her front door, she reached over and hugged him. It took all his control not to grab her and kiss the lips he wanted so badly to taste. Instead, he squeezed her shoulder lightly and watched as she entered her building.

Chapter Nineteen

riday night found Jack driving up the road to his island house with anticipation. He and Katerina had spoken numerous times on the phone. She had shared various color palettes with him electronically, and after getting his approval, she had started work. On their last call, she had been ecstatic about how the newly painted walls were bringing the rooms together, but this was his first chance to view the changes for himself.

He was spending the weekend at the house, and if some of his anticipation was due to the thought of spending two whole days and nights under the same roof as Katerina, well, he was a red-blooded male after all.

He pulled into the driveway and was getting his bag out of the car when Katerina rushed out of the house wearing an oversize T-shirt and leggings. Her dark hair was pulled back into a ponytail, and she had a splash of gray paint on her cheek. In her excitement, she practically launched herself into his arms. "Come here, come here!" she demanded, tugging him impatiently by the arm.

Laughing, he allowed her to pull him toward the back entrance. Stepping through the French doors that led into the kitchen, he had to admit that the paint she called *sea salt* was a beautifully subtle contrast to the white crown molding and the framing around the windows and French doors. The stainless-steel appliances and white painted cabinets seemed to come to life surrounded by the painted walls.

"Wow," was all he managed as she continued pulling him from room to room where the painted walls now reflected various shades of grays, creamy whites, and mushroom tones. The den/game room was painted the darkest hue—a charcoal gray called *iron ore*. "Wow," he said again. "Great choices and well done." He complimented her work, looking closely at how well she had handled the corners and angles where molding and framing had created painting challenges.

"Thanks—so you like it?" Kat's enthusiasm was contagious, yet underneath, he could sense her anxiousness to be reassured that he approved. "Absolutely!" he said, laughing and hugging her, feeling her release a sigh of relief. "I'm really glad you had this vision. I think it's a nice change from all of the plain white walls."

"Were they always white?" she asked.

"No, when my mom lived here, there was a lot of wallpaper. I pulled it down when my buddies and I moved in. Wouldn't do for a bachelor pad to be sporting wallpaper with flowers on it, would it?" he asked with mock seriousness.

"Of course not." Katerina teased back, "A bachelor's pad must stick to the manly man's code of decorating rules, featuring lots of dirty laundry and towering displays of empty beer cans."

"Wow, I didn't realize we'd had you over to the place," Jack said, laughing. "I would have thought I'd remember."

Katerina wrinkled her nose back at him and responded, "Okay, now that you've seen my hard work, I'm hungry. Can we order a pizza?"

"Sounds good, but are you sure you wouldn't rather go out?"

"I'm way too lazy for that, if you don't mind," she said. "I've been working my ass off, Mister."

"Well then, pizza you shall have." With a smile, Jack watched her leave the room. He enjoyed her quick wit and playful personality. *Yeah,* he admitted to himself, *I'm getting pretty hooked on this girl.*

Jack had insisted that Katerina stay in the nicest room while they were working on the house, so she had moved into the master bedroom upstairs. Stripping quickly, she stood under the hot spray of the shower in the adjoining bathroom, enjoying the warmth on her aching back and shoulder muscles. Painting was harder work than it looked—a lot of reaching. She quickly lathered and rinsed her hair. Besides being in a hurry to eat, she was excited to hang out with Jack. True, she had been left to her own company for the greater part of a week, but being a bit of an introvert, that wasn't usually a problem. *Be honest,* she told herself, *you like being with this guy.*

Jack was just opening the door for the pizza delivery when Katerina came bounding back down the stairs. She had showered and changed into another long-sleeve cotton shirt and leggings. Damn, whenever she wore those leggings, his body went into overdrive. *Does she have any idea how sexy she looks?* He watched her laying out plates and chattering animatedly, and decided she didn't have a clue. He set the pizza on the counter and turned just in time to see her reaching up for the wine glasses. As the fabric of her cotton shirt strained against her rounded breasts, he saw the clear outline of her nipple and almost groaned out loud. Great, if the leggings didn't kill him, the fact that she wasn't wearing a bra might.

They ate the pizza at the kitchen table, and Katerina kept up a steady stream of conversation. She had met Beth Milner, the former inn sitter, and had gotten some tips from her. She had checked out the local grocery store, farmer's market, and the gym. She had bought the paint they would need to finish the rooms over the weekend. She had started an inventory list of the attic contents.

When he finally found an opening to interject, Jack asked with amazement, "So do you always jump into projects with this much energy? No wonder you're tired."

Immediately the spark left her eyes. It was as if all of the vitality had drained from her. "I'm sorry, am I pushing where you don't want me to be?" Her tone was almost as flat as her expression, but he sensed anxiety that she couldn't completely mask.

Jack was floored at the change in her and equally surprised by a ferocious desire to protect her. It was almost as if she'd been conditioned to feel like her initiative and enthusiasm should be curbed. Without thinking, he walked around to her chair and reached down, pulling her to her feet and hugging her tightly. "Kat, honey, what is it—what did I say? Of course, you're not pushing where you don't belong. You're amazing and I'm impressed!"

Her small frame had been tight, but as he spoke, he felt her loosen up. When he finally went to release her, she squeezed him back. With a gentle finger, he tilted her chin up and looked intently into her eyes. "Are we okay?" he asked gently.

"Yeah, we are—thank you." Her husky voice was soft, but Jack sensed the iron strength of control she was exerting to mask her emotions. He wanted to demand an explanation but could see that she didn't want to talk. Despite her best efforts, he could sense her fragility. So instead, he pulled her by the hand in the direction of the living room.

When they reached the room, he turned the switch on the wall, igniting the gas fireplace. Next, he searched his phone's music library for a song. As the soft strains of an R&B song began to play, he pushed the coffee table up against the wall and turned to Katerina. "Ever since New Year's Eve, I have wanted to do this again. Will you please dance with me?" he asked quietly.

Katerina looked up at him in surprise, and when she saw the gentleness in his eyes, she allowed him to pull her into his arms. Clasping his shoulders, she leaned into him and rested her head on his chest. His arms held her tightly but tenderly as the fire cast flickering shadows, and the music played softly.

Without the heels she had worn to the holiday party, the difference in their heights was further exaggerated. Holding her body as they danced, Jack was painfully conscious of her near-naked breasts pressed against him and the skin-tight spandex leggings, but surprisingly his strongest feelings were tenderness and a desire to see her flash her big genuine smile again.

After a few songs, Katerina lifted her head and smiled up at him. Sensing a lightening of her spirit, he suggested more upbeat music and offered to teach her some swing dancing moves. It wasn't long before he had her laughing out loud as she fought to extricate herself from the tangle of arms and legs caused by their missteps.

Finally, she turned to him. "You don't really know how to swing dance, do you?" she asked suspiciously.

"Not a single step," Jack admitted with a completely straight expression. Katerina collapsed in laughter, giving him a big hug.

"You know, for such a sexy guy, you're awfully sweet."

"So, you think I'm sexy?" he asked, leering suggestively at her.

"Don't press your luck, but I am going to go get a glass of wine and whatever happens, happens," Katerina teased.

Laughing, Jack grabbed her hand and pulled her toward the kitchen. "I'll pour."

They ended up sipping their wine and arguing over which movie to watch. Finally, they agreed to a quarter toss, and Jack lost. Katerina selected a sappy chick flick, and he figured her choice had more to do with gloating over winning than any real desire to see the movie. Halfway through, he looked over and caught her sleeping. He was tempted to wake her up and demand that she continue watching the bad show but decided instead to switch movies to one of his choices, which also gave him the extra benefit of watching her as she slept. *I like to look at her.* Yeah, he had a thing for this girl.

When his movie ended, he decided to call it a night. Leaning over Katerina, he tickled her cheek. She opened one eye and grinned sleepily at him before closing it again. "Oh, no you don't, you are paid labor, and I have a busy day planned for you tomorrow." He heard a muffled obscenity, but she let him pull her to her feet. She was still grinning at him with a sleepy expression when he planted a quick goodnight kiss on her lips, and, turning her in the direction of the stairs, smacked her on her delicious little rear end.

Chapter Twenty

He awoke in the morning to the sound and aroma of coffee percolating. Throwing on a comfy sweatsuit, he ran his fingers through his hair and headed in the direction of the kitchen. He reached the door just as Katerina was reaching up into the cabinet to get some sugar. He was treated to a repeat of last night's performance, except today she was wearing only a skimpy tank top and flannel shorts, and he not only got the outline view of her breasts but a significant shot of her cleavage as the material bunched up. *I'm going to need to move things to lower shelves or just stop coming into the kitchen at all.*

When she heard his footsteps, she gave him a big smile, and he figured her for a morning person. "Coffee?" she offered.

"Sure, thanks," he replied as she came around the corner to hand it to him. That's when he got to see her legs, and they looked just as great as he had imagined they would—very toned. He took a quick sip of his coffee, burning his tongue, but at least it gave him something besides her legs to focus on.

Katerina set her coffee cup down near Jack and couldn't help but notice how sexy he looked when he was rumpled. His dark hair looked like he had been running his fingers through it again, and he needed to shave. She wondered what it was like to kiss a man with that much razor stubble. Somehow, it just added to the sexy, very maleness of him. His sweatshirt was only zipped partway up, and she could see enough to know that he had a nice chest. *Very nice, actually.* The whole package was very nice indeed.

"Well, I just came down to get some coffee. I'm going to take it upstairs and shower. See you in a few," Katerina said, heading out the door. That's when Jack noticed the ridiculous pig slippers attached to those incredible legs. The sound of his laughter followed her out.

"What's so funny?" she called back.

"What's with the slippers?" he asked.

"Oh, just my friend Marnie's idea of a bad chef joke. You know, pork, the other white meat." As she reached the stairs, she could still hear him laughing.

While she showered, her thoughts drifted to dancing with Jack the evening before. *He's sexy and sweet.* She'd felt a part of herself melt for him when he'd held her so gently in his arms. She realized she'd gotten distracted and had soaped herself up again. *Snap out of it, girl. This is a job, and you've got a busy day planned.*

⊷∘ᴑᴑᴑᴑᴑᴑᴑᴑᴑ◖◗ᴑᴑᴑᴑᴑᴑᴑᴑᴑ∘⊷

Katerina had already taped off most of the necessary woodwork, so they were able to get right to the painting. They were starting in Jack's boyhood bedroom. She had selected a rich, creamy taupe with pink tones, and a darker but still subtly pink-hued paint for the ceiling.

Jack got ceiling duty, which was very tiring on the arms. Occasionally, he would take a moment to rest and watch Katerina painting the walls. He was amazed at how much she had been able to accomplish. He hadn't thought about it until he watched her paint, but her petite frame meant she couldn't cover nearly as big of an area. Looking down at her, he noticed a new spot of paint on her cheek. "Hey, Splash, how come you always seem to get paint on your face?"

She rubbed at her cheek and scowled at him, but he could see the grin underneath her scowl. When they finished the second coat, she stood back and reviewed the effect with satisfaction. "I bet this ends up being my favorite room. I love how this angled ceiling looks with this color of paint and those great dormer windows."

"It does look good—you've had some great ideas," he said, getting down off the ladder and stretching his shoulders.

"Yeah, I think I'm going to raise my rates," Katerina teased.

"How about I buy you lunch instead?" Jack countered.

"Deal. I could do with a burger and fries."

"Wow, so far, you've been pretty easy to please, first pizza and now a burger and fries. You know, Splash, you're kind of a cheap date." He laughed as she swung playfully at him.

They carried paintbrushes to the laundry room sink and washed their hands. Katerina stayed behind, managing to get most of the paint off her face. Jack had already gone outside, and she was just locking the door behind her when she heard a car slowing down.

As she watched, a shiny black BMW pulled to a stop in the driveway behind Jack's Mercedes. A stunning woman emerged from the vehicle. Her look said expensive—from the top of her gleaming red hair pulled back in a sleek chignon, to the tips of her very expensive Prada shoes. As she got closer to Jack, Katerina was surprised to see that she stood maybe only a couple of inches short of Jack's six-foot-two frame.

Katerina was even more surprised when the woman reached over and, putting her hand on Jack's shoulder, gave him a very significant open-mouthed kiss. Katerina froze in her steps, not sure if she should return to the house or join them. Even as she pondered her decision, Jack turned and beckoned for her.

Noticing Katerina for the first time, the redhead gave her an appraising stare. As Katerina approached, she could see that up close the woman was even more stunning, with perfect skin and emerald eyes. Kat was mortifyingly conscious of how she must look in contrast with her hair in a ponytail and dressed in painting clothes. She knew the paint splatter was still partly visible on her cheek, and scrubbing at it had only turned the skin around it red and blotchy.

With complete ease, Jack turned to the two women and began introductions. "Nicole, I'd like you to meet Katerina Gascay. Kat is assisting me as an inn sitter, so you'll most likely be seeing her around. Kat, this is Nicole Reardon. Nicole is a friend of mine and she runs the local real estate office here in town." Both women smiled politely and murmured the expected greetings, but without any real enthusiasm.

Katerina was still struggling from the come-behind position of not being dressed or groomed at her best level. Nicole's demeanor conveyed the sense that she had categorized Katerina as entirely insignificant.

"Why don't you walk me to my car, Jack?" Nicole suggested, leaving no graceful way for him to refuse. She entwined her arm with his, commenting over her shoulder as she began herding him in the direction of her car, "I'm sure the inn sitter doesn't mind if we speak privately for a moment?"

"Not at all—take all the time you need," Katerina responded to their backs, feeling soundly outmaneuvered by the other woman. Not wanting to just wait behind like a lost puppy and watch them, she headed back into the house.

If she was really being honest with herself, she was put out by the other woman's preemptive attitude. *And yeah, by that kiss, too. What kind of friends kiss like that anyway? Get a grip,* she scolded herself. *Why do you care? You're in love with Michael.* But the irritatingly honest voice inside admitted that she did care.

"It's good to see you again," Nicole said, stroking her long manicured hand up and down Jack's arm. "We've both been so busy we've let altogether too much time pass. When I saw your car, I just had to stop. I trust that's not a problem." The tone of her voice held complete assurance of being welcome.

"It's good to see you, too, Nicole. I'm just out for the weekend doing some painting and prep work on the house. I have a guest coming in for a long stay, and we need to get the place decorated and in shape." He tried to keep his comments low-key, avoiding the line she had thrown out regarding letting time pass.

He and Nicole had fallen into a pattern of spending time together during his visits to the island. He enjoyed her company, and the sex was good, but somehow, when he was back in Seattle, he never had the inclination to invite her into his life there. Occasionally, she had called him while she was in Seattle and had even spent the night a time or two, but eventually, she had seemed to realize that Jack didn't intend to carry their relationship any further.

Nicole had handled the rebuff with class, and they had continued their island relationship, partly out of convenience for both of them. If he called during a visit and she wasn't available, or if he didn't call at all, neither of them took it personally. He couldn't remember the last time they had been together. Today, however, she seemed put out, and he guessed she wasn't thrilled to meet Katerina. Despite the limited relationship between Nicole and himself, she hadn't faced any female competition during his time on the island.

"You should have called me to help you decorate, Jack. I could have given you a lot of ideas for that space."

Jack pictured Nicole's condo with its monochromatic beige theme. Although he couldn't deny the result was beautiful, it was impersonal and cool, a bit like Nicole herself. "I appreciate the offer, Nicole, but I know you're busy with your own business."

"Well, I could have used the break. Sometimes all the provincialism of small-town life gets a little dull."

Although her words were spoken with light sarcasm, Jack sensed the truth behind them. "You could move your business to Seattle, you know," he reminded her.

"Ah, but then I would just be a small fish in a big pond—I prefer being the big fish in a small pond. I would have thought you'd have realized." The eyes she turned in his direction were reproachful.

Jack felt a moment of remorse. He had probably just seen more insight into the real Nicole than he had in all their previous time together. Sadly, he had never cared enough to dig beneath the confident, brittle façade she presented.

As if she could read his thoughts, she removed her hand from his arm, and leaning forward, gave him a quick kiss. While not as blatantly suggestive as the earlier one, it still left no doubt that she would be happy to continue where they had left off. "Good to see you, Jack. Call me sometime."

"See you, Nicole." He watched her get into her car and then turned back to his own car. Katerina had gone back inside, he realized, and as he approached the house, the door opened, and she emerged.

"Now, you owe me a chocolate shake too, for keeping me waiting." Katerina forced herself to keep her tone teasing and light. The fact that she was still bothered and maybe a bit jealous of the other woman wasn't something she was ready to admit.

"Fair enough," he said with a laugh. He was just as glad not to have to explain his past with Nicole. He felt he already knew Katerina well enough to be certain she wouldn't have wanted to be in a relationship like the one he and Nicole had shared.

They opted for the local island Burger Shack and returned to the house with their bags of greasy burgers, fries, and chocolate shakes. In no time, she had him back at work building wood panels that she wanted to cover in padding and fabric for one of the bedrooms upstairs. They had both agreed that his time was best spent on the construction-type work that would be most disruptive to the guest.

When he completed his goal for the day, he checked on Katerina's progress. She was removing the tape from the freshly painted walls in the master suite where she was currently staying. She had moved some of her things to a corner of the room, and his eye was immediately caught by a honey-colored stuffed toy dog.

"What's up with the dog?" he asked, reaching down to pick up the old and well-loved-on toy to study it closer.

"Oh, that's Buttercup," Katerina explained with a half-embarrassed grin. "I bring her wherever I go—kind of a stand-in until I'm able to get a real Buttercup. I've always wanted a dog."

"What's stopping you from getting a puppy?"

"Oh, I guess the obvious one is I need to be more settled in my life. I was gone for a year and now I'm inn sitting. Even when I'm at my place, it's awfully small for a dog, and there's no yard. Buttercup is a Golden Retriever, so she's going to need a lot of space."

"So, you never had a dog while you were growing up?" he asked, touched by her wistful expression.

"No, my parents traveled a lot and didn't want added responsibility. They didn't want anything that would slow them down from being able to just pick up and go."

She didn't say it, but Jack had the uneasy feeling that Katerina counted herself as one of the responsibilities that had burdened her parents. "So, don't tell me Michael and his family didn't have dogs either. What kind of a neighborhood was this?" he teased.

Katerina laughed. "No, Michael's dad is highly allergic to any kind of pet fur. You know, he always felt bad about that. He sat me down once when I was still quite small and explained that he was allergic, but if he could have, he would have given me a puppy that lived at their house. He's the one who gave me the stuffed Buttercup."

Katerina's smile was tender, and Jack could easily read the love that she had for Michael's family. He found himself fiercely glad that she had been lucky enough to have them. It also provided more understanding of the depth of the relationship he had sensed at the holiday dinner.

"You could start with a cat, you know. They're a lot easier to take care of and don't need a lot of room."

"I like cats a lot actually, but I want Buttercup. I want a warm, fat puppy who loves me unconditionally."

She said it in a light-hearted tone, but Jack felt as if he could again hear what she'd left unsaid, *unconditionally*, unlike the love that her parents and even Michael had given her. "Well, Splash, when the time is right, I think you will make one special puppy very lucky." He chucked her lightly under the chin and went back downstairs to clean the paintbrushes.

While he stood working the brushes under the warm water, his mind was on the woman upstairs. She touched him in a way no other woman ever had. Women had always come easy to him, and while he had dated more than his share, he'd never cared enough about any of them to hang in there when they started wanting more from him. *Funny, this time I'm the one wanting more.*

His thoughts were interrupted by Katerina's entrance into the laundry room. She was tucking that same chunk of dark hair behind her ear that always seemed to come loose, and she looked satisfied but tired.

"I'm beginning to feel hostility toward all paintbrushes," she said, watching as he finished cleaning the two in his hand.

"What took you so long?" he asked sarcastically, and she laughed.

"I guess I have been on a mission to get this done," she admitted.

"And again, it looks great, but remember, we can do some things while Jessica is here," he reminded her.

"Okay, I'm up for a break, so what's the plan for dinner?"

"Well, Splash, I can't take you anywhere with that paint on your face. No reputable establishment will have us," Jack teased, running his finger over a spot of dove paint and lingering to enjoy the softness of her skin.

Katerina put her hand to her face and smiled ruefully when she felt the paint on her cheek. "Not again! Okay, I'll clean up, and you can pick the place. Give me a few minutes."

❧

As she showered, Kat couldn't stop feelings of anticipation for the evening ahead.

The thought of spending another night alone in this house with Jack had her feeling slow tingles of awareness. She remembered the gentle, intimate feel of dancing with him in the living room and how sexy and rumpled he looked in the morning. All day, she couldn't help but notice that the guy could certainly fill out a pair of blue jeans.

She flashed back to the kiss she had seen between Jack and Nicole and wondered how recently their relationship had ended. In any case, Nicole seemed to be more than willing to pick up where they had left off. Even though she knew she had no grounds to complain, Katerina found that the knowledge bothered her.

Get a grip, she chided herself. *Don't forget the true goal.* Guiltily, she conjured up a vision of Michael's face, but when she chose to pair a soft, sexy, black sweater with her snuggest pair of faded jeans, it was all about the handsome man downstairs.

Drying her hair, she left it down and straight. When she applied her makeup, she took extra time to line her eyes with a smoky shadow and layered extra mascara on her already long lashes. A quick spritz of her favorite scent and an application of lipstick, and she was ready for a night out. Glancing in the mirror, she decided she liked what she saw and headed down the stairs to rejoin Jack.

"I thought maybe we could try Italian," Jack said, hearing Katerina on the stairs and heading into the entryway to join her. At his first sight of her, he stopped and just looked. "You look great," he finally said. And Katerina felt an entirely feminine satisfaction at the way his eyes turned smoky, and his mouth thinned into a straight line. He continued to stand at the bottom of the steps, simply watching as she made her descent.

"Thank you, sir, I'm just looking out for your reputation. I want to make sure those reputable dining establishments will open their doors to us." When she reached him, Katerina's laughing face was turned up to his, and her sparkling eyes and upturned lips made him catch his breath.

"Lady, I think with you on my arm, my reputation will be just fine." He moved closer to help her put on her coat and with a low growl, added, "Mmm, you smell great, too. I think you're trying to kill me."

In agreement on the choice of Italian food, they found themselves several minutes later seated in a cozy, dim booth with a beautiful view of the Sound. It was dark outside, but a handful of lights interspersed on the shoreline reflected off the dark water, giving it a mysterious and intimate feel. Their conversation was easy and light, but Katerina was aware of the blatant, sexual appreciation reflected in the heated gaze of her dinner companion. From her perspective, he was simply too sexy for her own peace of mind. She found herself focusing on the sensual shape of his lips, watching the way they clung to his glass when he sipped his Chianti. God, she really wanted to kiss this man. She found his complete ease in acknowledging that he desired her to be highly erotic. *When was the last time I've felt this wanted by any man? Has Michael looked at me like this since high school?* And even then, Michael had seen her through the eyes of a hormone-driven teenager, not with the heated, seductive gaze of a confident man. She knew there was more to the equation than this simple comparison, but tonight she simply enjoyed the escalating sexual tension.

They lingered over dinner, both of them enjoying the charged atmosphere. Katerina felt as if she could not break her gaze away from Jack's hypnotic one. A couple of times he traced a finger up her forearm or clasped one of her hands lightly in his, and wherever their skin met she seemed to burn.

She had counted on the intrusion of settling the bill and driving back home to break the spell she seemed to be under. But alone with Jack, inside the warm Mercedes, her senses seemed even more highly tuned. The steady pounding drip of the rain blurred the images outside until all she could think of was the man beside her. She watched him run his fingers through his dark hair, smelled the familiar citrus scent of his cologne, and felt the heat of his body beside her. Katerina sensed a loss of control, as if something had been started tonight that had taken on a life of its own.

--∞∞∞∞∞∞C(Ɔ)∞∞∞∞∞∞--

Jack pulled the Mercedes to a stop in front of the house, and reaching over with one hand, he placed it behind Katerina's neck, using it to pull her head toward his own. Leaning toward her, he looked deeply into her eyes, telling her without words that he intended to thoroughly and completely kiss her. He heard the soft intake of her breath, and her eyes focused on his lips as he brought them closer to her own.

His touch was at first light and gentle, but Katerina's response floored him. Leaning across the seat, she braced one hand on his chest and used the other to pull him closer. Her mouth was hot and tasted of wine, and when she deepened the kiss, Jack simply reacted. He teased her with his tongue and matched the soft little moan she made with a low groan of his own. His hand followed the seductive path down the soft skin revealed by the row of buttons on her sweater. Jesus, she had been driving him crazy with that sweater all night! His fingers managed to unbutton several of them, revealing even more soft, rounded flesh and an incredibly sexy scrap of lace, which seemed to have more to do with seduction than practicality.

He cupped her breast in his hand and felt her nipple already hard against his fingers. He lowered his head and trailed warm kisses down the enticing valley between her breasts. He felt her lips against his neck and her fingers digging into his shoulders. His lips moved to the soft fullness of her breast, and he pushed the lace aside to capture her nipple with his lips. He sucked and kissed the exposed flesh, feeling her response and hearing more delicious moans.

He shifted his body so that he could seek out her lips again, and looking down at her passion-filled eyes and swollen lips, he cursed the confining interior of the car. He needed to feel her entire delicious body wrapped around his own. His lips demanded access to all the seductive areas he longed to taste. Reluctantly, he broke the kiss off, trailing a finger down her jaw. "Hey, how about we take this someplace more comfortable?" he asked huskily. He leaned forward and teasingly captured her full lower lip lightly between his teeth before releasing it.

Her answer was a shuddering intake of breath, but looking across at her, he saw comprehension replace the passion in her expressive eyes. He knew without her saying a word that she wasn't ready to take this further. Her feelings for Michael stood between them. With a groan of disappointment, Jack tilted her face up and kissed her forehead. The simple, sweet gesture brought a sheen of moisture to Katerina's expressive golden eyes.

"I need you to know that I wanted this as much as you." She paused for a moment, still fighting to get her breathing back to normal. "Oh God, Jack, I'm so sorry. It's just that I don't take this lightly, and I guess… I'm just not ready… to be with someone else."

Jack tamped down hard on the frustration he felt at her words. But as if she could sense it, she reached over and grabbed his hand, clasping it firmly between her own. "I've spent my whole life in love with Michael, but somehow, I feel like you know me better already. I don't feel like I have the right to ask this, but I need you in my life right now." She made no effort to stem the tears that spilled down her cheeks, and Jack bent his head and kissed her salty skin.

"Katerina, I want to be here for you, but this situation isn't good for anyone." He squeezed her hand, bringing it to his lips briefly, before releasing it and opening the door of the car. Katerina inhaled slowly, and when Jack came around to open her door, she slowly followed him toward the house.

Inside, Jack grabbed a bottle of wine and a couple of glasses and then headed into the family room to see if there was anything on the television. He needed to take his mind off thoughts of how he would prefer to be spending the evening.

A few minutes later, Katerina joined him. She had changed into pajamas, and if she thought she had toned down the sexy look by selecting the full-length cotton pants with the drawstring and cropped T-shirt, she was mistaken.

Walking over to him, she reached up and rubbed his shoulders for a few minutes until she felt some of the tension release. "Hey, are we okay?" she asked.

He turned around to face her. "We are okay." Then, before he could stop himself, he lifted her chin and lowered his mouth to hers. At the first contact of his lips on hers, Katerina reached up and looped her arms around his neck. Jack groaned deep in his throat and deepened the kiss, enjoying the taste of her mouth and the feel of her petite and rounded body pressed up against him. With a low growl, he moved his lips reluctantly from hers and kissed the tip of her nose before releasing her.

"I'll be back in a minute. See if you can find something on TV or another movie," he suggested over his shoulder.

━━━━━━━━◦◦◦◦◦◦◦◦◦◦◯◯◯◦◦◦◦◦◦◦◦◦◦━━━━━━━━

Katerina absently switched from channel to channel with no conscious thought of what she was viewing. The intensity of her physical reaction to Jack had left her body in a state of arousal, and her peace of mind shattered. Her experience with men was limited, she admitted to herself, but still, she struggled to understand why she felt this hunger for another man who wasn't Michael.

She had moved to the couch and was sipping a glass of wine when Jack returned wearing the same tracksuit he had worn earlier in the morning. Katerina knew without asking that he probably slept in the nude, and just the realization sent her blood pumping harder. He accepted the glass of wine she handed him and then sat beside her on the couch. As soon as she set her glass down on the side table, he pulled her close against him but made no move to kiss her again. She sank in against him; it felt good to simply be in his warm, strong arms, and it felt good to feel alive with desire even if it confused her.

When the eleven o'clock news came on, Katerina stretched and began to pull away. Jack pulled her back and pressed a quick kiss on her forehead. "Sweet dreams," he said before releasing her.

"Goodnight, Jack." Katerina turned away before he could read the mixed feelings in her expression. Alone in her room, she washed her face and tried to remember the last time that she and Michael had made love. It had been the previous year, before her trip to Australia. It had been before he had suggested that they take another of his famous breaks to re-evaluate things. Katerina felt sad to be unable to recall any specific details about the night. Shouldn't something as important as the last time you made love with the man you have always loved be branded on your consciousness in some significant way? *That isn't the way life works,* she mused. You rarely know the significance of events because you don't see that your fate is about to change. Maybe that was kinder, she decided, staring at her reflection in the mirror. *Imagine the pain of making love with someone, knowing that you were in the midst of losing them.*

She patted her face dry with a towel and climbed into bed. She felt downcast, and a small voice reminded her that this was just more of the same. She knew Michael did love her, but not enough, apparently—never enough to stay for the long haul. In a twisted way, she felt safer with Jack, as if he was more likely to be there for her. As if he already knew the real her, better than perhaps Michael did. He seemed comfortable with her independence and respected her for it. And he made her feel desirable and sexy, and that felt good. *It feels really good*, Katerina decided as she drifted off to sleep.

Chapter Twenty-One

By the time Katerina awoke, she could already hear Jack's shower running. She forced her mind off the sexy image of his tall, firm body slippery with water and soap, dark hair slicked back from that ruggedly handsome face. Making her way downstairs, she discovered that he had the coffee ready. "Jack, you're a good man," she said out loud in appreciation. Sipping her coffee, she wandered around the newly painted rooms, visualizing how they would look when she had made some changes to the furniture and accessories.

Jack had arranged for a couple of older teenagers to come over and help them move furniture around and carry down pieces that Katerina had selected from the attic. She intended to put many of the items in a central staging area so that she could take her time rearranging things and make sure that she found the right mix. Filling her coffee cup, she headed upstairs to shower.

An hour or so later, when she came back down fully dressed in jeans and a sweatshirt, ready to attack the attic, she found Jack and the younger men already gathered in the living room. Jack's back was turned, so he didn't immediately notice her arrival, a fact for which Katerina was immediately grateful. At first sight of his dark hair and broad shoulders, she found herself unprepared for the immediate feeling of self-consciousness. She flashed back to the feel of his lips and hands on her body, and she felt her breath catch. Hoping she sounded more normal than she felt, she called out a quick "Good Morning" as she entered the room.

Jack turned at the sound of her voice, and smiling broadly at her, waved her over for introductions. The two brothers, Kevin and Chance, were neighbors from a couple of houses down. With Katerina directing and the three guys carrying and relocating items, they made fast work of setting up her staging area. She had selected several small tables, decorative pillows, pictures, candlesticks, and other accessory items that had caught her eye from the boxes upstairs. Also included in the space was the charming chest she and Jack had uncovered the other day. Looking around at her stash, she was anxious to find new uses for the lovely items.

It was harder deciding on items that she wanted to remove from the rooms. As Jack had admitted, many of the rooms lacked a sense of style. It wasn't as if there was anything wrong with most of the items; they simply didn't pull together and complement other pieces. Still feeling uncomfortable, she lacked her usual confidence and couldn't seem to keep her attention on the matter at hand. Finally, she decided to remove a chair and an end table from the living room. In the family room, she removed the coffee table, another chair, and a floor lamp. Upstairs, she asked them to remove the dresser from Jack's boyhood room. She wanted to leave more room to replace the furniture with more impactful pieces. "I think that's it for now," she decided, her face wearing a frown of concentration as she studied the room with a critical eye.

"Hey, I think I hear a phone ringing," Chance said, and recognizing the ring tone, she headed off toward her cell phone. The ringing had stopped by the time she retrieved it from her purse, but the message indicator was on. Punching in her passcode, she closed her eyes as Michael's voice filled her ear. He had already called her twice on Friday, leaving her two short messages. Today, his voice sounded tired and resigned—gone was the frustrated and irritable tone of his earlier voicemails. "Call me, please, Kitten." His use of her childhood nickname made her feel broken. With a sigh, Katerina replaced her phone in her purse and headed back to the men who were gathered near the front door. Jack had been so right when he'd said this situation couldn't go on.

"Hey, there you are," Jack said when she rejoined them. "Kevin and Chance have offered to swing by anytime if you decide to move some other items around. I don't want you trying to haul heavy stuff around by yourself, okay?" Jack cautioned her.

"Deal," Katerina responded with a smile that she hoped didn't look as forced as it felt. "And thanks, you two, for the offer—I may take you up on that. It's hard to visualize everything right now, and I'm guessing there will be more changes."

As Jack paid the two boys for their help, Katerina headed to the kitchen to get herself another cup of coffee and try to get her emotions under control. She heard the front door shut and the sound of Jack's footsteps heading in her direction. She braced herself mentally. Now that they were alone, she doubted she would be able to keep up her façade that everything was okay, because somehow it just wasn't, and as ridiculous as it sounded, she didn't even know why.

"Good idea—I could do with another cup of coffee, too. Any left?" Jack asked, entering the kitchen, walking over, and lifting the pot to test it. "Ah, good," he remarked, filling his cup. He turned to look at Katerina, who was standing against the counter, sipping her coffee and gazing intently out the window.

Jack glanced out the window, wondering what was so interesting, and finding nothing out of the ordinary, he focused on her still profile. Katerina didn't seem like her usual happy self. *But how well do I really know her?* They hadn't spent much time together—the sense of knowing her came more from the connection they seemed to have. But still, he felt he knew her well enough to figure out that something had upset her, and the odds were, it had something to do with her recent phone call.

The realization that he was so in tune with and concerned with her emotions frankly scared the hell out of him, and he fought against a strong desire to jump in his car and put some serious distance between them. Lately, he seemed to be putting in overtime dealing with emotional women, between Kat and his sister. Could anyone blame him if he didn't want to go there? More importantly, he couldn't guarantee that he would be able to hold his temper if Kat was feeling guilty for kissing another man besides Michael. Yeah, he decided for both their sakes, Kat was just going to have to work this one out on her own.

So instead, he focused on a safe subject and kept his expression even. "So, we have two weeks before Jessica arrives. Unfortunately, as we discussed, I am working both days next weekend in the office. Are you going to be okay up here, finishing the staging and decorating? Shall we run through the last-minute details on your end?"

"No worries, Jack—we are in good shape," Katerina responded, turning toward him. Jack wondered if maybe he had just imagined her mood. "There are a few small painting touch-ups. I need to try to find a home for the items we just pulled from the attic, and I am sure I will be back up there to retrieve more stuff. I need to do menus and grocery shopping. Oh, and I thought I would go into Seattle sometime to do some shopping for linens and some decorative items." Her gaze met his but then slowly slid away.

Looking down at her dark head and averted eyes, Jack felt a hot burst of anger and frustration. She was a beautiful, sexy woman, and sure, maybe he had taken advantage of the opportunity to move things along last night, despite knowing that she probably wasn't ready. But he had backed off the moment she'd asked, and—she had played a significant part in heating things up. Part of him wanted to pull her toward him and make her tell him what her problem was, just so he could see her beautiful smile again.

But that thought collided head-on with the frustrating awareness that he was getting more involved than he had ever intended with the abandoned ex-lover of his sister's fiancé. *What a fucking mess,* he mused. Yeah, he needed some distance—he needed to get his head straight.

As he walked to the sink to rinse his coffee cup, he called over his shoulder. "Sounds great. I'm going to meet Jessica Saturday after next here at the ferry dock and bring her up to the house. Is there anything else I can do to help you?"

"There might be some items you can help with," Katerina answered slowly, "and I guess I would like you to see the house before she arrives—you know, just to make sure that you are comfortable with everything." Katerina's face reflected her genuine concern that he be happy with the end result.

"Absolutely. How about I drive up the Friday before, mid-morning, and we can spend the day finalizing everything for her arrival on Saturday?" Surely by then, he would have had time enough to rationalize this mess and have his head on straight. It also gave Katerina time to deal with her guilt or whatever the hell her problem was.

He ran a hand through his hair. "And now, I should be getting out of here. I have a client dinner to go to tonight and need to do some prep," he explained, brushing past her on the way to his room. Katerina nodded her understanding and watched him disappear around the corner. In a moment, he reappeared, carrying his overnight bag, and she walked with him toward the door.

Once there, he turned toward her, determined to keep it light. "Kat, the place looks great—I can't thank you enough for all your hard work and good taste. Also, I had a great weekend. Let me know if you need anything during the week." He held her gaze for an extended moment, and despite the frustration that still simmered in him, he hated to leave her. If he was honest with himself, he had to admit that he'd enjoyed her company very much and didn't want to end on a bad note. "Promise?"

"I promise," she said softly. "Jack, thank you. I enjoyed being with you, too." Jack had the impression that she wanted to say more, and against his better judgment, wished she would, but again, her eye contact slid away, and she remained silent. So, he simply gave her a quick hug before opening the door and closing it behind him.

Katerina watched as Jack's Mercedes pulled away from the house and eventually out of sight on the winding road. The house suddenly seemed too quiet with him gone, and Katerina finally had to admit to herself that for the first time since moving to the island, she felt lonely. *Well, I was probably responsible for him leaving earlier than he'd planned.* He had done a good job of putting up a front, but she suspected he had been frustrated with her and had decided to leave her to her own crummy mood.

She made her way back to the kitchen and poured herself another cup of coffee. She considered returning Michael's phone call but wasn't sure she felt stable enough to deal with the emotional rollercoaster. She spilled some of the liquid on the counter. "Damn," she muttered, aware that her mood was increasingly gloomy. *What is wrong with me?*

She finished her coffee and wandered back to the newly formed staging area. She picked up various items and too quickly set them back down. She couldn't seem to concentrate; all of her creativity was stifled under the weight of her bad mood.

Disgusted with her inability to be productive, Katerina headed off to change for a long run. Exercise always helped her to clear her mind, and God knew she needed that help right now. She changed quickly into sweats and her sneakers and headed out the front door. The sun was warm on her shoulders, and the repetitive sound of her footfalls on the pavement helped her unwind just as she had hoped it would.

There was such a difference between running outside rather than the treadmill in the gym. She ran on side streets where she was able to get a feel for the other neighborhood houses. She enjoyed the fact that the houses were truly originals and did not give in to the bland sameness that so many planned communities resorted to. It was a comfortable and homey neighborhood where the owners cared about their homes and their yards. *Of course they did— they have a view of Puget Sound!*

During the run, she had let her thoughts spin randomly, hoping the underlying cause for her moodiness would become clearer. The weekend had been more fun than she had imagined, and with all their hard work, she was much closer to seeing her vision for the space come together. Jack had been appreciative of her work and her ideas. It had been so fun to bounce ideas off each other, and not once had he made her feel like she was controlling or making too many decisions.

Was she in a bad mood because being with Jack put a spotlight on the issues between her and Michael? Jack's driveway came into view, and she automatically slowed her pace and let her mind shift back to all the tasks she needed to accomplish in the next week.

Chapter Twenty-Two

Katerina reviewed her to-do list, and with a sigh of satisfaction, checked off another item. There was still a lot to accomplish, but she was feeling more comfortable that she was on track for her deadline. She was very much looking forward to meeting Jessica Lowry. She had finished Jessica's first book and really liked it. She hoped that Jessica would like the space and be able to enjoy her time on the island.

Knowing she couldn't put it off any longer, she grabbed her phone and dialed Michael's number. He answered on the first ring.

"Kat, what's going on?" The frustration in his voice was evident.

"Michael, if you're referring to my helping Jack out with his B&B, it's going pretty well."

"I am concerned about why you're spending time with this project and not looking for a real job. Jumping into this impetuously is so like you—what do you know about running a bed & breakfast inn? It doesn't make sense to me."

Kat found her own frustration rocketing. "I still don't know what I'm looking for career-wise. I want to make a change, but it just isn't clear to me yet. This gives me a chance to experiment a little without being back to a pressure-filled restaurant schedule."

"I wish you would look for something outside the food industry. You need regular hours, a 401-K, and steady benefits. You should go back to school."

"Michael, food is what I've always wanted to do. I know I need to figure it out, but I'm not ready to turn my back yet on what I love. I know all of those things are important, and I intend to make sure they are in my long-term plan."

"Well, you know how I feel about it—I just don't think that way of life gives you any security or a long-term path to success." He finished in a tone that to Katerina signified a closed mind. He had never been interested in working with her to address concerns; he'd just wanted her to do something else. "As for Jack," he began, but his voice sounded uncomfortable, and he began talking faster as if he wanted to get the topic over with quickly. "It also doesn't make sense that you and Jack are becoming chummy. He doesn't have a great track record on staying with any one particular woman."

Katerina swallowed hard; there was a lot to unpack from Michael's comments. She wanted to retaliate with the fact that he, himself, didn't have a great track record of staying with *one* particular woman, but she knew that would just start a fight.

"I just don't want to see you get hurt—you two seem friendly, and Amy tells me he hasn't been a guy to settle down." Michael's voice wound down awkwardly.

Katerina closed her eyes as she listened to him talk. She felt hurt, lost, and angry, and she wasn't sure which emotion ruled. "Michael, if you're concerned about my relationship with Jack solely because you don't want me to be hurt, then we should probably not discuss this further." Unable to choke back the words, she blurted out, "Michael, why did you propose to her and not me?"

The long silence made her wonder if he'd hung up. Finally, he said sadly, "I don't know, Kat. I'm just trying to protect you."

"Damn you, Michael," she said and disconnected the phone. She set her phone down on the counter and leaned against the wall for a sense of physical support. Her mind was going in so many directions, it seemed important to distill the conversation as much as possible. *This matters, Michael matters. Did I learn anything from the conversation?* He still didn't respect or understand her decisions, and he couldn't tell her why he was marrying another woman. Despite the hurt, a new, fledgling sense of awareness registered as well—Marnie and Jack telling her that she mattered, too. She needed to factor that into her plan.

Michael slammed the phone down on the counter and swore out loud. The call had gone as poorly as he'd expected it to. He'd heard the raw pain in her voice and was conscious of a matching pain in his stomach. From their brief conversations during her apprenticeship, he'd known that she didn't think the role she had at the resort was one she wanted to replicate when she returned to Seattle. He had hoped that she would finally set her sights on another profession, and that she would just settle down and be… be… what? Michael shook his head, not with frustration this time, but with dawning clarity. Kat would never have been happy with the changes he'd wanted her to make. Their differences went beyond a career choice. He was steady, predictable, and, okay, maybe a little controlling. Kat was creative, much more of a risk-taker, and too stubborn to back down. That stubbornness of hers just might have saved them both, he acknowledged. He looked at his watch. Suddenly, he wanted to see Amy and tell her how much he loved her.

Chapter Twenty-Three

Katerina called Kevin and Chance a couple more times to help her with the furniture and staging area. The three of them had just finished moving back to the attic all the items that didn't seem to have a purpose. After the boys had left, Katerina went into each room, inventorying what she should look for in the short term to fill some of the space. Jack was going to need to buy additional furniture down the road, but for now, she could still add some life and style to the house. At any rate, it was going to be a full day of shopping, and she was looking forward to it.

Katerina and Jack had spoken on the phone several times to refine their planning for his next visit, and each time the conversation had flowed naturally. Any leftover frustrations from the earlier Sunday seemed to have evaporated. Also missing was any sense of intimacy, but that was probably for the best—she didn't know how to handle it, and it could only complicate things. She had to acknowledge she had been overwhelmed by an attraction she hadn't expected and felt guilty for having said one thing to Jack and then acted in a completely different way.

She caught the first ferry off the island and relaxed with a cup of coffee, enjoying the beauty of the commute. Most of her fellow passengers looked to be heading to the office, lending credence to Jack's opinion that living on the island and working in Seattle was doable.

Her first stop was an art shop in Pioneer Square. She wanted to find some unique and colorful pieces, and she knew this place well. When she opened the shop door, the bell over it tinkled, and Katerina saw Shane enter the shop from a back workroom. He hooted in recognition and hurried over to give her a big hug. "Kat, what a treat! What can I do for you? And of course, how is your mother?"

"Mother is thriving. She and Dad are traveling, but I will make sure to tell her you asked for her."

"Your mother will always thrive. She's built for that," Shane said dryly.

Katerina laughed in agreement. "There is no doubt about it! So, I'm looking for some bright and modern paintings for a B&B that I am helping to update. The house is pretty much a blank slate. The paint is a series of neutral gray and cream colors with darker hues, so I think it's a flexible canvas for art. What do you have?"

It turned out that going to Shane's shop had been a great idea, and Katerina was over the moon with what she found. Bright, modern, and large, the pieces would look amazing in the house, and since they were all done by relatively unknown but talented artists, the prices were a steal. Shane wrapped her packages and helped her stow them in her car. She hugged him goodbye and headed to an upscale linen store.

"This is going to hurt you, Jack," she said out loud. She was right about the hurt, Katerina decided, looking around. These were the splurge items she had warned him about; guests appreciated a comfortable, plush bed. She found a very deeply padded mattress cover, good quality sheets, a feather duvet, and fluffy down pillows, and then went in search of the duvet cover, a throw, and additional decorative pillows. She decided to keep all the bedding white to maintain the luxurious resort feel, but she made sure the throw and decorative pillows had texture. Despite the all-white coloring, the result would be layered and luxurious. *For these prices, it better be.* Jack had told her to treat the bedding in the inn sitter's room the same, but she didn't have the heart to do it. She could make the room look very nice but scale back the luxury.

Her last stops were for accessories, books, towels, and lampshades. She selected thirsty, thick towels, again in white and in various textures for the master. She found large organic accessories—some stone, some wood, some metal, also a few ceramic pieces. She located serving trays to put on coffee tables and in bedrooms to hold books, candles, drinks, etc. She selected updated lampshade shapes to replace the existing ones. It was amazing how modern an old lamp could look with just that simple switch. Loading the last of her purchases—used hardback books for the library—into her Jeep, she was thankful to be done.

She was both exhausted and excited. The day had gone better than she'd expected, and she couldn't wait to put all these items in their new places. After arriving back at the house and unloading her treasures, she was too tired to even think about making dinner, or going out for it, either. She poured a glass of wine and, after staring in the refrigerator for a few minutes, finally decided to pair it with plain Greek yogurt, a handful of walnuts, and honey. A weird combination with the wine to be sure, but it was easy, and that was a good thing.

Chapter Twenty-Four

Amy sat down at the kitchen island where Michael was grading some student papers on his laptop. "Michael, I need to talk to you about something."

A glance at her stormy blue eyes told him she was either stressed or angry, maybe both. "What is it, babe?" he asked, reaching for her hand.

"I looked at our phone bills online, at the recent activity." Amy sniffled, and her blue eyes began filling up. "I saw some calls to Kat."

Michael maintained a firm grip on her hand he held, but his mind was racing. "I did leave a few messages, and finally she called me back," he admitted hurriedly.

"I thought we agreed that you weren't going to be in contact with her?" Faced with his admission, even though she'd already seen evidence of the calls, caused her sniffles to escalate to sobs.

"Amy, honey, I called her because I knew you were upset that she and Jack were spending time together, and you weren't happy she was helping with the B&B. I thought I could help by telling her it was stalling her career, and that Jack isn't a good long-term dating option."

Amy's face showed no sign of clearing and she tugged on her hand he was still holding. "If that was your reason, you should have talked about it with me! I felt like something was off—you've just seemed so distracted. I know it wasn't good for me to look at the bill before talking to you. I didn't want to be suspicious. I wanted to be wrong," she said, reaching for a napkin to wipe her eyes and nose.

"I thought I was helping you both," Michael said sadly. "I'm sorry I hurt you, and you're right. It was wrong of me not to tell you."

"I have to be able to trust you, and—and—" sobs interrupted her words "—I don't think you should be so invested in taking care of her. She's not your responsibility, and I'm pr—pr— pregnant!" The force of her sobs shook her entire body.

"You're pregnant!? Amy... that's amazing!" Michael grabbed her and held her as tight as he could, "I love you, Amy, and I'm so happy we're going to have a baby." His mind went into overload—a baby, his love for this woman, the family they would be, more responsibility. And then it hit him; there could be no more conflicting loyalties. He acknowledged the relief, deep, honest relief.

"You're really okay with it?" Amy asked, the relief in her voice clear and her tears slowing.

The sound of her voice pulled him from his thoughts, and he hugged her again to reinforce his delight. "Honey, I'm more than okay with it. I'm thrilled. And Amy, you can trust me—I was wrong, and you deserve to be sure it's only you that I want to take care of," he said.

"Can we keep this to ourselves for a while?" she pleaded, wiping at her eyes. "There's just been so much going on; I want to savor this and keep it private. It's early in the pregnancy to share, and I'd rather reveal it later when our baby news can get the attention it deserves. I love you, Michael, and I'm so glad you're happy about this. I can't wait for us to be a family."

"We're already a family," Michael said, kissing her and holding her tightly.

Chapter Twenty-Five

When the alarm went off, Katerina was ready to go. *Today feels like Christmas, and I can't wait to start.* She hadn't unpacked a single package the night before, so the day was going to be a busy one. Jack was going to be there soon to help her, but he also had some work of his own to accomplish. Jessica had requested a printer be available, so Jack was bringing one with him, in addition to a couple of large, flat-screen TVs to hang on the walls of the master and inn sitter's rooms. Katerina had been able to get the cable company out to install the outlets, so hopefully the setup would be easy.

She jumped in the shower before even getting her coffee, and in record time, she was dressed in a sweatshirt and jeans, with her hair in a ponytail. As she drank her coffee, she began unwrapping the purchases and organizing them by room. She also unwrapped the art and leaned each piece against the target wall. She carried the bedding up to the master, and the remaining bedding she put in the inn sitter's room, which was now her room. She had already made the bed in the other large bedroom that Jack was using. She would need to buy new bedding for that room, too, but she wanted to finish the fabric wall first.

Grabbing another cup of coffee, she went into the living room and began her work. She had already cleared the rooms of their lampshades and unwanted accessories, so it was really just an exercise in addition. *But keep in mind, less is more*, she reminded herself, smiling.

When she heard Jack's car pull up, she felt a mixture of anticipation and anxiety. If she was honest with herself, she felt those butterflies again. Walking to the entry, she greeted him and was rewarded with a big smile and an even bigger hug. "Kat, the entry looks great. I can't wait to see the rest of the place." He pointed to the corner. "This is the chest we found upstairs in the attic, right?"

"Yeah, it is. Kevin and Chance were a big help—we found rugs, too. There were a lot of great things up there. You're probably going to want to shop for some specific pieces and maybe change up some items that I took from the attic, but it's a start."

"That makes sense." He nodded. "Let me get the stuff in from the car."

As he left to retrieve the televisions and printer, Kat went into the kitchen to make more coffee. He joined her there in a moment, and with an appreciative smile, accepted the mug she offered him. "Kat, this place already looks better, and I know we aren't done with our day's work—thank you." He walked over to look at a row of terracotta pots she had placed near the window. "Are these herbs?"

"Yes, it's nice to have a supply that I can just grab from for recipes, and this kitchen has the perfect amount of light and plenty of space for them."

Jack leaned in and sniffed at the basil plant. "They smell nice."

"This island has a great farmer's market—flowers, produce, even meat and dairy. Not that many reasons to go to the grocery store," Kat said, smiling. "I'm planning to head over there tomorrow morning and stock up. I have a general idea of what I'm planning for this week's menu but let me know if there are any changes from your most recent discussions with Jessica."

"No, we left it at three meals a day but agreed to play it by ear. She may want to go out to a restaurant some night or maybe even over to Seattle. She was pretty excited to hear you are a chef. I can't blame her—I would be happy eating your food, three times a day, too." Jack grinned as he reached past her to get another coffee. "What's the plan for the day?"

"I'm on accessories, you're on electronics, and maybe we can hang the art together? You can help me make Jessica's bed, if you don't mind. As I mentioned, I'll review groceries before tomorrow's farmer's market, and… she does drink wine, right? So, I should get some wine."

"Yes, she did mention that she's a wine drinker. If we have time, why don't I take you to my friend's winery? I can introduce you to Adam, and you can find a good, varied selection there," Jack offered.

"Ah, that sounds nice, and not a bad way to end a busy day. Oh, and I have some stuff to make sandwiches for lunch if that works for you."

"Great. Thanks, Kat." He rinsed his coffee cup, and the two of them went their separate ways. Kat returned to the living room, and Jack headed to the library with the printer. He and Kat had agreed it was the best room for Jessica to use for her writing space. He noticed that Kat had added a rug, moved the two leather chairs from his man-cave den into the room, and added a small table. With the bookshelves and built-in desk, the room felt cozy. *She's talented at this.*

By lunchtime, Kat was finished with the accessories, and the rooms looked both modern and comfortable. When Jack joined her in the living room, she was placing fresh flowers on a dark gray leather tray set on the coffee table. The tray also held an assortment of magazines and a pretty glass bowl filled with wrapped chocolate truffles from the island chocolatier.

"I can't believe how nice this place has turned out—the rugs work, and it just really looks good," Jack said, smiling at her.

Kat sighed in satisfaction. "It does look pretty good," she admitted.

For lunch, Kat made tomato, fresh mozzarella, and homemade basil pesto sandwiches on crispy toasted bread with an arugula and lemon salad. Jack groaned in appreciation. "So, tell me about the art. You got some cool pieces—where did you go?"

Kat laughed and asked, "Are you sure you're ready for this? I can't tell you the place without sharing the back story."

He reached for another piece of cheese and said, "I'm ready."

"My mom is a very pretty woman and loves to be appreciated for her looks. She always bemoaned the fact that she was too petite to have a career in modeling. She tried to find petite fashion shows locally, but there really wasn't much of a market for them, so she was frustrated. I'm not entirely sure how she found out about the Art Institute, but she began doing face modeling for young art students. She liked the attention, and they had a pretty model. It's not uncommon for art students to display their work for sale in the park near the university, so it follows naturally that we would often see my mother's likeness on various portraits for sale or display—a fact that my mother was very proud of and my father tolerated. She probably has two of her favorites still hanging in their house to this day. One day, a friend of my mother's informed her that there was a nude painting of her for sale in the park. My parents rushed over there to see it, and my mother's reaction was horror that her face was on a body that did not meet her high standards. My father, on the other hand, found that his tolerance for the art world had hit a wall. The result of the nude painting was that my mother's modeling career came to an end."

Jack's unrestrained burst of laughter made Kat laugh again, too. "Later, when I wanted to find art for my condo, I went down to that area and I found out that a former student from that time runs an art store, where, in addition to other works, he features student art. The former student is named Shane, and while he had painted my mother, he promised me that he was not the one who had painted her head on the nude body."

"Oh my God," Jack said, laughing again. "That is hilarious, and I like the art even more now!"

After lunch, they went upstairs to make up the bed for Jessica. Putting the padded mattress top and even the fitted sheets on the heavy king-size bed was much easier with two people. The room looked every bit as luxurious and rich as Kat had hoped. It also had fresh flowers, magazines, and candles, and in the attached bath, she had placed the thick towels and a basket with luxe soap, bath salts, shampoo, and lotion.

The last project was the art. Jack looked at the pieces and where Kat had suggested they be hung, and after some discussion and walking from room to room, he agreed with her. They hung the art, and Jack gave her a big hug. "Feels good to be ready, right? You have worked hard these last two weeks."

"It does and I did!" Kat agreed, smiling up at him.

"Are you up for the winery? And then how about dinner at a local, laid-back seafood restaurant?"

"Deal," Kat said. "Let me change, and I'll be right with you." She exchanged her sweatshirt for a thick cable-knit sweater in gray, added some jewelry, and touched up her makeup. She swapped out her sneakers for boots and headed to the kitchen, where Jack was waiting for her.

"Alright," he said, smiling widely when she joined him. "Let's celebrate your hard work and success with a little wine tasting." Katerina followed him to his Mercedes and the two of them drove a few short miles and pulled into a small parking lot in front of a chateau-inspired building. Beyond it, she could see grapevines and a garden with seating. When they opened the front door, a bell chimed, and a man sitting behind the counter, doing paperwork, looked up with a smile of greeting. "Jack, stranger! How are you?"

"Good, good, Adam. Meet Kat Gascay, a friend of mine from Seattle who is helping me out with my B&B. Kat, meet Adam Binder. He owns and runs this place." Adam and Kat greeted each other, and Jack added, "I promised Kat some wine tastings, and then we want to get a few bottles to serve to our guest who is arriving tomorrow. Kat's a chef, so I'm sure she'll appreciate any insights you have on wine pairings."

"Of course." Adam waved them over to an area of the bar and reached below the counter to select various bottles for tasting. "Let's do the friends and family version where we just taste whatever we feel like," he said, smiling. They tasted a crisp white wine with citrus and grass notes and another white, which was drier and had more acidity. For reds, Adam poured them a pinot noir and then several red blends featuring pinot noir grapes, merlot, and other varietals.

Kat enjoyed the chance to unwind, sip wine, and be in Jack's company again. It was fun to listen to him interact with Adam. They had a history together on the island, and she was able to get another perspective on what kind of man Jack was. He was a generous friend, Kat decided—he asked Adam a lot of questions about his life and work and listened with genuine interest.

To close off the tasting, Adam poured them some sweeter wines, which were fun and bright. Ultimately, Kat decided on a mixed case, and Adam boxed up the selections while Jack paid. After thanking Adam and saying their goodbyes, Jack carried the box of wine to the car, and they headed to the seafood restaurant.

The restaurant was loud, crowded, and fun. They toasted their shared accomplishments with icy cold beers while slurping on appetizers of oysters and clams. They each had the grilled trout special for dinner and were both too full for dessert.

When Jack pulled his car up to the house, he reached across the seat and grabbed Kat's hand. "I had a nice time with you today."

She turned to him and spoke. "Jack, I really like being with you, too."

"Unfortunately, I have some work to catch up on this evening, so I'm not going to be very good company. I need to review some agreements since tomorrow is going to be another busy day. I'm just going to head to my room if you don't mind."

"Of course I don't mind," Kat said, shaking her head. "I'll probably just review my shopping list and read for a while."

Inside the house, Jack hugged her before going upstairs to his room, and Kat went into the kitchen and reviewed her shopping list for the morning. Most of the items she could get at the local farmer's market, but she needed to make a run to the grocery store for some chocolate and a couple of other staples. She put the wine away in the pantry before making her way to her room.

She lay in bed with the book open, but her mind couldn't seem to focus on the words. Instead, she was thinking about the man upstairs. He had seemed different tonight—friendly, invested, all those things that she usually felt from him, but yet something was different. He had treated her more as a good friend than a romantic interest. *Honestly, that's how he acted on the phone all week, too.* She had told him that she wasn't ready for more, so obviously, he was just honoring her request. *And now I'm feeling paranoid that he is already losing interest—wait, what?* Her mind had just gone to a place her heart couldn't catch up with. She tried to replace thoughts of Jack with a mental image of Michael, but she was too unfocused. She turned on the television. *I need a distraction.*

Chapter Twenty-Six

Katerina awoke with a start. Had she heard something? Her bedroom was dark except for the flickering images from the TV she had fallen asleep to. She was quite certain that the sound that had roused her had not come from the TV. She clicked the remote off and lay still, struggling to hear the unfamiliar sound again. *Footsteps?* Had she forgotten to lock the kitchen door to the patio?

Easing out of bed, she crept slowly to the door and cracked it open, peering out into the dim hallway. Suddenly, the kitchen light came on, and she heard the faucet running. *Of course, Jack's here tonight—the footsteps belong to him.* Katerina felt relief, followed quickly by a crushing need to see him, and she started down the hallway. The TV had not been the distraction Kat had hoped for, and before she'd gone to sleep, her mind had continued to focus on the possibility that Jack was truly losing interest in her. Without understanding exactly why, that possibility made her feel vulnerable.

Jack turned from the sink and saw Katerina come into view beyond the kitchen island. He set his untouched water glass down as she came closer. She was wearing the long pajama pants with the drawstring and the crop top he had seen before. Her hair was loose and tousled, her beautiful eyes looked into his own, and he lost all his good intentions of leaving her alone.

He wasn't certain who made the first move, but suddenly she was in his arms, and he covered her hot, sexy mouth with his own. Her arms came up to wrap around his neck, she pressed that incredible body against him, and he just reacted. Still kissing her, he managed to direct the two of them back to the open door of her bedroom, and when his knees felt the mattress behind him, he pulled her down with him onto the bed.

Jack kissed her urgently, deeply, and she kissed him back with her own matching need. Finally, he broke apart, and resting his weight on his forearms, he rose above her to look into her eyes. "Kat, is this what you want?" he asked hoarsely, needing her reassurance for both their sakes.

Kat nodded. "Yes, Jack. I want this, I want you."

He answered her by leaning in for another sexy kiss but more demanding this time. "I want to watch you take off your clothes for me," he whispered while still kissing her.

●•◦◦◦◦◦◦◦◦()◦◦◦◦◦◦◦•●

Kat felt the dizzying heat of being desired. She had never been asked to strip in front of a man, and the idea that Jack wanted her to tease him made her pulse race.

He lay back against the pillows, his dark eyes hooded and focused only on her as she pulled at the drawstring of her pajama pants, pulling them down her legs and revealing nothing but a lacy thong, her rounded hips, and a glimpse of her bare bottom. Jack's strangled groan of appreciation ignited a burning sensuality within Kat. She had never before felt so desired and so powerful. Slowly, she teased him by lifting her crop top and exposing the underside of her small, shapely breasts, and then pausing before finally removing it and baring her breasts for him.

Jack reacted by pulling her back down on the bed and covering her mouth again while his hands roamed over her thighs, pulling at the strap of her thong to remove it. In return, she yanked at his clothing, and with Jack's help, they were both soon naked. He turned to her, pushing her long, dark hair off her face and looking deeply into her eyes. "You are absolutely beautiful, and I am going to take my time with you," he growled. Kat sighed in eager surrender. His hands and mouth were everywhere, and Kat writhed, needing and wanting more. She tried to pull him toward her, but he refused, continuing to tease her.

Finally, when he could delay no longer, he positioned himself above her, and looking deeply into her passion-filled, golden eyes, he slowly entered her. Kat shattered immediately, and Jack began moving slowly. As Kat's breathing slowed, it was her turn to use her hands and lips to tease and arouse Jack. Her sexy body rose to meet his, matching his tempo—she was everything and more. Jack held off until he felt Kat's matching urgency, and when she cried out, he gave one last thrust and found his own dizzying release.

Jack pulled Kat's body into his arms and pressed a kiss on her forehead, smelling the familiar melon scent of her shampoo. She looked at him, and he could sense the questions and uncertainty about what had just occurred. He hadn't meant this to happen, and he knew that there were still issues and uncertainty between them, but he wouldn't be sorry he had made love with the woman he knew mattered to him. "Shush," he said, kissing her again, softly on the lips this time. "Kat, I know this was unexpected, but let's not regret this."

She nodded, and to his surprise, she nestled closer to him and closed her eyes, drifting off to sleep. He looked at his watch: 3:00 a.m. He forced his conflicted thoughts to the side and tried to relax and enjoy holding Kat.

—————⊙⊙⊙————

Jack awoke to the sound and smell of coffee brewing in the kitchen and the realization that he was waking up in Kat's bed. He lay there for a moment, remembering the night before and realizing that he had better stop that line of thought, or a cold shower would be in his future. Instead, he forced himself to dress and prepare to face Kat. This was not simple, but he was determined that the two of them see the previous night as a positive.

When he entered the kitchen, Kat was dressed in the pajamas he had watched her remove the night before, and again his body began to react. *This is going to be a tough morning.* She looked up at him, smiled shyly, and reached for a coffee cup to fill for him.

Walking over to her, he thanked her, took the cup from her hands, and brushed her hair back from her face, catching her gaze with his own. "Kat, we will figure this out," he said gently.

"Jack," Kat said. "I've never felt that way before—last night was amazing." Her lips were curved up in a smile, but her gaze slid away again, as if she were shy or embarrassed.

Jack half-groaned, half-laughed, and pulled her toward him in a tight hug. "You're killing me," he said, breaking away. "Damn Ms. Lowry for showing up today!" He headed toward the stairs with his coffee cup, and Kat watched him leave, smiling at the clear signs of his arousal.

She couldn't begin to make sense of the emotions spinning around in her mind—happy, vulnerable, excited, confused, and add to that, too busy to focus on the situation for long. It was complicated for sure, but she liked how Jack had handled it on his end.

Chapter Twenty-Seven

Katerina loved Jessica Lowry at first sight. She all but bounced into the house, her brown eyes sparkling with life, her arms filled with flowers. Jack followed a few steps behind, carrying what looked like a couple of heavy backpacks and rolling her suitcase behind him.

"Hello, I'm Jessica, and these are for you," she exclaimed as she handed off the bright pink camellias to Kat.

"Welcome, Jessica. I'm Katerina, but you can call me Kat. These are very unexpected and appreciated!" She took the bouquet and laid it on the counter while she looked for a vase.

"Jack told me you're an actual chef, so I immediately wanted to get on your good side," Jessica explained. "To be honest, there's a lot of self-interest here."

Both Katerina and Jack laughed, and the glance they shared was a mix of relief and 'we've got this.' Jack offered to show Jessica the house and to make sure that her printer and laptop were connected and working properly. Katerina exhaled a sigh of relief that her short-term project might be a good time, as well as a good learning experience.

Earlier, she had made a batch of cookies, and the oven was preheated, so she took the opportunity to put the tray in the oven to bake. As the smell of the hot cookies began to waft through the kitchen and likely further into the house, she wasn't surprised to see both Jessica and Jack show up with expectant faces and take a chair at the counter. Laughing at the two of them, she pulled out a platter and three small plates. "Just a snack, since I know you've already had lunch," she said over her shoulder as she started transferring the cookies from the cooling rack to the platter.

"Mmm, these are delicious. What kind of cookie is this?" Jessica asked after taking a quick bite. "I can't quite place what I'm tasting. And for the record, I can't remember the last time I had a glass of milk."

"They are chocolate, sea salt, and thyme cookies," Katerina replied. "It does add something unique to the mix."

"Delicious," agreed Jack. "I can't remember the last time I had a freshly baked cookie." After his second, Jack pushed back his chair and stood. "Ladies, I'm sad to be leaving this party, but I need to head back to Seattle tonight. I have a client presentation early on Monday, and I need to spend most of the day in the office tomorrow. Jessica, is there anything else I can help you with before I leave?"

"No, I think I'm all good—your lovely home is the perfect place to push through the last phase of my book. I appreciate that you were willing to take me in on such short notice. Now, I'll let you two talk behind my back, while I call my husband to let him know I'm all settled in."

They shared a laugh as she left the kitchen and headed upstairs to her room. Jack turned to Katerina, grabbing her hand and squeezing it tightly in his own. "She seems like a great person, and you two should have fun." As he rose to his feet, he pulled on the hand he still held, forcing her to stand, too. Undercurrents from the previous night seemed to swirl in their shared space. "We are a good team," he said, looking down at her, his gray eyes serious. Then he smiled. "And you, Kat, are a very talented woman, and you impress me more each time I see you."

"Ah, Jack," he watched as her eyes filled up. "Thank you, that means more than you can know."

He squeezed her to him tightly, and holding on for a long moment, he kissed her tenderly on the lips before heading upstairs to grab his things. Katerina savored the touch of his lips and felt the internal warmth from his compliment—no, his confidence in her—long after they said their goodbyes.

Shortly after Jack left, Jessica came back into the kitchen and sat down at one of the kitchen island stools. Katerina was perched on her stool reviewing menu ideas, and the two women shared a smile. "I appreciate that you're willing to handle three meals a day—I know it's a lot. When I'm in the final editing stage of a book, I need to bury myself and just fight through to the end. I've also found that if I remove myself from the distractions of my regular life, I do better."

"That makes sense to me." Katerina nodded. "I understand from Jack that you prefer healthy meals with the occasional splurge. I put together a sample of breakfasts, lunches, and dinners, along with desserts, and noted the splurges. Please feel free to suggest any changes—I have the basics on hand and it's not a big deal to make modifications."

"Perfect, Kat. And please join me for meals. It would feel pretty silly to sit off by myself, and I would love to get to know you better. I am very nosy—it comes with the occupation. I make up stories for a living, and I can't help but pry into everyone else's life. I'm very serious—you may have to call me off. I've been told I'm incorrigible," Jessica admitted, smiling unrepentantly, pushing her curly brown hair back from her face.

Katerina laughed out loud. Having Jessica around was going to be a good time. Katerina got up and made salmon piccata served over herby olive oil pasta. They shared a bottle of chilled white wine, and despite Jessica stating emphatically that she did not want Kat to make a dessert, they ended up getting back into the cookies.

"I'm concerned about where this friendship is going," Jessica said, licking some melted chocolate from her finger.

"We could have oatmeal for breakfast to make up for the cookie binge," Kat suggested.

"Not that concerned," Jessica said hurriedly with a grimace.

Jessica offered to help clean up, and when Kat adamantly refused, she admitted that she was tired and took herself upstairs to relax. Kat cleaned up the kitchen and was also happy to relax. *It's been a long day, but a good one.* She knew she had some thinking to do, but she was too tired to dwell on it now.

Chapter Twenty-Eight

*J*essica was as good as her word; she got up early and immersed herself in her work. Kat kept self-service coffee going throughout the day. She tapped on the library door to offer her breakfast around 8:30, and lunch was served at 1:00. Jessica would usually emerge around 5:30, and they would share dinner in the kitchen.

In the evenings, they watched TV together in the living room and often took a glass of wine to the hot tub. It was relaxing to sit in the hot water and steaming jets, sheltered from the Puget Sound drizzle by the partially covered trellis Jack had built.

The two became good friends, and both lamented the eventual end of their mutual break from their normal lives. Jessica had shared the hilarious story of meeting her husband-to-be at a book reading that his then-girlfriend had forced him to attend. The book reading hadn't featured Jessica's book, but how could anyone not notice Jessica? The other girl hadn't stood a chance!

Kat shared her background with Michael and the emergence of Amy, but omitted Jack's presence in the story. Partly to protect his privacy and partly because she just didn't know what to say. Jack texted her every day to check on her, and while the tone was always friendly and engaged, it was hard to interpret his feelings from a text. Worse, she didn't even know what she wanted from him.

What she did know was that she couldn't stop thinking about him, and it was making her crazy. Sometimes late at night, she would allow herself to relive their shared night and remember how hot the sex had been. Was he thinking about her, too? And she would have to remind herself that marrying Michael had always been the future she wanted, right? In the darkness of night, everything seemed more confusing.

But the return of morning and common sense didn't mean that she had any answers, either. Maybe because of her own feelings for Jack, she had even stopped thinking of Amy as the "Interloper." Honestly, she was so confused about the four of them that her still-unformed plan seemed like a murky maze

Chapter Twenty-Nine

Shopping, making meals, and handling the linens were an easy day for Kat, leaving her a lot of time to research and plan her next career steps. She looked into the licensing requirements for opening a catering business in Seattle and also into the availability of commercial kitchens. Her initial focus was on catering for private parties and small businesses, but as she continued to research, she began to see opportunities for home chefs. There were a lot of overlaps between the two areas, so she might be able to combine them into a cohesive business plan.

Jessica decided to take a break from writing on Saturday and join Kat on her trip to the farmer's market. Kat routinely used some of her own money to cook a few dishes she might offer in a catering or home chef capacity. She valued the chance to practice her culinary techniques, and she enjoyed sharing the finished dishes with her favorite farmer's market vendors. As they shopped, Katerina chatted with each of them—the organic fruit and vegetable farmers, the goat farmer where she got cheese and eggs, and the fresh seafood and meat vendors. She had gotten to know them over the weeks she had been on the island, and already she counted them as close friends. They all shared a love and respect for healthy, good food.

Kat and Jessica were stowing their bags into Kat's Jeep when Rhonda, from the fruit stand, waved for her to come back over. "Hey Kat, I didn't get a chance to tell you earlier, a bunch of us from the market are going over to Adam's winery after closing, say around 7:30, to have some wine. We're all going to bring something small to share and just hang out. Would you and Jessica like to join us?"

"That sounds great! I'm definitely in, and I bet Jessica would like to join as well."

"Great, Kat—see you later!" Rhonda turned back to her busy booth, and Kat walked back to her Jeep.

Once inside her vehicle, she turned to Jessica, "Are you up for wine and apps tonight with some of the market purveyors? They're getting together tonight around 7:30 at Adam's winery. You haven't met him yet, but you've been drinking his wine!" Kat said with a laugh.

"Oh, that sounds very fun, and, at this point, I should probably just give Adam a big hug."

Back at the house, Jessica went back to the library and Kat to the kitchen. Kat put the groceries away while considering what she could make to share with the group later that evening. She decided on a flatbread with figs, goat cheese, and arugula. She also opted to bake some lemon and rosemary shortbread cookies. That would cover both the sweet and savory side, she decided.

Her phone rang and she could see Jack was calling. "Hey," she answered, smiling even as she acknowledged anxiety building in her stomach.

"Hey, Kat." She thought she could hear the smile in his voice, and she began to relax. "I know we've been texting, but I wanted to hear your voice and ask how you're doing. You've been too understanding about me leaving you with all the responsibility, weekends and all—that is not how I sold the job to you."

"Jack, please, no worries. I am doing great, and as you know, Jessica is the best. I really don't need a break. How are you doing? I know you've had early days and late nights for a couple of weeks now."

"Thanks, Kat. It's been a lot, pitching for this project, but the optimist in me says we're close to signing a deal."

"That's good news. Are you working all weekend?"

"I am—we have another meeting scheduled for Thursday. After that, I'm hoping my schedule will free up and I can join you next weekend. I want to see you and give you that break."

"I'm pretty sure that I will choose to spend my break right here with you and Jessica. I hope you can make it because it will be great to see you." As she said the words, she knew it was true. His presence just made her day better, and she felt her pulse racing at the thought of him being in the same house.

"What are your plans for tonight?" Jack asked.

"Jessica and I are joining some of the local farmer's market team at Adam's winery after closing. We're all bringing something to share. I've been getting to know all of them, so it should be a lot of fun."

"Are you enjoying the island?" Jack asked.

"I really am. It's everything you said. It's casual and yet urban, too. The people I've met are friendly, and I do like it here." Kat had already admitted to herself that she wasn't in a hurry to return to her big-city life in Seattle.

"I'm glad you're happy there, Kat, and I wish I was there, too. Enjoy yourself tonight. That's a great group. I know—I went to school with most of them. I should hop, but I will be in touch and planning to see you next Friday night."

"I'm looking forward to that," Kat said as she hit the end button on her phone. She was grateful for Jack in her life. It was complicated, but it *was* something. She was ready to admit that.

While the cookies were cooling on the rack and Kat was rolling out the dough for the flatbread, Jessica came into the kitchen for coffee. She snagged a cooling cookie and took a bite. "How fun, I love that you put herbs in your cookies! It's so good and so unexpected, it's elegant somehow. I wish it also meant fewer calories, but it doesn't work that way, does it?" She looked over at Kat.

"Unfortunately, my friend, it doesn't work that way. Do you want me to lighten up our dinner tonight since we will be munching later in the evening?" Kat offered. "I could make us grilled fish tacos and come up with something light on the side."

"Deal. That sounds delicious and like a good idea." Jessica snagged another cookie and her coffee, and went back to her writing.

Slightly after 7:30 p.m., Kat parked her car, and she and Jessica opened the winery door carrying the flatbread and cookies. She saw a few familiar faces and Adam behind the bar, opening a bottle of red. He directed them to put the food at the end of the bar, where there was already a cheese tray, hummus with vegetables, and what looked like some fruit tarts. They took a seat near the others, and Adam handed them each a glass of wine.

The door continued to open, and more seats filled. A pretty woman with curly blonde hair and freckles joined Adam behind the bar, and more glasses were poured. After a few minutes, Adam raised his voice above the small talk and spoke. "Welcome, friends. I have been wanting to do this for a while, so thank you all for joining me tonight. It feels good to spend time with friends and keep our connections strong. Cheers," he said, raising his glass.

"Cheers," the group chorused back, and then the small talk resumed.

It was a welcoming crowd, and between the laughs, Kat learned a lot of interesting information about the island's food scene and its agricultural community. Jessica was a hit, both for her infectious personality and the fact that she was a published author. Kat learned that the woman behind the bar was Jill, Adam's wife. Almost everyone else, Kat, had already met at the farmer's market.

Adam wound his way through the crowd and approached Kat and Jessica. "Hey, is Jack going to be around a little bit more?" he asked her.

"He's been busy with a big project, but he's expecting to be here next Friday night and will likely spend the weekend."

"We miss him around here—he's a good guy. I understand the need to spend more time in Seattle, but we were sorry to see him get a place over there. How did the two of you meet?"

"I met him through Michael, his sister Amy's fiancé," Kat said with as much nonchalance as she could muster. She could feel the sudden and fierce attention from Jessica, but the other woman didn't say a word.

"Right," Adam said, nodding his head. "I heard that Amy was engaged—good for her. We don't know her that well, since she never really lived on the island."

Jill came over to join them, winding her arm around Adam's back. He smiled down at her and introduced her to Kat and

Jessica. "The rumor mill moves fast on the island, so I'd already heard that you both were here, but it's great to put a face to the gossip," she said, smiling widely. "I've already purchased your two books, and I can't wait to start reading," she said to Jessica. "And you, Kat, are you going to be staying on the island or is this a temporary visit?"

"I'm just here to help Jack out during Jessica's stay, but I can tell you, it will be hard to leave. I like it here."

"Well, I hope you change your mind and stay. You're a chef, right? That flatbread over there is delicious."

Jessica chimed in, "You have no idea what a pleasure it is to eat her food every day. She even makes healthy food that tastes good. But on that note, I'm going to go grab one of her cookies." Grinning, she headed to the food area.

"There are several restaurants in town—you might check in with them?" Jill offered.

"Actually, I'm considering going into catering. I want a little more control of my menus and a closer relationship with the customer," Kat explained.

"I get that. Adam and I found that opening the tasting room gave us some of that same satisfaction—we can see the customers and help guide their experience with our wine." Jill reached over and gave her a quick hug. "Welcome to the island!"

Shortly after nine, Kat made her way to Jessica and offered to take her home. They had both enjoyed the evening, but she suspected Jessica would want to be up early, writing. They thanked Adam and Jill, said their goodbyes to the rest of their friends, and drove the short distance home.

The minute they walked in the front door, Jessica surprised her by pulling a bottle of wine out of her purse. "This one's on me, my friend. I think you need to come straight with me. You left out the part where Jack is connected to Michael. That must be interesting because I could feel the sparks igniting between you and Jack."

Jessica was smiling broadly as she set the wine bottle down and opened the cabinet to retrieve two wine glasses. She poured them each a glass, kicked off her shoes, and perched on the kitchen island stool, smiling expectantly, her brown eyes alive with curiosity. Kat laughed and looked fondly at her new friend. It had been a long time, she realized, since she'd discussed her romantic life and been able to laugh.

Kat took a sip of wine and set the glass down. "It's complicated. What I told you about Michael before is the truth. I have loved him my whole life and never considered that we would not be together. There were signs I should have seen, I guess—I know this sounds crazy, but I don't know that I ever stopped to consider whether either of us was happy. Even as we began to grow apart, I just thought it was a phase. The issue that keeps haunting me is that I made this mess—this engagement came into play because I felt like he was going to ask me to give up being a chef. I was so afraid that I would give in to him that I just grabbed a chance to postpone the fight. I assumed he would wait for me, but he didn't. And now, I just need to understand where we really are. He's not a great communicator, so sometimes I feel like I'm getting mixed signals, and I wonder if he's truly happy with Amy."

"That is confusing," Jessica admitted. "So, you said that you weren't sure you and Michael were happy. If you were to find out that he isn't happy with Amy either, would you want him back?"

"Oh, Jessica—a future with him is what I always wanted. I'm really confused."

Jessica nodded, sipping her wine. When she reached over to pat Kat's hand, her brown eyes were filled with understanding.

"So, something recently happened that made you see things differently?" she asked.

"I think it's been a lot of little things with Jack—he's helped me see what a healthy relationship could be. I know he means something to me, it's just I didn't expect to feel a connection with him, and it's confusing. I mean, Michael is about to get married—if there was ever a time to pull together a plan, this is that time. I feel a lot of anxiety about it, but I can't seem to focus on the plan."

Kat paused for a moment, then said, "Sometimes I picture the situation with Michael and Jack as opposite sides of a scale. On Jack's side are all the ways he shows that he believes in me, respects me, and, of course, our chemistry! But on Michael's side are all our years together, and I just see the scale crushing under the weight of our history."

Jessica took a sip of wine and gave Kat a small smile. "Take this for what it's worth—but in writing, there is a concept around the lie the character believes. That false belief creates an obstacle in their life. Uncovering the lie is what allows a character to grow. Think of it like this—what if the man you have always thought you wanted to be with ends up not being the man you need?"

Jessica sighed and continued. "So, Kat, I'd say be easy on yourself and give yourself credit for looking at your relationship with Michael with fresh eyes. That sounds like a big step forward. Enjoy that you're hurting less and be open to new possibilities with Jack."

"Thank you, Jessica. You've given me a lot to think about. Cheers, my friend," Kat said, raising her glass.

"Cheers! Now, one last sip, and I am off to bed."

Before falling into a restful sleep, Katerina lay awake feeling both at peace and hopeful. Despite all the turmoil, was she finally getting more clarity? A lot was going on in her life right now that felt good. Jack was a positive for sure, and Jessica was right—she was hurting less.

Chapter Thirty

ack left the meeting and went straight to his boss's office. He rapped on the partially open door, and Don looked up, waving him in. "How did the meeting go?" his boss asked.

"As we hoped, they signed and we are good to go," Jack said with a smile.

"Congratulations, Jack. This is a big win for the firm, and an even bigger accomplishment for you, personally. I know how hard you've worked on this one."

"Thanks, Don—I've been lucky enough to learn from the best."

The two men exchanged a warm smile. Don had been best friends with Jack's stepdad. After college, when Jack had decided he wanted a career in real estate—but on the development side rather than on his stepdad's construction side—Don had welcomed the younger man into his firm and mentored him. The death of Jack's stepdad had only brought them closer.

"This is going to be a lot to manage. I know you've got a very talented team but let me know where and how I can help. I'm proud of you, Jack." The older man smiled again. "This project is going to change the landscape of Bellevue."

"As always, I appreciate your confidence, Don. You can bet I will keep you posted, and I'll make sure to use all the resources available."

Don nodded, and Jack left the other man's office, heading back to his own. He sat down in his chair feeling keyed up, and reached for his phone. He texted Kat.

Jack: Got it done, the deal is signed.

After a minute, he heard his phone chime and reached for it, seeing Kat's name.

Kat: Congrats, superstar! Celebratory home-cooked meal on Friday night?

Jack: Great idea, thanks. See you tomorrow.

Kat: Can't wait!

Jack put down his phone, smiling. *I can't wait to see her again.* His smile faded as he remembered it wasn't that simple. He had been thinking about the two of them for a while. He had feelings for Kat that he knew for a fact he'd never had for another woman. He also knew he had told her they would figure things out, but he had his sister to think about, too, and recent phone calls with Amy had convinced him that she was feeling vulnerable. He respected that Kat was experiencing a tough time, too, but for everyone's sake, he wanted her to resolve her issues before he got too mixed up in her life. He had never felt at risk in a relationship before, but this one was different, and he knew it. He forced his attention back to his work and reached for the phone again. High-end condominium skyscrapers in the largest bedroom community of Seattle did not just build themselves.

Chapter Thirty-One

Driving from the ferry to his house on the island, Jack's thoughts were filled with Kat. A mix of anticipation just to see her again, and unease because he knew he needed to have a conversation with her. When he opened the front door of the house, he stopped, again aware of the difference she made in his life. The house looked like a home, and his senses were flooded with the mouth-watering smells of her cooking. Time to put aside his worries and just enjoy the evening.

He went straight to the kitchen, where he found both women. Jessica was lounging on a stool, sipping a glass of Adam's white wine while watching Kat slice a French baguette. He squeezed Jessica's shoulder and walked to Kat, giving her a quick hug. She looked up at him with her beautiful smile and offered to get him a glass of wine.

"I'll get it," he said, and she turned back to laying the sliced bread onto a sheet pan.

"We have champagne to celebrate with, too," Kat said. "And I can time dinner for whenever you like. We wanted to give you time to unwind."

Jessica snickered loudly. "That's the sign of a professional— she just offered to let you choose the timing for dinner. In my house, dinner determines the timing, and sometimes that timing comes in unexpected and confusing stages."

Jack and Kat both laughed. "I'm happy to unwind for a few minutes," he finally answered, sitting on the kitchen island stool beside Jessica with his glass of wine.

"You must be tired—long week, right?" Kat asked, smiling at him.

"Tired, yes, but it's good to be here with the two of you, and dinner smells great." It *was* good to be there, and it never got old, watching Kat acting right at home, in his house. She was wearing snug, faded jeans and a round-necked tee with a layering of different delicate chains around her neck. She looked eclectic, casual, and sexy.

After finishing his wine, Jack left to take his bag up to the second floor, and when he came back, they decided to start dinner. Kat put in the bread to toast and a few short minutes later, she layered the toasted slices with whipped feta, followed by a drizzle of honey and topped them with fennel fronds. She set out appetizer plates, and Jack opened the champagne and poured three glasses.

Kat raised hers and spoke, "Congratulations, Jack, on your hard work and your success! Cheers!"

"Cheers," Jessica and Jack said in unison.

Kat served dinner in the dining room, where the table was dressed with candles and fresh flowers. They shared a delicious meal of roasted pork loin accompanied by cannelloni beans with broccoli rabe. For dessert, she had made lemon bars, which she knew were Jack's favorite. They finished the champagne and another bottle of Pinot Noir, and then Kat kicked them out of the kitchen and dining room so she could clean up in peace.

When the last wine glass was dried and the dishwasher started, Kat wandered into the living room to see that Jessica had already headed upstairs. Kat smiled inwardly; no need to wonder what was behind that move.

Jack was stretched out on the couch, and his eyes were closed. She enjoyed the chance to simply look at his handsome face without interruption. She remembered waking up to that same sleeping face, and she felt a definite flash of heat. She hated to wake him but knew he needed his rest—and in a comfortable bed. She could only imagine the hours he had worked over the last few weeks. She bent down and stroked his arm. His eyes opened sleepily, and he smiled at her. She smiled back, and he slowly sat up.

"Sorry, I fell asleep and left you with all the dishes," he said with a yawn.

"I think sleep is what you need, and no worries about the dishes. I am the hired help," she teased.

"Thank you for dinner, Kat. Thank you for making it special—it's nice to have someone to share good news with."

"I enjoyed celebrating with you," she said, and he smiled again.

"On a lighter note, Jessica is a riot. You two must be having a blast," he said with a chuckle.

"You have no idea! I'm really going to miss her."

Jack stood and pulled her close. "Sweet dreams," he said, giving her one tight squeeze before releasing her and heading for the stairs.

"Goodnight," she called after him. She waited until she was in her own room, and then she felt the tears well up and acknowledged her disappointment. Jack hadn't kissed her, and he certainly hadn't suggested they spend the night together.

Did that mean he regretted their shared night? She had made a mess of this. While dealing with her conflicted feelings for Michael, she developed feelings for Jack. She froze in the middle of reaching for her pajamas. *Did I just acknowledge my feelings for Michael are conflicted?*

Chapter Thirty-Two

When her alarm sounded, Kat sat up groggily. She always made sure that coffee was ready early for Jessica. The writer did not give herself a break on the weekends, and Kat wanted to make sure she had what she needed. She brushed her teeth, combed her hair, and changed quickly into a sweatshirt and leggings.

The percolating coffee filled the kitchen with its aroma, and just smelling the roasted beans made Kat happy. She loved coffee and mornings—and this was going to be a good one. She poured a cup for herself and took an appreciative sip while considering her breakfast menu. Jessica usually selected her splurges for Saturday, so today, Kat was making smoked salmon hash with eggs benedict.

Still sipping her coffee, she laid out a tray with Jessica's cup, sugar, cream, and a flower she pilfered from the previous night's dinner table arrangement. She heard a sound behind her and turned to see Jack entering the kitchen. "Wow, I expected you would sleep in, but good morning!" Despite her uneasy musings from the night before, Kat was so happy to have him there.

Jack laughed at her cheery greeting. "Good morning. I think my schedule is pretty messed up—I've had a lot of early mornings lately."

"Coffee?" she asked, already reaching for a cup, and he nodded appreciatively. He sat down at the kitchen island stool, and she joined him. "Tell me about the deal you signed," she said, smiling. "I know it's condos, but what will it be like?"

"It's an integrated upscale urban living concept. A thirty-floor, high-end condo building with retail and restaurants, much of which is yet to be decided, but we have some anchor tenants like a spa already signed up." Jack smiled. "It's a good feeling to have most of the major signoffs in place."

"I'm really proud of you, Jack. That is impressive. It will be amazing to watch it come together and know that you had such a large role in it." Katerina turned her earnest face toward his and saw his satisfied expression.

"Thanks, Kat, which means a lot. But be patient, it's going to take a long time," he said, teasing her. "What are your plans today?"

"Cooking and the farmer's market. Oh, and I got the fabric to put on those wood panels you made for the accent wall in your old room. If I have time, I might start on that project." "What are you planning to do with your day?" she asked with curiosity.

"I thought, if you had time, we might walk around the yard. You mentioned that you had some outside ideas, and I'm interested to hear them. Other than that, I confess I might enjoy a low-key, no-pressure day. I have a few emails, but nothing major."

"Of course, whenever you like. Shall I include you in the meals today?"

"Please—I love to eat your food," he said with a smile.

After an indulgent and delicious breakfast, Jack insisted on cleaning up the dishes so that she could get an earlier start at the farmer's market. When she came back with her purchases, Jack was there to help her carry them in from her Jeep. He sat on the kitchen island bar stool watching her as she put everything in its place and then suggested they go outside to look at the yard.

They dressed warmly in hooded jackets since the Northwest drizzle was at its soggy, drippy best. "So, these are just ideas, and obviously, you know better than I how much you want to invest in this place," Katerina said, walking to the hot tub gazebo area. "What I was thinking is that you have a large yard, and it's pretty. However, I think you could make it more functional and even more attractive if you expand your hang-out space and give it different zones."

Katerina gestured to the area beyond the tub. "We could extend the pavers that you have around the hot tub and gazebo, and create higher and lower zones by putting in walls and steps. Zone one could be your existing hot tub, zone two, maybe a fire pit with chairs or a circular bench, and in the third zone, you could have a water feature with chairs and a small table for drinks or reading. You could put in large planters to further define the zones. I mean, come on, Jack, you have a view of Puget Sound!"

She turned to see his reaction, and he pulled her off her feet and gave her a big hug. "That is so clever, and I can imagine how great it would look! I hear what you're saying about cost, but those kinds of improvements are good for market value. I want to pursue something along those lines. It's a project better suited for later in the spring."

Jack looked at her face, so alive with creativity and pleasure at his appreciation of her ideas. He was also aware of a level of heightened tension on her part and knew she had felt his reticence. Suddenly, he just had to talk to her. He couldn't put it off any longer. "Hey Kat, are you okay to talk out here for a minute or are you too cold?" he asked.

"No, of course, Jack. I'm fine."

"Here, come with me." He pulled her closer under the gazebo to shield her from the drizzle. Kat looked at his serious face, and he realized she seemed wary, like she wasn't sure she wanted to hear what he had to say.

He spoke softly. "Kat, you are important to me. I know our situation is complicated. At the beginning, I thought I could enjoy pushing the relationship boundaries while giving you time." He stopped and took a breath, trying to read her expression. Her eyes were huge, and her hands were clenched. He grabbed and squeezed them, continuing to hold them as he spoke again. "I can't. I don't want to be in a relationship that can go hot and cold based on your feelings for another man. I just can't be anything more than your friend until you resolve your feelings for Michael. I want to feel at peace supporting my sister and her relationship. I don't want to resent and dislike the man she plans to marry. If we have a future, Kat, the next step comes from you, and you need to be finished with your past and ready to move forward. I know I just put this all on you, unexpectedly. I'm not asking for a response. I just needed you to know."

Kat nodded, tears filling her golden eyes. "Would you like me to leave today and give you some space?" Jack asked.

"No," she said, and raised a fist to wipe at the tears. "I don't want you to leave. Jack, I have felt you backing off, and I knew something had changed. My feelings for you are real and growing, and they make me question what I always thought I wanted. You're right to ask me to put that behind me before we can go further," Kat said solemnly.

Jack swallowed the disappointment that she still wasn't ready, but it confirmed to him that talking to her had been the right decision. "Kat, in all fairness, we haven't known each other long, and I know your life is in flux in several areas. But I hope we don't lose this chance." Taking her hand again, they headed back to the house.

oooooooooooO()Oooooooooooo

For lunch, Jessica had chosen BLTs with homemade rosemary potato chips. Kat performed the tasks by rote, making the homemade mayo for the sandwiches and baking the chips to keep them as healthy as possible. With no need to concentrate, her mind was still processing Jack's words. He'd been fair and had communicated his feelings. He deserved credit for that.

After lunch, Jessica went back to the library, and Jack headed off to handle some emails. Kat decided to take on her fabric project while she had the large staple gun rented from the hardware store. In addition to the fabric, she had purchased quilt batting to create the depth and dimensions she was looking for. The process was unwieldy, given the size of the materials, but fairly simple. After the noise of the first few staples, Jack came in and offered to help.

With the two of them, the process went quickly, and they both stood back to admire their work. They carried the panels up to the bedroom and leaned them against the wall, where Jack could affix them later. The geometric pattern in the darker mushroom-colored fabric looked amazing with the taupe-painted walls. Kat high-fived Jack, and he laughed at her.

And just like that, she felt herself relax. He had given her a lot to think about, and she needed to face some things in her life. "I think this wraps up my last project for your house," Kat said, smiling. "Beyond this, we identified that you would need to buy some items to outfit the game room, some new furniture for this room, and... anything else you want to look differently from what I have pulled together for you."

"Selfishly, I would love your help with those final steps, so maybe we can measure the rooms, take some pictures, and go furniture shopping when you return to Seattle?"

"Good idea," Kat agreed.

"Also, while you were cleaning up from lunch, Jessica told me that she estimates that her edits are on track to finish soon. We might only have her for another week. She suggested we all talk about it at dinner."

"Wow, I feel sad," Kat said quietly. "I don't want this to end," she admitted.

"It's clear the two of you hit it off. You'll have to stay in touch," he said, smiling. "Now, I'm going to return to my emails for a few minutes, and I'll check in with you after a while," Jack said, heading back to the living room.

Back downstairs, Kat checked her phone and noticed a missed call from Phillipe. She had reached out to him to see if she could work a few shifts in the kitchen or as a bartender at the Sorbonne. With the end of Jack's B&B job looming, she knew she needed to find another short-term income option while still figuring out the next steps in her career. *And it sounds like I'll be needing those shifts sooner than later.*

She hit the call button on her phone and waited, hoping Phillipe would pick up.

"Kat, my friend."

"Hey Phillipe. I see I missed your call."

"Yes, yes, I know we've been talking about getting you some fill-in jobs, but I had a better idea and reached out to a friend of mine, here in the city. My friend, James, has a catering business, and at first, I was thinking maybe you could just shadow him to see if you like the catering space while you worked here for the income you need. However, it turns out that he could use some help, so this could be a win-win for you."

"Phillipe! That sounds very interesting, really—thank you for reaching out to him."

"I have thought about this, Kat. You know how much I respect you, and I do not want to see you get discouraged with this industry. You're very talented, and this could be a less risky way to get your feet wet. It's still not cooking your food, but it may allow for more of your own creativity. James may be able to offer you more flexibility there. As you well know, a restaurant thrives on every dish tasting exactly the same every time a customer orders it."

"I feel so thankful to have had your mentorship over the years, and the fact that you put this much thought into my career path is more than I could have expected from you."

"Of course, my dear—I have watched you grow up in my kitchen." Kat could hear the sincerity in his voice. "When we hang up, I will text you his contact information, but before you go, I spoke with Antoine. If you want to cover some bartending shifts in the evenings or weekends, we can use your help. The pay and tips could come in handy for capital needs down the road."

"Phillipe, again, thank you so much. I would appreciate that."

"Let me know when you are back in town, and we will talk schedules. Antoine and I both feel that with your beautiful face behind the bar, business may pick up." Phillipe was laughing as he ended the call.

Kat smiled. This was good news, and she enjoyed the burst of optimism the call had given her. She felt her phone vibrate and noted that Phillipe had sent James's contact information, as promised. Her recent research into catering had felt right to her, and she knew this was a good opportunity. *This could finally be where I want to grow my career.*

Jessica had chosen Italian for her splurge meal, and Kat was planning on caprese salad, garlic bread, and spaghetti with red sauce, meatballs, and sausage. She would make tiramisu for dessert. Depending on how the discussion went tonight, this might be the last time she got to enjoy dinner with the two people who had quickly become very important to her.

With a sharp pang, she realized that when she went back to Seattle, she and Jack might very well see less of each other, too. Glancing at the clock, she realized she had no time to waste—she needed to get the tiramisu made so it had enough time to set up in the refrigerator. It was a relief to turn off her churning mind for a while. The smell of garlic and tomato sauce brought Jessica into the kitchen. It was kind of their ritual—she always showed up when she smelled the early stages of dinner and then sat at the island enjoying a glass of wine and watching Kat cook. The sound of their laughter brought Jack in to join them, and he poured a glass of wine and took his seat at the island.

"What was the most unexpected thing you learned in culinary school?" Jessica asked, watching as Kat layered sliced tomatoes and fresh mozzarella, topping them with basil leaves, sea salt, and a drizzle of olive oil.

"That I needed to lift weights and build some muscle," Kat said with a laugh. "Pots, pans, and kitchen equipment are heavy, and working kitchens are competitive. No one wanted to help me get my work done."

"Oh wow," Jessica said thoughtfully. "I would never have thought of that, but it makes sense. Are kitchens as male-dominated as we see in the media? And if so, how did you deal with that?"

"In my experience, yes, they are. I have been lucky to work for good head chefs, but in a kitchen, everyone—male or female—has to prove themselves. We all work as a team, and at the end of the day, it's about earning respect from your team. It's a fast-paced environment, and poor decisions start a domino effect. You have to pull your weight."

"Okay, interesting," Jessica mused, and then she caught Jack's curious expression. "Oh, right, it sounds like I'm interviewing her, right? I kind of am. Kat has inspired me to use a female chef as my new lead character, so I am taking advantage of her experience. As a matter of fact, I'm planning to use her goat cheese and thyme cookies laced with poison as my murder weapon."

Jack's sudden laugh caused him to choke on his wine. When he recovered, he pointed at Katerina and said, "And seriously, look at Kat's face—she is so proud to have inspired the murderous cookie."

"All right, it's true, I am!" Katerina said, wiping tears of laughter from her eyes.

Dinner was delicious, they all drank too much wine, and mixed with the laughter came Jessica's bittersweet announcement that she would leave the upcoming Thursday. Her edits were done, and she was ready to send the novel back to her publisher. The three of them toasted Jessica's accomplishment and called it a night.

Chapter Thirty-Three

After breakfast, Katerina and Jack shared another cup of coffee and discussed the process for Jessica's departure. They decided Kat would drive Jessica to the ferry, and on the other side, Jack would have a car service pick her up and take her to the airport. Katerina would then close up the house and take any perishables with her.

Kat set down her cup and reached out to touch Jack's arm. "Thank you, Jack, for offering me this opportunity. You showed incredible faith in me, and I am thankful for my time here."

He smiled at her. "Having faith in you was not the stretch you give me credit for—I had already tasted your cooking and seen your place."

She laughed lightly. "I wanted to share with you that Phillipe has introduced me to a friend of his in Seattle who runs a catering company. He needs some help, so I'm going to talk with him this week and start next Monday. I'm excited because I will get to see how he runs the business. I really think catering is the space I want to work in, but I'm trying not to get my hopes up too high."

"Kat, that's great news. I know how much you want to find the right fit. Nice that it's a friend of a friend, too—that always makes it easier."

"Agreed." Katerina nodded. "I also wanted to let you know that I'm going to be bartending at the Sorbonne for extra money, on the weekends, so if you find yourself with nothing else to do, please come see me."

"Only if you promise to wear something sexy," he said, grinning.

"Jack, I don't want to lose you," Katerina said around the lump in her throat. She felt emotional knowing that he was leaving soon and this phase for them was ending.

His face sobered. "Kat, go back to Seattle and find your work passion and think about what you deserve from a relationship and how to make that happen. You know how I feel about you. I'll wait as long as I can, but my terms won't be changing. I will come and see you for sure, and we will be in touch, I promise you."

When he put his cup down and stood, she knew he was ready to return to Seattle. Katerina got up from her chair, too, and followed him to the door. He gave her a big hug, but as she shut the door behind him, she felt lost.

⟶∞∞∞∞∞⟨◯⟩∞∞∞∞⟵

Katerina hadn't expected the end of the B&B experience to pull so hard at her emotions. She had never imagined that she would bond so much with Jack and his house, the community, and with Jessica.

As Jessica pushed herself to wrap up all her loose ends on her book, Katerina took time to meet her farmer's market friends, including Adam's wife, Jill, for a goodbye coffee date. They were all interested in her upcoming plans, and she shared that she was going to be working for a caterer.

"I'm sure you can find clients in Seattle, but don't forget us here on the island," Jill said. "Adam and I have had conversations about whether we could expand tastings and bottle sales if folks had food options enticing them to stay on-site longer. I know a lot of the bigger wineries in California have food options. I will call you if we get serious about it, and ladies, let's keep other ideas in mind for Kat, too." The women nodded their heads in agreement.

"We'd love for you to come back here—you will be missed," Rhonda added.

As they were finishing their coffees, the door opened, and Nicole Reardon entered the shop. As before, the striking redhead was impeccably dressed. She walked over to their table and greeted them with a vague smile and indifferent small talk before heading to the counter and ordering a coffee to go. She waved again briefly on her way out.

"And that might be the best reason for you to come back," Jill said, laughing. "Adam told me Jack couldn't keep his eyes off you. I, for one, would hate to see Nicole sink her hooks into him, so you need to save him." Loud laughter erupted at the table as the women rose and hugged their goodbyes.

On Wednesday night, Jessica insisted on ordering a pizza so the two of them could just relax and drink wine. She assured Kat that ordering delivery was critical to helping her transition back into her real life. They ordered a sausage pizza with salad and took their usual spots at the island. They reminisced about their time together; both were sorry to see it end.

After the cleanup, Katerina poured them another glass of wine. "I can't wait to read your book—I'm so proud of you!" Kat said after a sip of her wine.

"Sure, up until you read something that a true Northwesterner will recognize as not quite right—" Jessica said with a scowl.

"Yeah, you're right, up until then," Katerina admitted, laughing.

"But now," Jessica said, turning serious, "keep me posted on your catering adventure. You are such a talented and creative person. Take chances. It beats regret. Lastly, and more importantly, Jack. Sometimes an outsider can see things more clearly because they aren't in the weeds. You two are good together. I see respect, laughter, and chemistry—that's a lot to build on, my friend."

"It was really hard for me to see him leave on Sunday. I felt heavy-hearted and anxious about when I would see him again," Katerina said quietly.

"I think that says a lot about what's important to you." Jessica reached over and squeezed Kat's arm. "I'm coming back here, with my husband Jeff in tow. I want him to meet you and Jack."

"That will be so fun, and I'm glad you said that. It makes knowing I have to say goodbye easier." Kat smiled at her friend.

"It does, doesn't it?" Jessica said with her usual good humor. "I better call it a night—tomorrow morning will come fast."

In her room, Katerina felt unsettled and glum. She knew she had good things to look forward to. She had spoken briefly to James, and she was looking forward to meeting him on Monday. She was going to be back in her condo that she loved, busy with catering during the week, and with bartending on the weekends. *And I'll see Jack soon, won't I?*

Chapter Thirty-Four

Amy reached across the table to clear the breakfast dishes, and Michael trapped her hand with his own. Laughing, she allowed him to drag her to the couch, where he pulled her down on his lap. "Have I told you how happy I am that you're living here now, and I get to see you every day?"

"Actually, I'm quite certain you haven't said that, and I like hearing it," Amy said, putting her arms around his neck and leaning in for a long, sweet kiss.

"How are you feeling?" he asked, rubbing her stomach.

"I feel great. The fatigue and nausea symptoms seem to be behind me, thank God. I've been thinking it might be time to start telling folks our news. Should we look for announcement cards to send? And right before we send those, we can tell our close friends and family?"

"Sure, babe, I'm good with that. Why don't we share that we are having a boy at that time, too?" Michael said with a satisfied smile.

"Yeah, good idea. I think it's time we introduce Michael Scott Doran Jr. to all our family and friends." Amy snuggled closer, and Michael squeezed her tightly.

"Amy, we should talk about how to handle the wedding. Do we want to postpone the date a little to cover the risk that Michael Jr. is a little late? Or just keep the date we already have?"

"That's probably a question everyone else will be asking, too." Amy wrinkled her nose in thought. "How about if I talk to my doctor again before we decide? It's cutting things close, in any case—I'm certainly not worrying about wedding dress fittings right now," she added with a smile.

"If the little guy is going to come before the ceremony, we can always have a quick civil ceremony to cover the logistics," Michael offered.

"Oh, that's a thought. I do want the birth certificate to reflect your last name."

"You're going to be an amazing mother and a beautiful bride," Michael said, sliding her off his lap and setting her on her feet with a long, gentle kiss. "I have to get to the school for a lacrosse drill, so I better hit the shower."

"Right. I'm going to have lunch with Deanna, but I will see you later in the afternoon," Amy said over her shoulder, heading back to the kitchen to deal with the breakfast dishes.

In a minute, she heard the shower start, and she sat down on the kitchen stool, hugging her stomach with her arms and trying to stop the feeling of panic that had been coming over her in waves lately. It wasn't good for the baby, so she had to get a handle on this. *Michael is being so unbelievably sweet—I only have myself to blame for screwing things up.*

Chapter Thirty-Five

James and Kat had agreed that she would meet him at his catering shop at 7:00 a.m. on Monday. She was sitting in the parking lot at 6:40 drinking a coffee and feeling as anxious as the first day of school. She wanted this to feel right; she knew that James's operation was much larger than what she was interested in, but the chance to learn from him was invaluable.

She heard her phone chime.

Jack: Have fun today! You've got this.

Kat: Ahh…thanks for thinking of me! In the parking lot now ☺

Jack: Call me later?

Kat: Absolutely!

Katerina smiled and dropped her phone into her purse. This was going to be a good day. When she opened the entrance door, James was waiting by the receptionist's desk. He greeted her with a friendly and harried smile. "Welcome, Kat! I'm happy to see you, and I'm going to throw you right into the thick of things."

"Great to meet you, too, and happy to help as needed." He led her down a hall to what looked like a staff break room. "You can put your things in a locker and feel free to keep your phone on you. Here's a coat and a hair net. When you are settled, my office is two doors down on the right."

Moving as quickly as possible, Katerina slipped into the coat. With her hair secured, she stepped into his office to see him waiting for a document to finish printing. He motioned her to a seat at the round table in the corner of his office and joined her there, passing her the document.

"As I promised Phillipe and told you earlier, I will give you oversight into any areas of my business as time allows. I am not concerned about competition. There is a lot of work to be had in this industry. My business is quite large, and as I understand it, your interest is to begin in a smaller space."

He took a breath and continued. "Right now, as I also mentioned, I am down my head caterer on Hot Cater, and another staff member called in sick, so we are pushing hard. We have our breakfast orders already complete and packed up. The delivery team is loading them now, and deliveries will begin soon. So, lunch is where I am going to put you. On tap today— we are providing soups, salads, and sandwiches to various businesses, as well as one hot catered lunch for twenty to a law firm. The sheet I just gave you is the menu for the hot catered lunch. I'm going to introduce you to Pete, who is on the catered meals team, and you can step into the role of head caterer. Let's walk through the menu and make sure you don't have any questions, besides the obvious, 'I just got here and don't know how any of this works!'" James said with a good-natured laugh.

Katerina laughed in return, appreciating his attitude. *This is being thrown in the fire, but I can handle it.* She studied the menu and noted common entrees of salmon piccata, chicken marsala, garlic smashed potatoes, sautéed zucchini and mushrooms, rolls, and green salad. "I'm familiar with these menu items," she said, nodding.

"Good," James replied. "Pete and the rest of the team have made these before under our former head caterer's direction. I am just looking for you to oversee, help if questions arise, perform taste tests, and give feedback. You will expedite at the end, making sure everything looks good, and counts and packaging are correct. I will have Pete assist you today to make sure you know where everything is and help you with the transition process to delivery. Handoff to Delivery will be at 10:45 and then you will supervise cleanup of the station. Lunch will be sandwiches and salad in the break room. After lunch, why don't you come back to my office so we can have a conversation about the big picture? Does that sound reasonable?"

"Absolutely," Katerina replied, smiling.

"Let me print out the recipes that go with that menu. They will be posted in the Hot Cater space, but it might be helpful to have your own copy. I'm going to call Pete, too," James said, getting up and crossing back to his desk.

Pete showed up just as the recipes finished printing. James handed Kat her copies and introduced her to Pete. He was tall and lanky, and his arms were covered in tats. His smile was friendly, and his handshake firm. Katerina liked him immediately. She followed Pete through a cavernous open space divided into different zones by large overhead hanging signs. The signs labeled the zones as Soup & Sandwiches, Salads, Hot Cater, Special Orders, Bakery, and Groceries. Toward the outer perimeter of the space, there was a zone labeled Delivery & Servers. Each zone was manned with personnel, but Katerina didn't have time to register how many people were in each.

Pete led her to the Hot Cater zone and introduced her to Diego and Jim. They smiled and greeted her while continuing to perform their roles. "Shall I give you a big-picture overview of our area, and you'll stop me if you have questions?" Pete offered, and she nodded.

"Okay. Diego, Jim, and I are assigned to this area as primaries. Every day, when we arrive, we come here and check the schedule. This team can handle two catered lunches for small groups if the menus are different, or larger groups if they all share the same menu. If there is too much demand for the three of us, we're assigned help from floaters. Likewise, if our assignments are light, then one or more of us becomes a floater. Before our shift starts, management assigns the float status, and you will see it noted on our schedule. Once Diego, Jim, and I have the workload covered, we take the menu to Groceries, and they pull our inventory. We bring it back and begin prepping and cooking the hot dishes. We rotate proteins, starches, and vegetables periodically so that we all get practice. Based on our menu, Bakery, Salads, and Soups & Sandwiches may have orders on their schedule, for us at Hot Cater. If that's the case, we will go retrieve those completed items in time to combine them into our expediting process." Pete added, "Today, we technically have a light day with only one order for a group of twenty, but James is giving us a break to bring you up to speed. He has asked me to guide you through the process. So, no worries, this should go pretty smoothly."

The morning was busy for sure, with a lot of new systems to learn, but Katerina appreciated the high level of organization and cross-checks built into the process. Pete had already picked up from Grocery and validated the receipt against the inventory while she was talking with James. So, upon her arrival, Diego was pounding out chicken breasts and James was cutting up zucchini, mushrooms, garlic, and onions for his own dish, garlic and mushrooms for Diego, and garlic for Pete's salmon dish. Pete, Diego, and Jim were good guys, but their skill sets were not as refined as the line cooks she was used to working with, so she was able to show them some techniques in each of their areas.

The recipes looked and tasted good, and Kat enjoyed thinking how she would have tried to elevate them, but for now, that wasn't her place. With Pete's guidance, the expediting process went smoothly, and the cleanup was efficient. After returning all unused inventory to Grocery, Kat joined Pete, Diego, and Jim for lunch in the break room. They were very interested to hear about her experience in the restaurant industry and culinary school since none of them had formal training or restaurant experience. The three of them, just like her, felt that working with food was where they wanted to be.

After lunch, the three men went to their secondary roles at the bakery, and she found James in his office. Again, he waved her toward the round table in the corner and joined her there with another handful of papers. "How was your morning?" he asked with a smile.

"Good, thank you. I'm impressed—you have some really solid processes developed here."

He laughed, "Trust me, they were born from chaos. I printed some menus and advertising that you are welcome to take with you for reference. They may just help with jump-off points for your efforts down the road."

James spoke with Kat for a full hour. He shared that as a trained chef himself, he had moved to catering for the work-life balance. He recommended developing a niche space where she felt confident making consistent cash flow, allowing her to expand her market further. His example was starting with small coffee shops. They all needed similar baked goods, and he'd been able to differentiate his offerings to make them unique even though they required similar ingredients, timing, and effort. From there, he had expanded to soups, salads, and sandwiches, which he could prep in advance.

He stressed that her relationship with her vendors was critical, and good, consistent inventory was a must-have. He also encouraged her to check in frequently with her customers and not wait for them to reach out to her. He had started with renting space in a commercial kitchen and would suggest the same for her. Along with the menus and advertising, he gave her supplier ideas for disposable packaging and serving materials.

She left his office with her head full of ideas and possibilities, and the satisfaction that what she had heard only bolstered her confidence. *With the smaller scale and the chance to have more creativity in my offerings, catering is feeling like the right thing for me.* Before leaving for the day, she checked in with the scheduling department, and Gina gave her an advance printed schedule of Hot Cater's orders for Tuesday. The schedule listed two orders—the first for fifteen catered lunches and the second for twenty. The menus had different proteins, and the second order had soup as well as salad. With a smile and an acknowledgment that Katerina was new, Gina assured her that the team should be able to handle the orders. "One caveat, though," Gina cautioned, "when you get here in the morning, double-check the schedule posted at Hot Cater. There are times when we get a late call, and if we can fit in another order, we will. At that point, floaters will be added as needed." Gina clarified that with Kat's chef credentials, her secondary responsibility would be on the Special Orders team.

Katerina nodded and thanked her, heading back to the breakroom to remove her chef hat and coat. Her regular shift would remain at 7:00 a.m.; her first day had been typical. She smiled fondly in recollection of her line cook days on the breakfast shift.

Back at her condo, she laid out the information James had given her, and after reviewing it, added it to the information she had gathered on licensing. His feedback on starting with a niche client base made a lot of sense to her. He had also given her some good tips on selling food items through the mail and even marketing ready-made items like sauces and soups for customers to use for dinners at home. She made some notes and questions for follow-up. She felt deep gratitude for all who were supporting her in this venture.

With a pang, she thought of Paul and Helen. They meant so much to her, and she had missed them terribly while in Australia. Since coming back, she had felt awkward over Michael's engagement and then left for inn sitting on the island. She wanted to be able to talk to them about her catering plans, and she was sure they would ask about her time on the island.

That reminded her to call Jack. Grabbing her phone, she hit the call button, and he answered after the second ring. "Hey, how was your day?"

"It was busy and interesting. The place is like a factory. Much larger than I ever aspire to be, but there are still a lot of things I can learn. James was very forthcoming with ideas and his philosophies on catering, and my teammates are good guys. I enjoyed it!

"That is great to hear. So, are you staying on the early morning shift?"

"Hah! My start time is 7:00 a.m., and that's for the lunch shift! There is a full-size bakery and a breakfast team that starts at 4:00 a.m."

"Not the career for me," Jack said with a laugh. "You're going to need a nap on Fridays if you're bartending that same night, right?"

"So right. I can't lie—this schedule is going to be an adjustment, but the offset is it's nice to get off early. How was your day? Are things going to pick up quickly?"

"Yes, there's going to be a lot of meetings, plans, approvals, and red tape, but it's an exciting time and my team is pumped up, as am I."

Kat could hear the smile in his voice, and it made her smile, too. "Jessica texted me. She is home safe and wearing sunglasses because the sun seems so bright after the Northwest."

Jack laughed. "There's probably some truth in that. She picked the worst time to visit if she wanted to see the sun."

"I know you're busy, Jack, and still at the office. I just wanted to let you know how things went and to say thanks again for texting this morning. It was sweet of you to think of me," Kat said.

"It's good to hear your voice, and I'm happy that you're excited about your day. Stay in touch, and I am planning to drop by Sorbonne's Friday night."

"Perfect. Talk to you soon, Jack."

"See you, Kat."

Jack ended the call and set his phone down on his desk. He picked it back up after a minute and scrolled through his recent pictures. He had taken a couple of Kat and Jessica this last weekend, and Jessica had insisted on getting a few of Kat and him. He looked closely at the pictures she had sent him. In the first one, he had his arm around Kat's shoulders, and she was laughing, likely at something Jessica had said. The picture perfectly captured the life and vitality her smile brought to her already beautiful features and those incredibly colored eyes. The second picture was of the two of them sharing a piece of tiramisu, and her grin was playful and just so distinctively her. He knew he had been right to tell her to figure out her issues, but now she was back in Seattle and meeting new people. She was going to be bartending. *God knows who she could meet there.* With a start, Jack realized he was jealous. He wasn't sure he had ever cared enough to be jealous before, and he wasn't sure he liked the feeling.

Chapter Thirty-Six

The rest of the week flew by for Katerina. She enjoyed the fast pace and found her time in Special Orders to be an especially valuable learning experience. With her intent to have a small catering business, her model would likely be much closer to this area. The Special-Order kitchen was a fully equipped commercial kitchen since they made everything from quiche to lobster mac & cheese and numerous other specialty items. She was thankful for the experience and grateful for the money that she was earning there and with bartending.

Her list of notes in the catering file at home was growing exponentially—and her excitement along with it. She had filled Marnie in on her catering work and longer-term plans, and her best friend's confidence and validation meant the world to her. Marnie and she had gone to culinary school together, and her friend now ran her own business, so her feedback was invaluable.

Driving home on Friday, Kat was filled with excitement to see Jack. She had so much to share with him and wanted to hear about his week, too. It was almost impossible to take a nap when she got home, but she knew she needed to. She was scheduled for 6:00 at Sorbonne's and she would work until 11:00ish. It was going to be a long day.

Katerina jumped when her alarm went off and smiled at the realization that she had actually managed to fall asleep. She showered quickly and dressed in the Sorbonne's unofficial bar uniform of a black pencil skirt and a white button-down shirt. She added comfortable black wedge pumps, a simple silver chain, and large silver hoop earrings in addition to her diamond studs. She wore her hair up in a high ponytail and applied more smoky eye makeup than usual to fit with the bar atmosphere. She needed tips, after all, and, she admitted to herself, she wanted to look good for Jack.

Entering Sorbonne's, she went to the kitchen to find Phillipe, and the reception from her former co-workers was a mix of catcalls and derisive comments about front of the house vs. back of the house. Laughing, she threw up her arms in self-defense.

She found Phillipe in the back room and hugged him. "Phillipe, thank you again for helping me get a spot with James and for letting me join Greg at the bar. I'm so grateful."

"Ma chérie, it is my pleasure! You are learning and enjoying yourself?"

"I really am, Phillipe."

"Wonderful, I will find you later and we can talk more. It will be fun to hear what James's place is like," he said, giving her another warm hug.

Walking back out into the hallway, she bypassed the dining room and entered the separate bar area. She greeted Greg, the long-time bartender, and listened as he filled her in on inventory and gave her a quick update on trending drinks.

Her night started with a smattering of businesspeople, mostly men coming in for a drink before heading home, and a few folks having apps and a cocktail at the bar, plus parties coming into the bar for a drink before being seated for dinner. She found the rhythm pleasant, making small talk, and pouring wine mostly, but also the occasional martini or old-fashioned. She was aware that she was keeping an eye out for Jack but still managed to enjoy herself.

Around 8:15 p.m., Jack walked in dressed for the office but without the jacket. His tie was loosened, and the top button of his shirt unfastened. Katerina felt her stomach drop and chided herself for feeling nervous.

•••◦◦◦◦◦◦◦◦◯◯◦◦◦◦◦◦◦◦•••

Jack took a seat toward the end of the bar where there was the most open space and gave her a big smile. She smiled widely back, grabbing a menu and a glass of water. "Great to see you, Jack," she said, putting the water glass down and handing him the menu.

"Glad to be here," he said. "You look amazing."

"Ah, thank you. You had dinner, right?"

"I did—I had a sandwich at my desk. I took this opportunity to work late and got some things done."

"Then you deserve a drink. What can I get you? I'm really glad to see you, Jack." It was clear to them both that her last statement was weighted with unspoken meaning.

"I've missed you, too," he said seriously, and then he lightened the moment with a smile. "I'll have a martini up."

"Certainly!" She smiled back and then left him, returning in a moment with his drink and placing it before him.

"Excuse me for a moment," she said, moving away to greet new customers. He sipped his drink and enjoyed watching her.

Kat was a beautiful and sexy woman. Her manner was professional and self-possessed, and she clearly knew her way around a bar. He had seen her dressed up before, but the short skirt was very nice. Also, he felt a strong personal connection to her now, so the experience felt different. He was aware of the admiring glances she received from the other men sitting at the bar, and he tamped down what he now recognized as jealous possessiveness.

After a few moments, the bar crowd settled down enough to allow her to come back to his corner. "So how did the entire week go for you?" he asked, truly interested.

"I had a really good week." Her voice was animated and her eyes sparkled. "James keeps sharing ideas for me to consider, which is priceless. I'm so impatient to move forward, but it's great to be earning some money here and there. How was your week? Clearly, you're busy if you stayed at the office late."

He smiled. "We are busy, and it feels great—a lot of planning and negotiating with all the stakeholders. I'm pretty pumped up, too. I'm going into the office tomorrow for a while."

"I plan to sleep as long as possible. I'm going to be dragging if I don't make up some sleep," she said, grimacing.

•◦◦◦◦◦◦◦◦◯◯◦◦◦◦◦◦◦•

Jack ordered another martini, and they managed to talk frequently between her other customer responsibilities. She was sorry when he finished his second drink and told her he should be getting home. When he pushed back his chair and stood, she came from behind the bar and gave him a big hug. He hugged her back and gave her his sexy grin as he headed toward the door.

She watched him leave, feeling somehow untethered. It made her uncertain and anxious.

Chapter Thirty-Seven

Katerina awoke the next morning and just lay in bed appreciating the fact that she had nowhere she had to go that morning. She'd arrived home around midnight, exhausted, and had gone straight to bed. She wished she'd been able to sleep longer, but the early weekday mornings had shifted her body clock.

The night before had been good; the tips had made it worth working. *Saturday night tips may not be as good.* There'd be more dating and married couples and fewer business professionals and singles. Oh well, she would welcome whatever she got.

It had been good to see Jack, too, but seeing him outside the bubble of their time on the island had been disconcerting. The uncertainty of knowing when he would show up, the wondering where he might go afterward. She probably wouldn't see him tonight—would he come into the bar next weekend? Would he come if she didn't ask him to?

Groaning out loud, she pushed back the covers and got out of bed. She made coffee and got ready for the day, intending to do some laundry and straighten up her condo. On a whim, she group-texted Paul and Helen to see what their schedule looked like. In a minute, she heard the familiar chime.

Paul: Would love to see you. Helen's off with her sister for a girl's weekend. Come on over.

Kat: Perfect, heading for the car now!

When she pulled up to the familiar home, she looked next door at her childhood home. It was still dark and shuttered, as her parents had decided to go directly from their Mexican cruise to their winter home in Arizona. Her mother didn't like the Northwest's overcast winters.

Before Kat could ring the doorbell, Paul opened the door and gave her a big hug. "Ah kitten, it's good to see you!"

Kat laughed at the childhood nickname. "It's so good to be here! I've missed you." She followed him to the kitchen, and sitting down at the familiar kitchen table, she accepted a cup of coffee. She handed him a bag of his favorite doughnuts for the two of them to share. They exchanged guilty grins, knowing that Helen tried to keep sweet treats away from Paul.

"Tell me what's going on in your life?" he asked, pulling a chair up beside her and immediately reaching for a doughnut.

"You knew I was on Bainbridge Island, helping Jack with his B&B, right?

"I did hear that. I heard you were cooking and decorating—both of those activities are in your wheelhouse," he said, smiling.

"I did enjoy it, and Jack's house is lovely. It was fun helping him update it, and well, cooking is what I love to do. The author guest ended up being amazing, so honestly, I was sorry to see it end." Her voice quieted, and she said, "I'm sorry if my decision to help Jack caused stress for Michael and the rest of you."

Paul reached over and took her hand in his own. "Kat, you deserve to make decisions that work for you. Jack asked for your help, and you wanted to provide it. If that decision made anyone else uncomfortable, that's their issue to work out."

"Oh Paul, I appreciate you saying that, but I do feel awkward. I know Amy wasn't happy—Michael told me. And I don't think he liked it either." Kat was horrified when her eyes filled with tears.

Paul pulled her close and hugged her tightly. When he drew back, he waited until she met his eyes with her own. "Kitten, you are the daughter that Helen and I couldn't have. We just want to know that you are making decisions and plans that are good for you." Katerina's shoulders shook, and tears dripped down her cheeks. Paul just held her until he felt the shaking lessen. He stood up and reached for a tissue, handing it to her. "So now, you're back in Seattle. Tell me what you're doing."

Katerina inhaled deeply. She recognized that Paul was trying to refocus her attention so she could calm her emotions. Finally, she was able to speak. "I'm interested in using my culinary background to start a small catering business. I really want to make my own food creations. Right now, I'm working for a large catering business and bartending on weekends to make some working capital."

"Good for you," he said, patting her hand. "I know how much you love food, and I'm really happy to hear you're trying to find the right fit. Both Helen and I were hoping you wouldn't give up on your dream. So, you're enjoying the catering company?"

"I am. The owner is a friend of Phillipe's from Sorbonne's, and he's been very generous with ideas and pointers. I am so excited. I feel like this will give me the creativity I couldn't seem to find in the restaurant world."

"How long do you think it will take to build up the working capital you need?"

"James, the owner of the catering company, advised me to work on getting some niche clients at the beginning that will bring in a regular cash flow, and he's offered to let me only work part-time at his place when I get to that point. That's a generous offer, so I'm trying to research what niche might be best for me. I'll need to be able to cover the commercial kitchen rental, packaging, etc. I'm working on a budget now. With the part-time help from James in the beginning and the bartending from Phillipe, it should be doable soon. The downsizing of my condo has given me some financial cushion."

"I'm proud of you, Kat. I know you're talented, but I also know that you have worked very hard and haven't always gotten the support you deserved from the ones you love."

Kat nodded. "My parents and Michael were never fans of me going into the culinary field, but it's where I want to be."

Paul reached for her hand again. "Kat, I know you and Michael have struggled in your relationship over the years, and I imagine his engagement has been an adjustment. Do you want to talk about it?"

Kat could feel her eyes welling up again, and Paul handed her another tissue. "I feel like it's all my fault—I should never have reacted to his time-out by going halfway across the world. I knew we weren't happy, but I shouldn't have done something so drastic."

"Helen and I have talked about this many times, and we both feel like you did the best thing for the two of you. You gave both of you some space to breathe. Neither of us wanted to interfere because we love you both, but we have watched your relationship over the years and had our concerns about the cycle the two of you were in. Do you mind if I share some insights with the hope that it helps you see another perspective?"

Kat nodded, and Paul spoke quietly. "I know my son is a good man. I also know that he has felt like your protector and sometimes in that role he could be rather judgmental. And you, my dear, are an amazing, strong woman, and you are loyal to a fault. You will go down with the ship," Paul said, smiling gently at her. "Maybe because of your upbringing with your parents and the closeness that you have with Helen and me, you felt the need to hold on to the romantic idea of you and Michael longer than you might otherwise have. There is no doubt in my mind that the two of you love each other dearly. I'm just not sure either of you want to be a couple."

Katerina choked back a sob and wiped at her eyes. It was hard to hear Paul say the words, and she needed to process everything, but she recognized some truths. "Do you think Michael is really happy? Does he want to be with Amy?"

Paul patted her back. "I think Michael enjoys being the decision-maker and likes that Amy looks for him to play that role. I think they share a lot of common interests and life goals. Yes, honey, to answer your question, I do think he loves Amy."

Katerina closed her eyes tightly and gripped Paul's hand. "Thank you for that, I needed to hear it. It's important to me that he's happy, and I'm sorry if I tried too hard to hold us together. I've been confused, feeling like I needed a plan to fix all of this, but then I wasn't always sure I wanted to fix it."

"Shush," Paul said, holding her as she let the tears fall. "You both played this out—maybe as you both needed to. There is no blame. Are you going to be okay?"

Katerina nodded, wiping at her eyes. "I will be. I heard what you said, and I know much of it rings true to me. It's just still hard. And then, I've had feelings for Jack that have confused me, too."

Paul chuckled. "Helen told me at the holiday dinner that he spent a lot of time looking in your direction. From what we've seen of him, he's a good man, but you do like a complicated path, my dear."

"Yeah, that seems to be the case," Katerina said, mustering a teary, rueful smile.

Later that evening, behind the bar at Sorbonne's, Katerina's mind seemed to be working separately from her body. Going through the motions of greeting and serving customers, she spent every spare minute rehashing her morning with Paul. His unconditional love had felt like a lifeline to her earlier five-year-old self when she had gone to that same house for love as a child, and now Paul had made her feel secure that the door was still open. His unbiased feedback helped her see both Michael's and her own actions in a new way. But most importantly, if Michael was happy, could she now let go?

Chapter Thirty-Eight

*S*unday was the sleep-in day that Katerina needed. She didn't even stir until 10:30 a.m. She checked her phone and saw a call and voicemail from Helen. Hearing the love and compassion in Helen's voice brought on a storm of tears to rival those from the day before.

Katerina got out of bed to grab tissues and start the coffee. With her hot coffee in hand, she padded back to her bed and crawled right back under the duvet. Sipping her coffee, she let her mind process the recent events. Today, the tears felt like a cleansing of her soul. So many of the answers had been there in front of her all along, but she had been too caught up in her fear and long-standing habits to see them. Some of the answers had crystallized in the life she had been building since her return from Australia.

She spent the morning cleaning her condo and doing laundry. She left a heartfelt voicemail for Helen, thanking her and promising to make plans for the following weekend. In the early afternoon, while she was deep in her catering budget, her phone rang, and she picked it up to see Marnie calling her. She was surprised because they had a long talk the day before, just after she'd gotten home from her morning with Paul.

"Hey, you," she answered.

"Hey, yourself. I am calling to introduce you to the new short-order cook at the Sunshine Beach Grill," Marnie said, chuckling.

"No, way! That's the place you get your morning rice, spam, and eggs, right?"

"Yes. They've had a sign posted for a while, and the owner and I have gotten friendly over my visits. This morning, a group of tourists came in and they got totally swamped. I offered to help, and one thing led to another."

"So much for living the life of leisure. How much are you planning to work?"

"Just the breakfast shift, and it was fun—it'll give my day a little structure which I will appreciate, and hey, I will learn more about Spam!"

"Is that a good thing?" Katerina asked with a laugh.

"I don't know, but I am kind of getting fond of it. I threatened my brother with developing a new bagel-with-Spam recipe, and my idea wasn't exactly met with enthusiasm."

"Well, not all culinary migrations are successful," Katerina mused dryly.

Marnie laughed. "What are you up to today?"

"I am budgeting for the catering business. The tips were pretty good this weekend, which was helpful, and I feel like I'm getting close on the basics. Figuring out the niche business will help narrow down the provisions and packaging costs."

"Right… any thoughts?"

"I thought I might look around the Fremont area. I feel like I might have more opportunities in areas that embrace independent coffee shops and small bookstores."

"That's a good idea. Any thoughts on reaching out to the friends you made on Bainbridge Island? If you could get in early at the local wineries, that could be your niche. And maybe like Fremont, it's more of a small business community?"

"That's interesting—I do like the pace there, and to be honest, Seattle seems busy and noisy after being on the island. It's a commute, but not a long one. I will add that to the mix. Maybe I'll call Jill and find out if they are serious about adding food, and I can talk to Jack about it, too."

"Whoa, wait… talk to Jack about it, why?"

"Just because he's from there and I want to make sure he's okay with it." Even as she said the words out loud, Katerina knew Marnie would pounce on it.

"Kat, please don't let another man hijack your intentions. Remember how you wasted a year of college trying to be something for Michael instead of going to culinary school to be the chef you wanted to be? Talk to Jack if you want his advice or help, but not for permission—promise me?" Marnie's voice was soft, but Kat knew she would follow up on this conversation if need be.

"You're right." Kat surprised both Marnie and herself with her quick acknowledgment. "I want to be confident and drive my own future."

"That's my girl! So now that we mentioned Jack, are you ready to tell him that you want to give the two of you a chance?"

"I am—just not sure how exactly to do it," Katerina admitted.

"Well, good for you! I'm really happy for you, Kat. Oh, I have to run but keep me posted!" Marnie was laughing as the connection ended.

Smiling, Kat laid her phone down and added Bainbridge Island to her catering notes. As she worked through her budgeting calculations, the idea of starting her business on the island began to take form. As Marnie had pointed out, there were the wineries to target. She also recalled that Beth Milner had mentioned some of the B&Bs wished they could offer dinners—especially when customers were staying at their place to celebrate special occasions. James had mentioned prepared items that might fit in with the farmer's market. She had also noticed the island had a commercial kitchen, so that box could be checked. Her ideas so far were all over the catering spectrum. *This is going to require a lot of organization, but I can handle it.*

Chapter Thirty-Nine

Katerina's week was a blur— there were two days where she needed floaters which was good and bad—it was extra help, but in both cases, it was their first introduction to Hot Cater so more supervision was required. In her Special Orders role, she was assigned several different kinds of quiche and a seafood tower, all of which were time-consuming, in addition to the usual mac & cheese and lasagna dishes. Still, she was happy for the practice, and the fast pace kept her energized.

In the evenings, she started brainstorming menu items to present to Adam and Jill. She assumed they would be able to provide a small, dedicated refrigeration unit, so she focused on chilled or room-temperature items. She and Jill had been exchanging emails, and she wanted to give Jack a heads-up. With her newfound personal clarity, Katerina was feeling nervous to call him. He answered on the second ring.

"Hey, Kat! How are you? You beat me to it—I was going to call you." His voice was warm, and picturing his smile reassured her just a little bit.

"I'm good. Very busy week in the catering world, but all good. How are you doing? Getting a break at all?"

"No, this is a big push time—that's why I was going to call you."

"Oh, what's up?" Katerina asked, her stomach tightening with anxiety.

"I was planning to come by the bar to see you tomorrow, but I need to entertain some out-of-town business folks, who today just requested an on-site meeting. Timing is tight, so we will all be spending the weekend working in our office. We are negotiating some of the remaining retail space, and it's gotten rather political on who goes where and who else is on the site, etc."

"Oh, I'm disappointed for sure, Jack, but I understand." Kat tried somewhat unsuccessfully to add a bright tone to her words.

"Well, I'm disappointed, too," Jack said with an audible sigh. "There is some good news, however. I booked dinner for eight at your restaurant, and I will guide the group to the bar before we are seated so I can at least see you."

"Jack, thank you. That makes me happy." Suddenly, she couldn't stop herself. "Jack, I really miss you," she blurted out in a rush.

"Kat, I miss you, too." His voice was soft, and she could hear that he meant it. "I am unfortunately tied up this whole weekend with work."

"Maybe next weekend we can spend Saturday or Sunday together?" she asked, holding her breath.

"I would love that," Jack said. "I could do dinner during the week, too, but I am pulling some late hours right now, and you have early mornings, so maybe the weekend is easiest?"

On an exhale of relief, she responded, "Probably. While I would love to see you sooner, I would hate to fall asleep over dinner, and it could happen. My internal clock is confused," she said dryly. "On another note, I wanted to let you know that

I'm planning to talk with Adam and Jill about some catering ideas for their winery and hopefully contact some other island wineries. While I was inn sitting, Jill mentioned some interest in expanding their tastings and we have been emailing ideas back and forth. I will likely be heading out there this Sunday to take them some samples." Katerina swallowed hard, waiting for his response.

"Kat, what a great idea, and good for you! I am bummed that I can't go with you. I would love to see them both, and of course, I would love to eat your samples." She could picture his grin, and she warmed with happiness as she recognized again his support and belief in her. "You know you are welcome to use the kitchen in my house to do your prep if it's easier than doing it in Seattle. I don't know if transit creates a problem?"

"Jack, thank you—that's very generous of you! Let me think about my plan, and I will let you know Friday."

"Sounds good, Kat. Again, I am happy for you, and it will be great to see you on Friday."

"Thanks, Jack. Good to hear your voice." Katerina ended the call, and with a burst of energy, she got up and paced around her small condo. She was disappointed about how little she would see him on Friday, but the weekend after felt like a date! She was also over the moon that he was happy for her to be talking to Adam and Jill.

Chapter Forty

When Kat got home Friday afternoon from her catering job, she again tried to take a nap to boost her energy levels for the long bartending night ahead. Like the previous week, it was hard to turn her mind off and relax. The money was good, but she had been tired all week, and she looked forward to getting her catering business off the ground. Working part-time at James's catering company and part-time for herself would hopefully allow her to give up bartending.

The first thing she did after arriving at Sorbonne's and getting settled behind the bar was to pour herself a cup of black coffee. Greg, the other bartender, smiled sympathetically at her. "Already feels like a long night?"

Kat smiled back. "Yes, it does, but that's what coffee is for." As she sipped her coffee, Greg updated her on inventory, and they reviewed the restaurant's reservations for the evening to get a rough prediction of busy times for the night ahead. Kat noticed Jack's party of eight at 7:30 p.m. and appreciated again that he had made the reservation at Sorbonne's so that they could at least see each other briefly. The bar began to pick up with the after-work crowd, and Kat, fueled by caffeine, got into her rhythm of mixing drinks and making small talk.

A few minutes after 7:00 p.m., Jack entered the bar with a group of men. They were all dressed in suits, and Jack led them to a table in the corner and then made his way to the bar. "Hey, beautiful," he said, flashing his grin.

"Hey, yourself," she responded, smiling widely. "Let me get some drinks in for your table." She grabbed some menus and exited from behind the bar to walk with him to the table. Jack made quick introductions and Kat took their orders, returning a few minutes later carrying a tray with drinks, and setting them down for each of the gentlemen at the table. He handed her his credit card, and she thanked him.

By introducing Kat, it was clear to his guests that he knew her at least peripherally. None of them made any outright comments, but he was aware of several appreciative male eyes following her movements behind the bar. He understood she was a beautiful and sexy woman, and he was still getting used to his feelings of possessiveness toward her. His mind flashed back to their call and the feeling he had that she was ready to move things forward. Reluctantly, he forced his attention back to his companions.

When Kat returned with his check, he grabbed her hand. "I'll stop by to say goodnight after dinner," he said, looking into her eyes. She gave him the smile that lit up her eyes, wished everyone an enjoyable dinner, and returned to the bar. Leaving her a very generous tip, Jack led the men toward the dining room.

Around 9:00, she was pleasantly surprised by a visit from Pete and Diego, who pulled up seats at the bar. "Welcome!" she said, smiling at the two of them. "Great to see you. What can I get for you?" Pete ordered a whisky sour with rye, and Diego ordered a Sazerac.

"We wanted to come see where you used to work in the kitchen," Pete explained.

Kat nodded. "This is it. I worked in a couple of kitchens before this one, but this is where everything clicked. I like the head chef a lot, and I felt good cooking his food. This is where I first really felt like a chef, I guess," she said, shrugging her shoulders. She knew Pete wanted to expand his expertise with food. During their primary shifts, he asked her a lot of questions and was always wanting tips and feedback on his dishes.

The three of them were discussing food trucks when she saw Jack enter the bar. With a smile, she waved him over, introduced him to Pete and Diego, and explained that they all worked for James Catering. He accepted a seat on the other side of Pete and ordered a cabernet. He took a sip of his wine and then said, "Please don't let me interrupt your conversation."

Pete said, "We were just discussing the food truck scene— Portland has a really big footprint. It's a cool thing for the city and for people to get their food noticed. I wish Seattle had something as big as theirs."

Kat excused herself and went to serve other customers and when she came back the three of them were having an animated conversation about the hottest new downtown restaurants and their cuisines. Jack sipped his wine slowly and stayed for at least a half hour talking to Pete and Diego.

Kat couldn't help making the comparison that in similar circumstances, Michael would have moved to another seat after being introduced to her restaurant friends, forcing her to choose him or them. Jack, on the other hand, made an effort to fit in—in fact, he seemed to be enjoying himself. When Jack finally set his empty wine glass down after paying his check, Pete said, "Jack, man, you look familiar to me. Did you grow up on Bainbridge Island?"

"I did," Jack admitted, looking closer at Pete. "No way; you're Rhonda Bright's younger brother!"

"Yeah," Pete said, "that's where I know you from."

"Ha, I know your sister from the farmer's market," Kat said, laughing. "Small world."

Jack said, "It's been great talking to you guys, but I need to get some sleep—big day tomorrow." He pushed away from the bar, and Kat came from behind the bar to hug him. Before releasing her, he looked into her eyes as if questioning, then he kissed her lightly on the lips. "Good night, Kat."

"Good night, Jack." She watched him leave while trying to commit the feel of his lips to her memory so she could replay that scene over and over. When she re-entered her spot behind the bar, Pete and Diego were grinning at her.

"So that's how it is?" Pete teased her.

"Maybe?" she teased back.

"Ditching the catering jacket and the hair net is a nice touch," Diego said dryly, and they all laughed.

Chapter Forty-One

Katerina and Helen had decided to meet for coffee on Saturday afternoon. When Katerina entered the shop, Helen enveloped her in her arms. Releasing Katerina, she sat back down, and Katerina noted that Helen had already bought them each a coffee, so she sat down, too.

"Kat, I know you've talked to Paul, and you and I have talked on the phone, but I did want to see you. I want to make sure you know how much we love you, and I guess see for myself that you are doing okay." Helen's blue eyes were sympathetic, and her love for Katerina was clear in her gaze.

"Honestly, Helen, I've had some time now, and it just seems to be getting clearer to me every day. I feel pretty good about things." Katerina surprised herself by being able to share those words without tearing up.

"I'm so happy to hear you feeling good and sounding optimistic," Helen said, patting Kat's hand. "In many ways, my son is a traditional, maybe even old-fashioned, man. I think you were a handful for him sometimes with your creative flair—you were always unique and independent." Helen's voice took on an earnest tone. "Kat, I know sometimes he made you feel like those traits were bad, but they are not; they were just uncomfortable for him."

"Oh Helen, I am so lucky to have you and Paul," Katerina told her, squeezing the older woman's hand.

"Paul and I are the lucky ones," Helen insisted. "Remember how we met you? Michael brought you to our house because he wanted me to help you with show-and-tell at school. I guess you were five. I was in the garden, and you asked about my herb garden, and we decided that could be your story. Do you remember how we sat on the ground and tasted every one of the herbs? Kat, you filled all the empty spots, and truthfully, sometimes Paul and I have felt guilty that we may have overstepped our roles and hurt your relationship with your parents," Helen said gently.

Katerina clasped both her hands and held on, squeezing them tightly. "Please, don't ever feel that way—my relationship with my parents would not have evolved any differently if we hadn't found each other. I honestly believe that, and I know how lucky I am to have found a family with you and Paul. Helen, I always felt that Michael saved me that day. I think he brought me to you because he knew I needed you and Paul. I have always loved him for sharing the two of you with me."

Helen wiped a tear from her eye. "So, tell me, honey, what is going on in your life?"

Chapter Forty-Two

Katerina drove her car off the ferry, or "boat" as the Bainbridge Island locals called it, and drove to Jack's house. She had decided to take him up on his offer to use the kitchen to make her samples for Jill and Adam to taste. Pulling up to the house, she felt homesick, and after retrieving the hidden key from its hiding place and opening the front door, she almost wanted to cry. This place was a part of her, and she had missed it.

Carrying her produce and groceries into the kitchen, she set them down and laid the items out on the familiar workspaces. It felt good to be back here and cooking. First, she whipped up a quick batch of herby cheddar cookies. She planned to use the savory cookies on a cheese platter. After also making a quick chicken salad with basil, she began to build her platters.

The platters featured various combinations of French baguettes, crackers, her savory cookies, both hard and soft cheeses—aged and fresh—for flavor and texture, a variety of nuts like walnuts, pistachios, hazelnuts, and pecans, charcuterie meats, soft briny olives, and apples, pears, and grapes. On future platters, the fruit could change with the seasons. She used sourdough bread to make chicken salad sandwiches, pairing them with fruit for a heartier option. She wanted to be able to provide unique offerings to each winery, so if Adam and

Jill made their selections today, she planned to remove those choices from her later presentations.

Satisfied with her work, she packed up the platters and cleaned the kitchen. Securing the platters carefully in her car, she replaced the hidden key and drove to Adam and Jill's winery. Adam met her at her car and gave her a hand carrying in the platters. After hugging Kat, Jill helped Kat place the platters randomly on the bar while Adam poured them each a glass of red wine. As they sat sipping wine and tasting samples, Jill explained, "We are trying to capitalize on the small-town resurgence to rebrand our business. We want folks to come for a tasting and then buy a couple of glasses or a bottle and eat inside, or outside when the weather is better. We are thinking of developing a marketing blitz to create interest for dates, lunches, parties, etc. We're working to reorganize the space to fit some small tables and add some personality."

Katerina nodded enthusiastically. "That sounds exciting, and I like your plans. This will help you bring in more business during the off season."

"Exactly," Jill said. "Adam's always been the driving force behind the wine, and I'm excited to focus on the front of the house."

Katerina left the island happy with her day. Jill and Adam had placed some orders for early May, and Jill had given her a list of contacts for the other local wineries and assured her that it was good for each island winery if the others thrived as well. She had also shared that the local bookstore owner wanted to serve coffee and tea on-site and had been inquiring about the cookies her friends from the farmer's market had been raving about. Jill gave her that contact information as well.

As Kat was driving home, her mind full of the day's events, she reflected on James's idea about shipping through the mail. She wanted to test how her cookies would stand up to travel, and she knew just the right person to be her taste-tester—Jessica, now that she was back in Colorado. She forced herself to go to the grocery store before going home so she could purchase the ingredients for her herb cookie recipes. She didn't have the energy to make them today, but having the ingredients on hand would be nice.

When Katerina got home, she was so exhausted all she wanted to do was go to bed. She was putting the groceries away when she heard her phone chime. Picking it up, she saw a text from Jack.

Jack: How did the meeting go?

Kat: First signed catering contract! And thank you for letting me use your house. I'd missed it—

Jack: Congrats! That must feel good, glad you miss the house. Gotta run, just wanted to check on you.

Kat: Thanks, Jack ☺ Good luck with your meetings!

Katerina put the phone down, musing about what he meant by being glad that she missed his house. *That seems like a positive thing.*

Chapter Forty-Three

Tuesday after work, Kat knocked on James's office door with a plate of cookies in her hand. He waved her inside, smiling broadly. "Hey Kat, how are you and what've you got?"

"I'm good, James, and this is a cookie bribe for your advice on shipping containers," she said, laughing as she set the plate down in front of him. "You have chocolate, sea salt and thyme, rosemary shortbread, brown butter and sage, goat cheese and thyme, and the last one is an olive oil, lemon, and basil cookie."

"Wow, these sound as good as they look," he said, reaching for a cookie. He took a bite and raised his eyebrows comically while chewing. He tried a second kind of cookie and then one of each of the remaining cookies before speaking. "Kat, these are good." His expression was intense, but then he smiled. "The flavors are unique, and they work. I'm happy to help you with shipping containers, but I would also like your permission to help you with some marketing around these.

"Have you ever tried making the dough and freezing it, then when you are ready to bake, adding the fresh herbs?" he asked. "If that works, you could buy yourself some flexibility. Experiment with it and see how it impacts the flavor and texture. You'll find that the freezer is your friend in the catering business. Here, have a seat." James waved her over to the round table and put the plate of cookies between them.

An hour later, she left with her head spinning. James thought her cookies could be a nice cash flow boost for her, maybe even a better niche market than other prepared foods. In addition to coffee shops and delis, he thought she might find a market for them in the restaurant and hotel industry. He cautioned her to have her licensing in order and be comfortable with her purveyors and commercial kitchen space because once the marketing began, demand could follow quickly, and she needed to be ready. He had also sent her home with the perfect container to ship her cookies to Jessica.

When she got home that evening, she packed up the cookies for Jessica and dropped them off for shipping. Then she sat down with an herbal tea and tried to visualize her future and how she wanted to work and live. The farmer's market in Seattle was second to none, and she already owned a home nearby and any last-minute ingredients or supplies were readily available. The commute to the island was not a big deal, and it was a reverse commute which meant it was faster to load and unload her Jeep off the ferry. She already had her licensing and permits for the state and City of Seattle and, impulsively, she'd decided to apply for Bainbridge Island permits as well. Being back in Seattle made her realize how much she missed the small-town community feel of the island. It couldn't hurt to have some flexibility, she reasoned.

Chapter Forty-Four

The rest of the week went by quickly. Katerina and Jack texted a couple of times and settled on meeting Sunday as that would give Kat the most time to rest and Jack was having another busy week himself. They didn't have a plan yet, but he was going to come by and pick her up at 11:00 a.m.

Knowing she wouldn't see him Friday night took the excitement out of the evening. She still made sure she looked her best, but the buzz and adrenaline were lacking. Greg handed her a cup of coffee, so she figured it showed. Her professionalism in addition to the caffeine helped her focus her energy and she managed to get her mind off Sunday and back to the bartending tasks at hand.

Around 10:40, Katerina was making an old fashioned and a vodka on the rocks for a couple of gentlemen at the bar. When she turned to set down the drinks, she saw Jack enter the room and head toward the back corner of the bar. Her heart rate soared, and her hands got clammy as she approached him. "Hey Jack, this is a surprise."

He looked at her seriously, without his usual grin, and simply said, "I needed to see you, Kat." She understood that he was asking her if she was ready to give them a chance. He had read between the lines on her request to see him and the comments regarding missing him, and he was here asking for an answer.

Katerina couldn't look away from his penetrating gaze. She felt the weight of the emotion and attraction he had been suppressing lately, and she knew it must be mirrored in her own eyes. She nodded, as if in a daze, and then finally murmured, "I'm glad you're here." She swallowed hard and asked, "Can I go home with you tonight?"

He nodded and then his expression lightened, and he smiled for the first time. "I'll wait for you. And how about a vodka up in the meantime."

"Coming right up," she said, smiling back at him. She could feel adrenaline shooting through her body. He sipped his drink slowly and she was aware of his eyes on her while she waited for the late-night patrons to cash out and helped Greg perform their closing procedures.

Finally, she was free. She left him sitting there while she grabbed her coat and purse. When she returned, he stood, reached for her hand, and walked with her toward the exit. The feel of her hand enveloped by his larger one was electric.

He walked her to her car and as she reached for her keys, he put a hand on her arm and pulled her in close for a long kiss. His mouth was warm, and he tasted of vodka. All her nerve endings were on fire. She reached for his shoulders and kissed him with her own urgency.

Breathing hard, he broke the kiss and stood waiting while she opened her Jeep door, not turning for his car until she had safely closed the door. She waited while he started his car and then followed him out of the Sorbonne's lot and onto the damp Seattle streets, heading toward his downtown condo. She found a parking spot close to his building, and he waited for her, opening his passenger door for her to jump into his Mercedes.

He drove into the below-building parking, and in a few short minutes they were in the elevator heading up to his condo on the twentieth floor. He unlocked the door, ushering her in first. Dim lights on a sensor came on as she entered, and she gasped at the beautiful space and the view of Puget Sound. The condo was decorated in dark camel leather with navy accents that proved both warm and luxurious. The kitchen on the other end of the large room was modern and large with fluted floor-to-ceiling cabinets that created a clean textural feel. She could see an outside deck that faced the Sound. As she gazed around her, he hit a switch and the lighting changed and a low, linear gas fireplace came to life.

"Wow, Jack, this is amazing," Katerina said, finally turning to him.

"You know, I had nothing to do with it," he admitted, smiling at her.

"Can I get you a drink?" he asked. "I have red, white, and a bar if you want something stronger."

"Sure, I'll have a glass of red," she said, following him toward the kitchen, running her hand over the soapstone island and admiring the high-end appliances.

"Jack, I can't believe how incredible your place is."

"I can't lie—I enjoy it here." With each of them holding their glass, he led her to the couch, and they sat down, sipping their wine and enjoying the ambiance of the fireplace and the view of the water.

The atmosphere between them was charged with what was to come and they both acknowledged it without needing to say a word. When Katerina put her glass down, Jack set his down, too, and shifted her body so she was leaning back against the head of the couch. Balancing his own body so as not to put too much weight on her, he leaned over and began kissing her. There was nothing gentle or soft in his kiss. It was all about need and desire, and Katerina gave as good as she got. She wrapped her arms around his neck, pulling him closer, and running her hands through his hair and over his back. After a minute, he pulled her up and guided her across to another door which she knew would be his bedroom. Again, a dim light came on as they entered the space, and Jack led her to a large king-size bed, gently pushing her down on it.

"Jack, I should have—"

He reached forward and put a finger against her lips.

After that, it was a frenzy of need and wanting and pent-up feelings. Their clothes ended up on the floor and Jack paused for a moment to just look at her. "You're so beautiful," he said, unfastening the clip that held her ponytail and running his fingers through the long, dark, fall of hair. "I've needed to see you like this again," he said. "I've dreamed about you this way." He trailed a finger from her cheek down between her breasts and lingered there for a moment before bending to taste one erect nipple. With a moan, Katerina arched her body, pushing her breast into him, and with his own groan, their lovemaking resumed its urgency. When Katerina felt Jack's fullness enter her, her last coherent thought was that being with this man was where she was meant to be.

Later, wearing a fluffy robe that Jack offered her, they went back out to the living room to retrieve their wine glasses, and topping them off, took them back to his bedroom, which, like the great room and kitchen areas, was both masculine and warm. He turned on another fireplace on the wall across from his bed. With his arms around her, she leaned comfortably against him, and they both sipped their wine.

"You must be exhausted," he said apologetically. "I lost track of what a long day you've had."

"It will catch up with me, I'm sure," Katerina said, "but right now, I am definitely not tired…" She said the words slowly, reaching back to kiss his lips suggestively. This time, their movements were slow and gentle, but the heat between them was just as hot, maybe hotter. Each of them savored and discovered while looking deeply into the other's eyes.

Later, they showered together, enjoying the jets in Jack's large walk-in shower. Back in his bed, he wrapped his arms tightly around her and Katerina fell asleep almost immediately. Jack lay there, watching her and feeling emotions he had never thought he was capable of. He loved her, he acknowledged. He leaned in to press a small kiss on her shoulder, breathing in her scent, and then he went to sleep.

Chapter Forty-Five

Katerina awoke with a start, recognizing immediately where she was. Looking beside her, she saw Jack was gone. Smelling coffee and hearing him in the kitchen, she relaxed and took a moment to remember the events of the night before. She smiled in satisfaction and happiness; she knew that Jack was the future she wanted.

Putting on the fluffy robe laid out on the end of the bed, she used the facilities and brushed her teeth with a finger and his toothpaste, then made her way out to the kitchen. When Jack saw her, he came over and gave her a long, sexy kiss. Reluctantly breaking apart, he poured her a cup of coffee and set it down on the counter in front of her. Grinning appreciatively, she thanked him before taking a sip.

"How about I make you some bacon, eggs, and toast? I would like to cook for you, for once," he said, smiling over his shoulder.

"I would love that, Jack, thank you." Katerina sipped her coffee and realized how happy she was just being with him. The sex had been amazing—she had never felt so wanted, and honestly, had never felt such hunger and desire herself. But it was so much more than that. Jack was the whole package.

━━∞∞∞∞∞∞C()D∞∞∞∞∞━━

Jack took eggs and bacon out of the refrigerator. He was cracking the eggs and dropping them into a bowl when his phone rang. Picking it up, he noticed it was Amy. She usually texted him rather than calling, so he answered rather than letting it go to voicemail—maybe she needed him. "Amy, what's up?"

"I wanted to call you with some good news," she said cheerfully. "Michael and I are having a baby, a little boy."

As Jack listened to her words, a dark, painful suspicion clawed at his gut. "Wow, Amy. Congratulations, this is unexpected but great news," he managed to say on autopilot. He couldn't even look at Katerina.

"You're the first person I've told," Amy's voice went on. "Michael is calling his parents now to let them know."

"So, you're just now sharing your news?" he asked, hating himself for using this chance to find out more information.

"Yes, we wanted to make sure it was a viable pregnancy before we announced it. We're going to be sending out announcement cards shortly. Oh, and the baby is due very close to our wedding, so we're going to have to figure out how to handle that, too."

"Congratulations, Amy, and tell Michael congratulations as well. I'm sorry, sis, I need to run."

"Oh, well, sure," Amy said uncertainly, and a bit petulantly before ending the call. He couldn't blame her, Jack thought, putting down his phone. He turned to face Katerina. He could tell by the way she looked at him that she knew what the gist of the call had been. He was struggling with her reaction which looked more surprised than devastated, but maybe that just lent more credence to his suspicion.

—∞∞∞∞∞∞∞◯◯∞∞∞∞∞∞∞—

"You knew, didn't you?" Jack asked, his voice was low, but he had the same look in his eyes that she had seen at Amy and Michael's engagement dinner—suspicion and judgment.

"That Amy was pregnant? Was that what she was telling you on the phone? No, of course not," Katerina protested with an impending sense of loss. It was in his voice, in his eyes, in his body language as he backed up physically, putting more distance between them.

"You knew that Amy was pregnant and that was the one thing you couldn't plan around, so you thought you would use me as a consolation prize."

"Wait, Jack. What are you saying? I didn't know!" Katerina protested wildly.

"I told you on the island that we couldn't move forward until you were ready to let go of the past, and Kat, you looked at me with tears running down your face. You told me you cared about me, but what you didn't say was, 'All right, Jack, I'm ready. Let's see what we have.' You weren't able to let him go then, but now, all of a sudden, you are? Tell me, Kat, that last night wasn't just because you knew you couldn't trump a pregnancy."

"Oh my God," Kat said, standing up and backing away herself. "How little you must think of me." She turned and walked back to his room. With shaking hands, she dressed in her clothes from the night before, ran a quick brush through her hair, and with her keys in hand, she walked back to the kitchen. She hoped that he would say something, that he would show he believed in her. She hoped that he would stop her. He was sitting at one of the island stools, and he didn't even look up as she walked by, letting herself out the front door.

She managed to hold it together until she got to her car, and then the sobs came. Deep, broken sobs. She let the tears flow until she was too physically exhausted to cry. She drove home, set an alarm, and went straight to bed. Later, when her alarm went off, she checked her messages—nothing from Jack and a voicemail from Helen asking her to call. It wasn't hard to guess that Helen wanted to make sure she had been told about the pregnancy and that she was okay. Even in her emotionally overloaded mental state, she had to appreciate the irony that Michael was having a baby with another woman, and she was only happy for them.

Still, she was in no shape to call Helen back right now, plus she needed to shower and get ready for her Saturday night bartending shift. After showering, she put cold compresses on her eyes, but there was only so much that could be done. Even with nice hair and makeup, she looked like a puffy, tired version of herself, but at least she was showing up for her shift. Emotionally she felt numb, and her body was exhausted—she prayed for an easy night.

Chapter Forty-Six

*J*ack had dumped the eggs from the bowl directly into the disposal and thrown the sheets on his bed into the washing machine. He wanted to erase all evidence of Kat's visit. He was angry. He had patiently given her time, and she had misled him. He hoped she had enjoyed her experiment of testing their attraction, the attraction that was always confusing her! He ran his fingers through his hair and tried to block her from his mind.

He showered and went to the office. He needed to call Amy, too, and make amends. Amy answered on the third ring, but her tone was cool. "Amy, I'm sorry. I saw your call and I answered it thinking it was an emergency, but I didn't have time to talk."

"It's okay, I guess I don't call very often," she relented.

"So, you're having a boy, and you're due around September? I'm happy for you, sis."

"Thank you, we're going to name him Michael Jr."

"That's great, Amy. I know you've always wanted kids, and you and Michael will be great parents."

"Thanks, Jack. We're both really excited."

He knew he should leave it alone, but he needed to know. "Amy, please forgive me for asking this, but do you think Kat knew about this before you told me?"

He heard Amy's intake of breath. "So, you're asking me if Michael told her?" Her tone was cool again.

"Yes, I guess I am."

Sounding resigned now, she said, "He told me he wouldn't, but I don't know. Back when she started helping you with the B&B, I confronted him about calls to her, and he told me that he had called her to warn her about getting involved with you." She paused for a moment and speaking slowly said, "I looked at the bill and it was true—there was only one call that had more than a few seconds. He promised me he wouldn't call her again, and I haven't looked at any more bills."

"I'm sorry, Amy," Jack repeated, feeling guilty for bringing her down and sad for her uncertainty in her own relationship.

"Why are you asking, Jack? Are you involved with her now?"

"Amy, it's complicated, and hey, my situation is not the news of the day. I am truly happy for you and Michael. Let me know when a good time is—I would like to take the two of you to dinner to celebrate."

"Oh, Jack, that's sweet. I'll talk to Michael and get back to you. And, Jack, take care, okay?"

"Deal," he said, ending the call. He sat at his desk and stared out the window, thinking about Kat. *She may or may not have known... Did I judge her too quickly?* Did it matter? Should he just take this opportunity to get out of a complicated relationship? He had always found it easy to find female attention and been just as happy to let it go when that female wanted more of him. What he had never done was sleep all night with a woman in his arms, a woman he loved, and then have her rip his heart out the next morning. Maybe the bigger question was, did he want anyone to have the power to bring him to such highs and lows?

Chapter Forty-Seven

One day at a time. Katerina grimaced at the overused phrase. Surely, she could come up with something better than that. *Put one foot in front of the other.* Frustrated with herself, she gave up. *Who needs a mantra anyway?* The truth was she actually did have a lot going on in her life, so she had no choice but to hold it together.

Even though almost two weeks had passed, and Jack still hadn't reached out to her, she tried to distract herself by building her new business. She emailed Kelly at the bookstore, along with the other three wineries on the island, and made plans to visit all of them on Sunday.

She did her shopping after her catering shift on Thursday. Putting all the samples together Saturday before her bartending shift and adding the finishing touches before driving to the island on Sunday kept her busy. She ruthlessly ignored the stab of pain that came with remembering that last time she had prepped in Jack's house.

She returned to Seattle with two contracts—the bookstore and a second winery. Another winery was still thinking about the right mix but was likely to do something. One winery had turned her down, too small to delegate space for food. She was feeling both energized and anxious about her future. James's offer to let her begin working part-time in May had taken a lot of pressure off her and also allowed her to have James's mentorship and guidance on the cookie marketing, which was going out next week. She had given her notice to Phillipe and Antoine for her bartending position at the Sorbonne. While grateful for the chance to earn extra money, she needed more sleep and weekend flexibility for her fledgling catering business.

During the week, she updated James on her efforts with freezing cookie dough, and they tasted samples together, discussing possible refinements to her process. She tentatively asked him how he felt about her using Pete for backup help if she needed support, and he generously agreed.

"Pete's a good worker, and I can see that he wants to grow," he conceded with a smile. "Just the two of you keep me posted, will you?" Kat fervently promised, so grateful again for his mentorship.

She arrived home from her Friday catering shift, and without the diversion of her bartending job, she felt the hurt and depression descend like a smothering blanket. She poured herself a glass of wine, knowing it was absolutely a bad decision, but regrets were overrated. Wait, was that another trite phrase? She shook her head in disgust and took a sip of her wine.

She was in love with Jack. It was so clear to her now that she had loved him for some time. It was also clear that Jack wasn't in a hurry to talk to her, so maybe she needed to be the one to take the first step. She needed a new plan.

As she thought about Jack's explosive comments, she had to acknowledge that he had given her only one ultimatum—that she be over her feelings for Michael. While she knew that she was truly over Michael, maybe the fact that she and

Jack had fallen into bed before talking hadn't given him the certainty he needed.

She was still hurt he had resorted to not trusting her, and judging her, but that shouldn't stop her from trying to fix this. Jack mattered.

Before she could talk herself out of it, she grabbed her phone and texted Jack.

Kat: Jack, I'm sorry about how things ended that Saturday. You were right, you only asked one thing of me, to be over Michael. I am. I'm sorry I didn't tell you in words that night, but I hope you can recognize I was trying to tell you in so many other ways. I didn't know about the pregnancy, and I'm actually happy for them. You could never be second best. I miss you—

She hit send and laid the phone down. By bedtime, she still hadn't gotten a response, and she tossed and turned. Frustrated and sad, she wiped the tears from her eyes and willed herself to a restless sleep.

Chapter Forty-Eight

*J*ack raised his glass of wine. "A toast," he said, smiling at Amy and Michael. "Congratulations to my beautiful sister and to you, Michael. I am thrilled to know that I will be an uncle soon, and I'm happy for you both!"

Amy clinked her glass of club soda against their two wine glasses and smiled contentedly. "Thank you, Jack. We wanted to keep it to ourselves for a while, but it feels great to be sharing it with family now."

Michael put an arm around Amy's shoulder and pulled her closer for a gentle hug. "My parents are beyond thrilled," he said, smiling broadly.

Jack was oddly aware of an almost omniscient perspective to the evening. It was as if his mind was running on dual tracks -the easy-going and friendly dinner companion and the observant, judging presence which seemed to be measuring them all for signs of inauthenticity and duplicity.

The evening progressed to its conclusion without any apparent awareness of his distractedness from either of his dinner companions. He did note that all three of them were careful not to mention Kat or the B&B—conversational landmines to be dealt with another time or perhaps to remain buried for good.

He was relieved when he was back at his condo with no further need for conversation. Pouring himself a glass of red wine, he sat in a chair viewing Puget Sound in the dark reflection of his window and letting his mind wander.

What did I put in motion? He was honest enough to know that the dynamic between Michael and him had shifted with his inclusion of Kat in his life. He had been so sure he could handle it, but he wasn't so certain anymore.

He had replayed his last moments with Kat that morning in his kitchen more times than he wanted to admit, and he was still shocked, both by his immediate reaction to distrust Kat and his equally cruel action to let her leave his condo without speaking one word to her. He had never imagined that he would be capable of being that kind of man. *But I was that morning,* he admitted to himself.

I love Kat. He felt his fingers tighten on the stem of his wine glass and forced himself to relax. But it was clear that including her in his life was much more complicated than he had imagined. Was it fair to risk the happiness of Amy and Michael and perhaps even put at risk his ongoing role in their life and that of his future nephew? Recognizing that he didn't have any answers, he rinsed his wine glass and made his way toward his bedroom, grabbing his phone off the counter on his way.

He stiffened when he saw a text from Kat. Reading it quickly, he felt his stomach clench. He knew she was hurting, and it killed him to know he was responsible, but he simply didn't know what to say. He needed a clear mind before responding. Sighing, he laid down the phone and prepared for a restless night.

Chapter Forty-Nine

The minute Katerina awoke, she reached for her phone and checked her texts, but there was nothing, and her heart hurt. She had expected some sort of response, even if just an acknowledgment that he had received her text and needed to think. She'd never thought of Jack as a cruel man, but maybe she didn't know him as well as she thought she did, based on the last two weeks.

She checked her phone several more times while making coffee and finally, exasperated with herself, she forced herself to shower. She had a busy day; she was planning on making several batches of cookies and experimenting with refining her frozen cookie batches based on her discussion with James. She had just finished mixing a batch of brown butter and sage cookies when she heard the chime of a text. Rinsing her hands quickly, she reached for her phone.

Jack: Kat, I am sorry for how things ended, too. Can we meet and discuss? I am happy to come to your place or meet you anywhere you like.

Kat read the text and, with a shaking hand, set the phone down. She knew it was risky trying to read too much into the tone of a text, but her gut feeling told her it wasn't good. It sounded curt to her, and he certainly hadn't said he missed her.

She felt a tear on her cheek and brushed at it angrily. Right now, she wasn't sure he deserved her tears. She considered waiting for a while before texting him back but decided that was silly. Better to get the answers she needed.

Kat: You're welcome to stop by here. I'm just doing some baking. Let me know when you plan to arrive.

Jack: Thanks, Kat. I will leave in 30 minutes or so. See you soon.

Kat didn't bother to respond and forced her attention back to her baking, but her hands were shaking, and her stomach was in knots. Unbidden, she remembered the happiness she had felt waking up in his bed. Most of her recollections from that night had been spent on moments of physical intimacy or at the devastating end of the following morning. But somehow, remembering the simple joy of that moment was the most painful memory of all.

She was making a new pot of coffee when he buzzed her intercom. She pressed the button to grant him access to the building and then poured herself a new cup and took a sip, hoping the warmth would calm her nerves.

When he knocked on her door, she opened it and fought the urge to look away when his familiar gray eyes locked onto her own. His expression was solemn, and she sensed that he was as unsure of himself as she was.

"Come in," she offered, gesturing toward the kitchen area, and he followed her to the island. "Coffee?" she asked as he took a seat. He nodded and waited to speak until she had joined him and handed him a steaming cup.

"Kat," he said finally, his voice quiet but intense. "I'm so sorry for the way I acted and for hurting you. When I think of that morning, I can't stand how I behaved toward you."

Kat swallowed hard and nodded; she felt tears beginning to pool, and she squeezed her eyes shut tightly, willing them to stop.

⚬⚬⚬⚬⚬⚬⚬◯⚬⚬⚬⚬⚬⚬⚬

Jack wished they could just be relaxing together in her warm kitchen filled with the sweet scent of cookie dough and spices instead of having this difficult conversation.

He spoke again. "I've thought a lot about it, about us, about the complications for all of us. I admit that you tried to warn me, and I didn't listen. Kat, I need you to know that our night together was everything I had imagined and more. What I have trouble understanding is how quickly I turned to doubt, suspicion, and anger. I hurt you and I hurt Amy, too, by not being in a place to share her happy news. I'm the only family she has." He paused for a moment, searching out her watery, golden eyes. "Kat, all of this has been a real eye-opener for me."

"What are you trying to say?" Kat's voice was ragged, and Jack felt certain she was bracing for his answer.

"Kat, I just need some time to think." He put his coffee cup down and grabbed her hand. He felt her stiffen, but she didn't pull away. "Kat, you make me feel things I've never felt, but we, the two of us having a relationship, it changes the dynamic of so many other relationships. I just need some time," he repeated. She nodded but didn't speak. She felt numb and also needed to process his words. He seemed to read her mind because he rose slowly to his feet. Looking down at her, he asked softly, the intensity gone from his voice, "Is there anything you want to say to me? You've been quiet…"

She shrugged and shook her head slightly. "You hurt me that morning, and your silence since has hurt me. I need to think about all of this. And I obviously can't refuse you time when you gave me that same benefit."

He nodded and reached down, gently squeezing her shoulder. "I'll let myself out and I'll be in touch," he said, walking toward the door.

Jack felt regret and sadness as he exited her building. Asking for time was probably the smart thing, but he missed her already, and he knew she was hurting, too. For all the times he had imagined that Michael had damaged her confidence, was he now doing the same?

When the door shut behind him, Kat allowed herself the luxury of tears before standing up and resuming her cookie dough preparation. She let the repetition of her familiar recipes, and the atmosphere of her cozy condo calm her mind. She had gained so much clarity from going through the experiences of the last few months. She would give Jack his time, but she had a role to play, too, she decided. For the first time since coming back from Australia, the steps to put her plan in motion were finally crystal clear.

Chapter Fifty

Katerina sipped her coffee and waited for Michael to arrive at his parents' house. After discussing her idea with Paul and Helen, they had agreed to help facilitate a way for her to be alone with Michael.

Katerina's "plan" had finally come together. It involved finding a new way forward for Michael and herself, but to be successful, that plan had to include Amy. But first things first, she and Michael needed to talk.

She waited until she heard him open the front door before grabbing the large Starbucks iced coffee and heading toward the entryway to greet him. Michael had just taken a few steps toward the kitchen when he spotted her.

"Hey, Kat. This is a surprise."

"Hi, Michael. Please accept my peace offering for using subterfuge to find time alone with you. Also, please forgive your parents' participation—I take full responsibility." Smiling nervously, she handed him the drink, which she knew was a favorite.

He reached out to accept the drink, and his expression was friendly but puzzled as he followed her toward the kitchen. "What's going on, Kat?" he asked when she took her seat at the table, and he realized that his parents were not there.

"Michael, I needed to see you—I need to tell you some things, and I hoped to avoid creating a situation where you needed to tell Amy that we were meeting in case it would upset her." Katerina could tell by the tensing of his jaw that her concern had been on point, but he only nodded and took the chair across from her.

"I hope you can be patient as I try to communicate this because I feel like my heart and my head are all over the place." Katerina's golden eyes were teary, and her expression was both fragile and determined. "I want to thank you for being my friend, my protector, and my first love." Her voice broke a little, but she continued, "It's hard for me to even imagine a life without you and your parents, and I am in awe that even as a child, you had the unselfish and caring nature to bring us all together. I see those same traits in you today with your teaching and coaching, and I know you will be an amazing father."

Michael reached out and covered her hand with his, and Katerina closed her eyes tightly to hold back the sudden flush of tears. "I know as children we always said that we would be together forever, but now that's not how it will be… and Michael, I give you credit again for knowing that we weren't meant to be romantic partners." She pulled her hand free, reaching for a tissue and wiping at her eyes and her nose.

Michael cleared his throat and said softly, "Kat, I made mistakes, too. My 'time-outs' just allowed us to put off what became inevitable. I know this has been hard on you. You need to know that I want you to be happy. Are you involved with Jack? Does he make you happy?"

Kat shook her head and looked down before meeting his eyes. "It's complicated. I do care for Jack, and he does make me happy, but I think it took me too long to realize that I was ready to move on. I think he also feels protective of his relationship with Amy, and with you."

Katerina paused, trying to summon her courage, and then, because she needed to know, she forced herself to ask, "Michael, may I call Amy and ask her to meet me for coffee?" She rushed on before he could reply. "I imagine she has concerns and fears about me and us. And I would like to hear them and help her get more comfortable. Michael, you and your parents are the only true family I've ever known, and unless Amy can trust me, I feel like my relationship with all of you, and even Jack, will be impacted. Can you give me that chance?"

Michael met Kat's anxious gaze and nodded slowly, reaching for both of her hands and clasping them tightly. "Kat, I want this for all of us, too. You've always been a better communicator than me, and you're right, Amy has questions and fears that I am sure she is not voicing to me. I assume Mom and Dad thought this plan had merit also, or they wouldn't have helped with the set-up," he said with wry amusement.

Chapter Fifty-One

Amy faced Jack as he sat on the other end of the couch in his living room. She had called, asking if she could come over, and when he had opened the door at her knock, she'd cried the minute she saw him.

He handed her the box of tissues he'd gone to retrieve and took her hand, waiting for her tears to slow. "Talk to me, sis," he said.

She sniffed and dabbed at her eyes. "Kat called and asked to meet with me. We met at a coffee shop yesterday." Jack felt a sharp stirring of anger toward Kat for upsetting his pregnant sister. He was sure the surprise registered on his face, but he tried to keep his voice even.

"What did she want to talk with you about?"

"She wanted to congratulate me on our pregnancy, and I think she wanted to reassure me—and build a path forward. She said that she hoped sharing some insights would be helpful to me. She feels that she and Michael had both outgrown the relationship years ago, but both had remained trapped, mired in history and established roles." Amy paused and wiped her nose again. "She explained how much his parents mean to her and how she had felt that ending a relationship with Michael would mean losing them, too."

Amy paused again and looked at Jack, who just nodded for her to go on. "She also told me she now realizes that Michael's lack of commitment to taking things further between them shows her that he wanted something else for his future, but his long-standing habit of protecting her kept getting in the way." Amy smiled forlornly. "I didn't want to meet with her, but I'm so thankful I did. What she said made sense to me, and Michael would never have brought it up or been able to communicate it as clearly as she did."

Jack felt shame again for judging Kat so quickly. "If you feel better, why are you crying? Did something else happen?" he asked Amy, looking at her in confusion.

"Oh Jack, I'm so afraid I've screwed things up with Michael. I was so paranoid and jealous of Kat that I let my fear override all of the reassurance that Michael was giving me. Don't get me wrong, I think he tried to protect her too much, but now I understand better, and I know he loves me, and—and now I've ruined things."

Fresh sobs erupted, and Jack patted the hand he held. Finally, he said, "Amy, honey, what did you do that was so bad?" She gulped loudly and gripped her hands together. "Shortly before New Year's Eve, I quit taking the pill, hoping I would get pregnant. I thought it would make our relationship safe from her." The sobs were even louder. "I thought if she got between us, he would pick me because of the baby. I've been feeling really guilty about this. At times, something small would happen that made me feel somewhat justified, but honestly, nothing he has done justifies what I did."

"Okay," Jack said, "how did he react to the initial pregnancy news?"

"He's been nothing but wonderful—you saw him the other night. He's as excited as I am, and he's treating me like a princess." She wiped her eyes and nose and looked at Jack.

"Amy, I know Michael loves you, and it sounds like he is genuinely happy about the baby. I think you should talk to him. He knows that the situation with Kat has been hard on you—he may be a lot more understanding than you think."

"Do you really think so?" Amy's tears stopped for the first time. "I had no right to take such a big step for the two of us into my own hands." Her voice wobbled. "I hope he can forgive me."

"Amy, talk to him. You need to get this off your chest. I've seen how he looks at you—give him a chance to tell you he understands."

"Do you really think he can forgive me?" Amy asked, looking to Jack for reassurance.

"I think you need to tell him and let him work through his emotions. But nothing good comes of you holding on to the secret." He squeezed her hand.

"Thank you, Jack. I know you're right, and I feel better just telling you. How are you doing? Kat didn't talk a lot about the two of you other than to say that her feelings for you helped her realize that she didn't love Michael. Are the two of you together?"

"It's complicated, but I'm thinking maybe I was hard on Kat, and I need to have some difficult conversations of my own," he said wryly.

"The Kat thing is still tough for me," Amy said carefully, "but she didn't have to reach out to me, and I know this has been hard on her, too. Part of me selfishly wishes you could be with anyone else, but I've never seen you interested enough in any woman to use the 'complicated' word."

"It is complicated and partly my own fault, and I'm sorry if my caring about her is uncomfortable for you, Amy."

"I'm glad someone caught your interest, Jack. Good luck with your situation. Now I need to go home and work on mine," Amy said, standing up.

Jack hugged her at the door and then went into the kitchen and poured himself a glass of wine. He made a quick ham and cheese sandwich and sat at the bar eating it. He had always admired Kat's strength. Reaching out to Amy had been an act of strength and kindness. For the first time in recent weeks, he felt a stirring of optimism himself. Maybe it was time for him to reach out to his brother-in-law-to-be. He couldn't foresee a conversation as open as the one between Amy and Kat, but he could still make some inroads.

Chapter Fifty-Two

Amy's stomach was in knots, and her eyes were already tearing up when she opened the door to the condo she shared with Michael. She'd told Michael she was meeting her brother, so he was expecting her to be late. She found him in the kitchen with a plate of pizza and an open beer.

When he saw her tear-streaked face, he immediately stood up and came toward her, his handsome face filled with concern. "Babe, what's wrong?"

"Oh Michael, I need to talk to you," she said.

"Sure, honey, sit down." He pulled up a chair for her and gently pushed her into it. "What is it? Why are you crying?"

"Michael, I guess I should start a few months back. I was a lot more worried about having Kat back in your life than you may have known. I struggled with talking to you about it because I felt like it might just make you see her good points all over again and want to be with her instead." Amy grabbed a napkin, wiping her eyes. "I know we talked about it a few times, but trust me, there were a lot more times when I just felt insecure and kept it inside me."

Michael reached over and hugged her. "Amy, is this about Kat talking to you?" When Amy shook her head no, he swallowed hard and continued. "I've made mistakes. I felt like the bad guy with Kat, and I guess I was trying to help lessen her pain so I could ease my guilt about falling in love with you. I put you through a lot, Amy."

"Michael, I deliberately got pregnant without telling you. I stopped taking the pill because I wanted to make sure you chose me." Amy knew her voice sounded shrill, filled with her fear of telling him what she had done.

As Amy's sobs erupted, Michael froze for a moment, taking in the news. Finally, he nodded slowly, and then he said earnestly, "I wish you could have talked to me, and I hope we can both do a better job of dealing with uncertainty and frustrations in the future. But thank you for being honest—and Amy, nothing you've said changes the fact that I love you and I am very happy about Michael Jr." Amy shot up from her chair, and Michael quickly reacted to catch her as she flung herself into his arms.

Chapter Fifty-Three

On Thursday afternoon, Kat had received a call from an established B&B owner on the island. Rob had been asked to host a dinner for some guests who were booking a weekend in early June. He had asked if she could meet him, see the space on Saturday, and provide a catering proposal. She had approached Pete to see if he was interested in making some extra money helping her out with the dinner, and he had given her an enthusiastic yes.

Saturday morning, after coffee and a quick breakfast, Katerina was ready to leave. She was meeting Rob at his home at 10:00 a.m., an earlier morning than she preferred. *But when you're trying to build a business, it's not about you.* She dressed in jeans and a sweater, grabbing a jacket, too. April was still damp and cool in the Northwest.

She checked her phone, hoping for a text from Jack, and finding none, forced herself to put it in her purse. She needed to focus on her upcoming meeting, but that didn't stop the sad, lonely feeling inside her.

Impulsively, Katerina decided to treat herself to a large Starbucks latte rather than just grab a coffee on the ferry. She knew there was a Starbucks close to the terminal, and when she saw it, she pulled in quickly. She opened the door and had taken a couple of steps toward the counter when she saw Nicole. The striking redhead was sitting at a table in the corner. She was laughing at something her companion had said. Kat's stomach sank, and she felt a surge of pure adrenaline as she recognized the dark hair and jacket. Nicole and Jack were here together.

Without conscious thought, her body turned, and she walked out of the shop and back to her Jeep. Clumsily, she turned the ignition and pulled recklessly out onto the street. She just wanted to get away. On autopilot, she pulled her Jeep into the ferry terminal and joined the line of boarding vehicles. Her breath came in gasps as she gripped the steering wheel tightly with white knuckles.

She had replayed their lovemaking countless times, and the thought that he could immediately replace her was a new level of pain. Despite her deep hurt and betrayal, feelings of anger began to surface. Was this really how Jack was spending *his time to think*?

With a jolt, she considered the fact that Nicole might be taking the same ferry as Kat, after sharing a night of passion with Jack. Why else would they be at the Starbucks so close to the terminal? With a furtive scan of the concession area, Kat entered the room and grabbed a large coffee, immediately climbing the steps to the top deck and going outside. *I won't run into Nicole out here.* There was no way the elegant redhead would stand outside and let her hair be disturbed by the wind.

Get a grip, she told herself, taking large sips of her coffee and feeling the calming warmth seep inside her. *This meeting with Rob is important to you.* A small voice inside her wondered if building a business on Jack's hometown island was a good idea after all—maybe too many memories and too small of a footprint.

Even as her insecurities took her in that direction, she pictured Marnie's face, and she tamped down those feelings. She had made these friends and business opportunities happen, and she couldn't let a failed romance stand in her way. Katerina had turned her phone on "Do not disturb" after arriving at the ferry terminal, and she refused to even look at it before her meeting.

She drove to Rob's house and parked her car, willing herself to stay focused and confident. "You've got this," she said out loud. She knocked on the front door, and Rob opened it right away.

"Good morning, Kat. Thanks for taking the time to meet with me." Rob was an older man with a friendly smile. As he led her through an entryway and into a sitting room, she recognized the interior from one of the pictures that she had printed for Jack's review. In person, the space was as she had imagined it—attractive but busy, and the style somewhat heavy in the way that B&Bs often are.

"Have a seat." He indicated a nearby table with two chairs. "Can I get you anything to drink?" he offered. "Coffee, juice?"

"Thanks, Rob, a black coffee would be great," she said, smiling and placing her leather portfolio down on the table. He returned in a minute with their two coffees and set one in front of her.

He referred to his notes before speaking. "The event will be a party for ten women who have grown up together. They meet annually for a small getaway, and they have requested a dinner on site and to combine it with wine pairings. This is the first time I've considered a dinner, but I like the idea of providing that service as an option to guests. I had thought of having the dinner catered by a local restaurant, but as I told you earlier, Adam and Jill suggested that I should meet with you."

Katerina nodded. "It's very nice of them to mention me, and I am excited by the opportunity to work with you, Rob."

She glanced at her open portfolio. "Last time we spoke, you mentioned that you would like me to handle the serving platters and dishes, but that you would cover the place settings and cutlery. Does that also include the wine glasses for the pairings?"

"Yes, Adam is providing the wines based on the final menu selections, and he is going to provide the wine glasses. I can cover the flowers as well," Rob said.

"Perfect, once we finalize the menu, we can touch base briefly to make sure that you have enough place settings to handle all the different courses." Katerina pulled some papers from her portfolio, handing them to Rob. "Here are the menu options you requested. As you asked, the cuisine is Italian but includes entrée choices for beef, poultry, and seafood, with a separate course for pasta. In addition, you will see appetizers, soup and salad, and desserts. I will provide you with a proposal based on an average for the menu selections as a placeholder, which will be refined if we proceed further."

"Thanks, Kat. Once I see that, I will know whether I am ready to take this event on or will decline. I will let you know either way."

Katerina nodded. "That works. Also, may I see the kitchen quickly on my way out to check on the dinner set-up?"

"Of course," Rob said, leading her to a room down the hall. It was a fairly large space with a double oven and plenty of counters for prep room and plating.

"Thanks, Rob. You have a lovely kitchen, and I can work with this," she said, smiling. She followed his lead back to the entry room, shaking his hand as she left. A few minutes later, she was back in her Jeep.

Katerina drove straight to the ferry and boarded the 11:30 a.m. crossing. Once on board, she headed back to the concession stand for another coffee. More caffeine would only give her the shakes, but she needed the comfort of a warm drink in her hand. She wanted to be seated and as calm as possible before she texted Jack to let him know what she thought of him.

Hot coffee in hand, she took a seat on the inside deck, pulling her phone out of her purse. The message light was lit, and she took a deep breath before pulling it up. There were two messages, one from Jack and one from Matt, the owner of the as-yet unsigned winery. She also had a missed call from Jack, but he hadn't left a message. Her stomach clenched, and she opened Matt's message first.

Matt: I would like to proceed further with the tasting room ideas you presented last week. I was talking to Adam and Jim at the other wineries, and I'm ready to go.

Kat: Perfect, I will send you a tasting menu so you can finalize your selections, and I'll also email you the contract for your signature. I look forward to working with you.

She tried to focus on the satisfaction of onboarding a new client, but Jack's unread message felt like a ticking explosive in her phone. She closed her eyes briefly and then pulled up the message.

Jack: Kat, I need to see you. It turns out that more time is not what I need. What I need is you. Can I see you today?

Katerina stared at the message, recognizing that everything had changed now. Those words on their own were everything she'd been longing to see. But knowing he had gone straight into Nicole's waiting arms was just too much. With her phone on "Do not disturb," she dropped it back into her purse and willed her nerves to calm down.

She drove off the ferry in Seattle and was home in a few minutes. It was still early afternoon, but she had no desire to go out or talk to anyone. She had no appetite but needed something to do, so she made pasta and a fresh sauce with cherry tomatoes, basil, and olive oil. She poured a glass of wine and turned on the television. She needed distraction.

As the night grew later, she poured another glass of wine and another. She refused to look at her phone—she couldn't deal with Jack. The hurt and sense of betrayal were too fresh. *Let him wait on a text and see how it feels.* She felt the tears on her cheeks and tried to let the anger take over. Maybe it was the wine, but instead, all she felt was sad.

Chapter Fifty-Four

Jack kept his phone with him, checking frequently to see if Kat had responded to his text. His conversation with Amy had opened his mind to the fact that, despite the complications, he could have Kat in his life without abandoning his sister. Eventually, he left her another voicemail, hoping that she would pick up. He acknowledged to himself that telling her he needed time to think had been another painful blow, but he hadn't expected her to shut him out completely.

By 7:30 p.m., when she still hadn't responded, he needed to do something. He decided to go to Sorbonne's and try to talk to her while she tended the bar. He wasn't sure it was a good idea to approach her while she was working, but he needed to see her. When he walked into the bar, he saw Greg, but another woman was behind the bar. He sat down in his usual spot. When the female bartender came over and introduced herself as Trish, he ordered a cabernet.

When Trish placed his wine in front of him, he asked if Kat was going to be working tonight. With an apologetic smile, Trish informed him that Kat had resigned. Jack thanked her, finished his drink, and left the bar.

Back at his condo, he paced in frustration. It had taken time for him to realize he'd been too quick to judge, and time to get his head around the fact that being vulnerable was uncomfortable and new for him. Now he could see that not having Kat in his life was infinitely worse. *Where is she?* He hadn't realized she was going to quit her bartending job. Letting time go by without talking to Kat meant he wasn't up to date on her life events, he realized with a pang.

He reached for his phone and texted her again.

Jack: Kat, please can we talk?

As the evening got later, he admitted it to himself. *She's not going to respond tonight.* When he went to his bedroom for the night, he put the phone on the bed beside him, just in case. Sleep was a long time in coming.

●●∞∞∞∞∞◖◗∞∞∞∞∞●●

Kat woke up to the buzzing of her alarm clock and, after turning off the annoying sound, she reached for her phone and re-read Jack's text, and his later text as well. She steeled herself to respond because she needed to put the drama behind her. The last few weeks had been hell, and she just wanted peace so she could heal. She didn't want to play games.

Kat: Jack, I don't know how I feel right now. Let's talk. You're welcome to come here. I think it makes sense to let you know that I saw you and Nicole yesterday at Starbucks. Let me know what time you want to meet.

The sound of the text awoke Jack, and he sat up abruptly, reaching for his phone. He read her text and groaned. *Damn, that didn't help my cause.* He glanced at his watch and quickly texted back.

Jack: Kat, I can imagine how that looked, but it wasn't what you might have thought. I would like to see you as soon as possible. Is 10 this morning too early?

Kat: No games, total honesty, 10 works.

Jack read her text and sighed. He couldn't blame her—look how he'd jumped to conclusions. He'd messed this up, and the situation was his to fix. He refused to even consider that he couldn't fix it. *I can't lose her.* He quickly texted back.

Jack: I understand. I'll see you at 10. Kat, don't give up on me.

He put down his phone and headed out to the kitchen to make some coffee. He needed to be sharp—he had made a real mess out of falling in love for the first time.

⋯⋯⋯⋯⋯○◯◯○⋯⋯⋯⋯⋯

Katerina was an emotional wreck, but she got ready anyway, dressing in leggings and a Seattle Seahawks sweatshirt, and leaving her long hair down and straight. She wanted to be comfortable, but applying her makeup was all about armor and non-negotiable.

Promptly at 10:00, she buzzed Jack into her building. When she opened her door, he handed her a huge bouquet of colorful tulips in a lovely glass vase. She recalled mentioning that tulips were her favorite flower. Mechanically, she thanked him, setting them down on the end of the island.

It hurt so much just to see him; she struggled just to catch her breath. Jack seemed tense, too. He hadn't tried to hug her, and she was grateful for that. Forcing herself to regain some sense of normalcy, she offered him a cup of coffee. Nodding, he took a seat at the island.

As she handed him the hot coffee, Jack looked into her eyes, and against her will, she could feel them welling up with tears.

He began talking quickly, the words tumbling over themselves, tension palpable in his voice. "Kat, I messed this up, and I need you to know how sorry I am. I would like to try and explain to you why I needed time to think." He paused for a moment, but Katerina didn't say anything, only nodded, breaking eye contact to try to control her emotions.

He spoke again, softer this time. "That Friday night when you were sleeping in my arms, I realized I was in love with you." He noticed Kat stiffen beside him, but he needed to keep talking to try to make this right. "I've never been in love before or felt vulnerable in that way. That next morning, when Amy called, I jumped to a conclusion and just reacted to protect myself. Kat, I couldn't bear the thought that the night we had just shared wasn't as important to you as it was to me. I know I took too long to reach out to you—I was afraid and in denial. I couldn't believe that you had that much power to hurt me, but you know what was worse? Last night I tried to see you at Sorbonne's and the bartender told me that you had resigned. Kat, not knowing what is happening in your life feels far worse than knowing that you have the power to hurt me. These last few months, watching you flourish and grow your business, I just want to be in your life so you can continue to amaze me."

Katarina set down the coffee cup that she'd been clutching tightly, and before she could speak, Jack said, "Do you mind if I clear up the Nicole thing?"

Kat nodded again and forced herself to meet his gaze. Despite how her heart had soared at hearing his words, she needed to know how he could have turned to Nicole.

"I had asked Nicole a while back to keep her eye out for any lots that came up on the island since I'm interested in large lots that have a good view of Puget Sound. A few lots came up recently that had been held as part of an estate. She's dating someone from Seattle and was planning to be here Saturday morning, so she asked if we could meet. She had some paperwork on the lots she wanted to give me and also wanted to fill me in on some background on the sale. Nicole and I have been over for a while, and once I met you, there was no going back."

"And Kat," he added, "Amy told me that you reached out to her. Thank you." He leaned closer to touch her arm again. His eyes locked on to hers and she could see the hope in them. "That took a lot of strength, and it was compassionate, and you made me realize that we can handle complications."

"Oh, Jack," she said with a sob, tears streaking down her cheeks. "I've done things wrong, too, and I've certainly wasted time by not being able to see what was right in front of me. I love you, Jack."

He pulled her out of her chair and into his arms, holding her tightly and giving her a long, slow kiss filled with promise. "So, the lot I mentioned," he said, still holding her tightly. "I was thinking that you and I could have a great time designing our new home together. And of course, we'll plan plenty of room for Buttercup, our golden retriever. What do you think?"

"Oh, Buttercup—that seals the deal!" Katerina said, laughing and leaning in for another long, forever kiss.

Epilogue

Jack bent down to stroke Buttercup on her soft, golden head, avoiding her beseeching brown puppy gaze and then tossed her the dog treats he held in his other hand. As Buttercup lunged for the treats, Jack quickly shut the door behind him. The whining would start again, he knew. They had clearly spoiled this puppy, but with Paul's fur allergies, a temporary detention was needed. Pete would be by shortly to pick her up for an overnight stay at his sister Rhonda's orchard.

At the bottom of the stairs, Jack turned toward the kitchen to see if Kat needed any help. She lifted her head when he entered the door, her lips turning up in a wide smile, and blew him a kiss. Amy and Helen were both bustling around the space, setting out appetizers and sandwiches. He figured there was no room for him, so instead he retreated toward the game room where he could hear a Seattle Seahawks game and knew a cold beer waited.

As he entered the room, Paul and Michael greeted him with similar expressions of disgust. "Denver just scored," Michael said on a sigh. Jack responded with his own sigh and grabbed a beer. On the way to his chair, he skirted the large couch to tickle the chin of the smiling baby on Michael's lap. Michael Jr. gurgled in appreciation.

As he sipped his beer, Jack took a moment to appreciate his life and all the changes that had occurred since he first laid eyes on a beautiful, dark-haired woman with golden eyes. She was so much more than beautiful, he mused. *She is strong, talented, and loving.*

Her catering business was booming, especially the cookies—so much so that Pete worked for her full-time now. Jack and Kat had just finished framing their new home on the island, and the plan was for Pete and his girlfriend Carrie to move into the B&B once Jack and Kat moved out. Carrie worked on Rhonda's orchard but was excited to add the role of inn sitter, and Pete was excited to do the cooking.

Jack's thoughts were interrupted by the entrance of Amy, Helen, and Kat, each of them precariously balancing plates heaped with food, and wine glasses, and still, Amy managed to deftly scoop up Michael Jr. The women headed toward a large table with an impressively complete jigsaw puzzle they had been working on most of the day. Jack stood quickly as Kat passed him, and catching her eyes, he said, "I love you, babe."

"I so love you back," she said, her golden eyes shimmering.

Jack squeezed her arm and turned to follow Paul and Michael, who had temporarily abandoned the football game to load up their own plates.

Back in the game room, Jack bit into his sandwich, appreciating the crusty bread and fresh herbs that always let him know he was eating Kat's food. He sighed with true pleasure, but he knew that it was more than the food; it was family. Paul, Helen, Michael, Kat, Amy, and himself had come from blended families and all appreciated what "family" felt like. Each of them had worked hard to make their new version of a blended family work.

"Yes!" Jack heard Michael shout, and he returned his attention to the screen in time to enjoy a Seattle touchdown.

THE END

If you enjoyed *A Change to the Plan*, please help other romance lovers find this book by posting a review.
Thank you!

About the Author

For years, Pamela Moulton, a certified public accountant, balanced a structured career in corporate tax with a creative mind filled with fictional characters. As you may suspect, the fictional characters ultimately won out, giving rise to her debut novel. While she currently resides in Philadelphia, Pennsylvania, *A Change to the Plan* is set in the Pacific Northwest—a place where she once lived and still loves.